WHERE THE THISTLE GROWS

PICT BY TIME
BOOK 1

MIA PRIDE

ARE YOU SIGNED UP FOR DRAGONBLADE'S BLOG?

You'll get the latest news and information on exclusive giveaways, exclusive excerpts, coming releases, sales, free books, cover reveals and more.

Check out our complete list of authors, too!

No spam, no junk. That's a promise!

Sign Up Here

www.dragonbladepublishing.com

Dearest Reader;

Thank you for your support of a small press. At Dragonblade Publishing, we strive to bring you the highest quality Historical Romance from some of the best authors in the business. Without your support, there is no 'us', so we sincerely hope you adore these stories and find some new favorite authors along the way.

Happy Reading!

CEO, Dragonblade Publishing

ADDITIONAL DRAGONBLADE BOOKS BY AUTHOR MIA PRIDE

Pict by Time Series
Where the Thistle Grows (Book 1)
Where the Stars Lead (Book 2)

Irvines of Drum Series
For Love of a Laird (Book 1)
Like a Laird to a Flame (Book 2)
Maid for the Knight (Book 3)
How to Save a Knight (Novella)

Pirates of Britannia Series
Plunder by Knight
Beast of the Bay

For my four dogs, Kirby, Lucy, Bonnie, and Clyde, who made writing this very complicated with their adorable need to constantly be on my lap. Nearly every word was written while they surrounded me with love!

CHAPTER ONE

THUNDER CRASHED AS sleet pelted the earth, muffling his echoing moans of pain. The cave's graveled floor chilled her flesh as she kneeled beside him, tears blurring her vision as she held her hands to his chest, feeling warm blood slip through her fingers despite her desperate attempt to stop its flow.

Blood coated her long, green tunic and puddled on the ground around her feet, a scene she felt all too familiar with. She had lived this moment a thousand times before and still never learned to accept the truth or numb the pain.

"Don't leave me," she whispered, bringing her face closer to his, blinking through blinding tears to get one final glimpse of the beautiful man she loved before losing him forever.

More agonizing moans escaped his cracked lips, his injured head thrashing from side to side. Wet tendrils of dark blond hair stuck to his forehead, perhaps from the relentless storm that raged beyond these colorless walls, or maybe sweat from fighting the battle that led him to this demise.

"I warned you!" she wailed, pain searing her heart as she pressed down, knowing there was nothing more to be done. Dying in this cave was his fate, the inevitable end to his reign. "You didn't listen!" she cried just as another flash of lightning lit up what little sky she could see through the cave's entrance.

His eyes flew open when the clash of thunder reverberated off the cave's walls, a look of confusion and sadness in his gaze before shutting his eyes once more—this time forever.

She shook his shoulder with one blood-stained hand, shrieking when a final gasp left his lungs. A visible wisp of breath curled into the chilled cave's air.

"No! Don't leave me!"

Collapsing onto his still body, she sobbed, hearing the rhythmic pounding of rainfall outside, and wishing it was his heart that beat so methodically instead. The rest of the world continued to turn, but her world lay dead at her feet—

"Caitriona." A deep, familiar voice echoed from the cave's entrance, pulling her out of the moment with a startling gasp.

Blinking rapidly, Caitriona looked around, squinting into the sunlight streaming through cream-colored canvas flaps. Sitting up in her cot, Caitriona rubbed her eyes and breathed deeply, trying to calm her rapidly beating heart.

"Cait? Are you all right?" The deep, authoritative voice of her mentor, Samuel, penetrated her panic and made her focus on her surroundings. Caitriona swallowed hard, nodding when she realized she was back on-site, safe within her tent.

"I'm fine, Sam." The ache in her stomach and the tightness in her heart contradicted her words, but she gave her mentor a reassuring smile just the same. This dream repeatedly plagued Cait, always leaving her shaken for days.

"That dream again?" Samuel asked, creasing his brow as he stood at her tent's entrance, holding one flap back. Light from the new day flooded the small space, and coastal winds shook its canvas walls, a stark reminder that she slept atop a cliff on the northern edge of Scotland.

Nodding, Caitriona took a deep breath. "Why do I keep having this same awful dream? I've had versions of it or other dreams about the same man my entire life. He looks so much like my ex-fiancé, Taylor, yet I know it's not him. This man is larger, his hair lighter, and he has a bull tattoo on his chest with a scar above it. Yet, the way I feel about him is... well, it's certainly not Taylor, despite the resemblance." Cait shuddered when she thought about Taylor, who relentlessly called and plagued her existence.

She ran her fingers through the tangled masses of her wavy hair, wincing when her fingers caught on a knot.

"Dreams are odd things," Samuel said with a shrug. "You're in Scotland excavating the caves you've been fascinated with your entire life. That explains the cave part. The man being your ex-fiancé isn't too strange if your mind is filling in the blanks. I admit, the violent death part is odd. If we could decipher dreams, that would take all the fun out of them, wouldn't it?" he said with a crooked smile.

"I suppose you're right." Cait decided that explaining the man's face had always looked the same, even before she met Taylor, would only be more confusing. There were other dreams, as well—ones that made her burn fever hot whenever she even thought about them. She'd once believed Taylor was her soulmate because his face had appeared in her dreams all of her life. However, it didn't take long for her to realize that Taylor was possessive, controlling, and had a temper large enough to scare off a grizzly bear. So, why did his face appear in all of her dreams, even when she was young?

She looked to her left, realizing Emilie's cot was empty and already well-made. "What time is it?" she asked her grad school professor. As one of Cait's first archaeology professors, Samuel shared her passion for antiquity, but he loved fieldwork most. It was hard to believe that after all this time, all this studying, training, and learning from the best, Caitriona had landed a position at her dream site in Scotland, excavating a group of caves off the coast of Moray—and already, she'd overslept on the first day.

"Don't worry. It was an exhausting trip here from California, plus all the set-up. I won't hold it against you." Samuel cracked a smile and looked at his watch. "Well, it's about that time. We have the equipment on-site, Emilie is mapping the space with her GPS equipment now, and the low tide is due in an hour. We should head over to the caves."

Nodding, Caitriona swung her legs over the cot and

stretched, thankful that Samuel was an old, gentle soul who cared just as much for the living as he did for the dead. He left, and she swiftly got dressed in her field gear, which was nothing more than khaki pants, a button-up shirt, and for this frigid location, a thickly lined black parka with a faux fur-lined hood.

Tying back her long hair into a ponytail, Caitriona stepped out of the tent and took a deep breath of fresh Scottish air as the chilled wind nipped at her nose. Dreams did come true, and that was evident as she stood atop this cliff, overlooking the sea. This was more than just an excavation. Her lifelong obsession with Scotland had always baffled her parents, whose roots reached back to this mystical land, but their family had been in America for the past 300 years and didn't care about their ancient roots quite as much as she did.

Scottish history was her passion, and one particular tale of an ancient Pictish King named Brodyn Mac Cuill enraptured her like no other. He'd lived over a millennium ago, and no trace of his existence survived except a story shared throughout the generations of the king who united all of the Celtic tribes against their southern enemies. His prowess in battle was legendary, as was his brutal death on the battlefield, when he was cut down by the enemy's blade. However, one part of Brodyn's legend always stuck with Caitriona. In a tumultuous time of violence, death, and instability, Brodyn was known to love his wife above all things. And before his final battle, somehow knowing his death approached, he bade her bury him in the cave where they first met as she wandered lost on the shore, from a distant land.

Caitriona wondered if her dream created this obsession or if her obsession inspired the dream. It was like the chicken or egg, for the two had simply always existed for Caitriona, and a life spent studying the Picts had made her one of the world's more comprehensive Pictish historians at the young age of twenty-five. Though no evidence of the tale's veracity had yet to be found, Caitriona was here now, hoping she would be the one to uncover some small clue or artifact within this set of caves, despite past attempts from other teams.

Standing atop a cliff overlooking the Moray Firth as the sun glittered off its surface, Cait prepared to excavate the very caves she had seen in her dreams for years, though last night's dream still had her off-kilter. Never had her dream been more vivid, and a chill ran up her spine as a gush of wind blew wisps of hair across her eyes. Even now, she grieved for the man in the cave. A specter who visited only in her dreams, the man only ever died in her arms, leaving Caitriona equal parts devastated from the loss of a man she never knew and confused by the depth of that grief. Somehow, though he looked just like Taylor, she always knew it wasn't him because her love felt transcendent; it was a love she'd never felt for Taylor. Her parents had pushed her to marry him, and she had hoped to feel more over time, but as their relationship continued, the angrier and more controlling he'd become.

Though she'd broken off her engagement with Taylor nearly two years earlier, he often called, determined to win her back despite her many rejections. He was a beautiful man on the outside, but inside hid a darkness, a possessive man who would do anything for Cait's honor, even if she did not wish him to. She knew he would never hurt her, but too many fights with random men for simply looking at her in what he considered the wrong way left a bad taste in her mouth. She could not live with such a man.

"Ready to go?" Samuel pulled up beside her in a small, rusted buggy they'd rented to travel between their campsite on this isolated strip of green land and the caves about half a mile to the east.

Nodding, Caitriona hopped into the buggy and gripped the side rail as they maneuvered across the rocky terrain, following a narrow path leading to the shore. "Thanks again for allowing me to be a part of this team, Sam. I cannot say what it means to me."

Smiling widely, Samuel dared to take his eyes off the path for a second before looking back. "Honestly, I cannot imagine it any other way. Your borderline obsession with the Pictish culture, especially King Brodyn, led you down this career path. When we set up this excavation, I knew nobody else could possibly respect and understand this history more than you. I'm happy to have helped your dream come true."

Another shiver crawled up her spine, and goosebumps covered her arms despite the huge coat she wore. Was it excitement? Anxiety? Caitriona wasn't certain, but the stakes were high. The momentous responsibility of handling ancient artifacts, discovering bones, or unveiling one of history's mysteries was not something she took lightly.

When they reached the shore, Caitriona saw Emilie standing beside some of the crew, chatting as she held a hot cup of coffee in her hand. Caitriona's stomach growled, and she cursed herself for not grabbing a coffee and pastry back at the campsite.

"Hi, Cait!" Emilie bounded over to her and Samuel, her blond hair tied back in a ponytail that did little to prevent the wild wind from whipping it around her face. "Hi, Sam. Low tide is almost here. We can access the cave soon."

"Great," Samuel said as he climbed out of the buggy with Caitriona in his wake. "Let's get set up. We will have six hours to work each day before the tide changes. Do not lose track of time. Once the high tide comes in, the water reaches just above the entrance, and we will be trapped until the next low tide."

Coming up beside Caitriona, Emilie, her college roommate, and best friend, linked her arm through Cait's. "Do you smell that? Fresh Scottish air." Taking a deep breath, Emilie grinned and looked up at the gray sky. "I thought you would be more excited to be here."

"I am. Maybe it just hasn't hit me yet, or maybe a part of me wonders how anything will ever compare to this excavation. When I leave here, it's back to California—back to reality, and my lifelong dream will have been met. Then what?" Caitriona shrugged as they walked toward the equipment area, grabbing her bag of tools.

A tall man with a slim build and dark hair came up to

Caitriona and Emilie with a hand held out. "Hey, I'm Rob. I've heard a lot about you both from Sam. First dig in Scotland?"

Caitriona nodded, observing the man. He appeared only a few years older, yet he seemed worldly as if he had already lived a thousand years. "Yeah, first time. I just finished a dig in Russia last month. You'd think I'd be used to the cold by now, but a few weeks back in California spoiled me," Caitriona said with a chuckle. Visible puffs of breath left her mouth from the cold, and she rubbed her hands together for warmth.

"Congrats. It's pretty amazing to land a dig this significant at your age, however, I've heard you're one of the world's foremost Pictish historians. That's incredible! These caves haven't been excavated since the 1940s, and there is a line of archaeologists pining to be here," he said with a kind grin and genuine interest in his dark eyes.

"Cait understands more about the Picts than the Picts did," Emilie proclaimed, nudging Caitriona on the shoulder. "She drove me nuts in grad school, but really, I wish I was as passionate about anything as she is about the Picts."

"My parents wouldn't agree," Caitriona said ruefully. "They wanted me to be an actress, not dig in the dirt. Not exactly what's expected of a little girl in the L.A. Hills."

Despite her anticipation, anxiety niggled deep inside Cait's belly. This dig would likely be heavily publicized, especially if they found anything of note—like the remains of a Pictish king. A lot of grant money was tied up with this project, and many eyes were watching their every move and awaiting every report.

"I don't think any of us were considered 'typical' children." Rob used air quotes and flashed a crooked smile. "Typical is overrated."

"Thanks," Caitriona said with genuine appreciation. She could tell Rob would be easy enough to work with, and her excitement bolstered.

Bags of supplies in hand, they walked along the shore as gulls flew overhead, and waves lapped at the ancient shores. If only this land could talk, what tales it would tell. Cait was determined to discover its secrets.

When the cave came into view, pulsing, searing pain tore through Caitriona's skull with the impact of a lightning bolt, making her stop in mid-step. Crying out, she dropped her bag into the rocky sand at her feet. Cradling her head, Caitriona gritted her teeth and closed her eyes as odd flashes of light flickered through her brain.

"Cait! Are you all right?" Emilie hollered, touching her shoulder, but the crackling sounds in her head nearly drowned out her friend's voice. Static buzzed in her ears like a poor radio signal, and she swore she heard voices speaking unidentifiable words.

When the pain subsided, Caitriona took a deep, steadying breath and looked up to see Rob and Emilie frowning at her with concern.

"Maybe you should sit this one out and check with the medic," Rob suggested softly.

"No, no…" she whispered and cleared her throat, grabbing her bag from the ground and standing straight. "I'm all right—just a headache. I get them often," she lied. Never in her life had she experienced anything like this. Emilie frowned and pursed her lips, yet thankfully knew better than to argue. Nothing was dragging Caitriona away from this excavation. She would be one of the first people to set foot in a cave presumed to be used by ancient Pictish people as a burial ground, and she intended to be there.

Grabbing Caitriona by the arm, Emilie pulled her aside, squinting her blue eyes with concern. "You're not acting normal. I know you don't get headaches like that," Emilie whispered. "I know you want to be here more than anything, but this is a several week's long excavation. If you're not well, then you should rest today."

"I'm fine, really," Caitriona persisted. "I just had another dream this morning. This one was… well, it shook me up a bit."

"The one where Taylor's the Pictish king in the cave?" Emilie questioned. "This isn't healthy. Cait, you realize that he lived almost 1,400 years ago. It's okay to be passionate about history. We all are. But, if you expect to find any trace of him around here, you will be disappointed. He isn't buried in any of these caves, despite the legend. He was likely buried in some old abbey cemetery with a headstone long gone, just like the rest of the Pictish kings. It's like the story of King Arthur. People may want it to be true, even if there's no evidence."

Swallowing hard, Caitriona looked over Emilie's shoulder and saw Rob waiting for them with concern on his face. "I know, Em. You're right. We won't find him, and I don't expect to. I'm not going back to camp. The tide is low, we are here, and we are doing this. There may not be a king buried here, but this isn't called the 'Cave of the Dead' for nothing. Many Pictish artifacts are likely here, and I, as you said, know more about them than anyone."

Nodding, Emilie accepted Caitriona's response. Having lived with Caitriona, Emilie understood her interest in a long-lost culture and a man of legend. Still, the depth of her interest was something not even Caitriona understood.

Approaching the cave, Caitriona saw a few other archaeologists buzzing around the entrance, some using brushes to dust the walls, others kneeling on the wet gravelly ground as they gently dug through layers of soil with small shovels or trowels. The Northern Scotland Coast Guild of Archeology had begun studying the shores surrounding the caves a month ago but only just now worked their way toward the Cave of the Dead, one of the more inaccessible of the lot. The cave was so often submerged and so little studied that few bothered to seek its secrets until now. Once the team came closer and realized the cave could be excavated during low tide, Samuel had called Emilie and Caitriona to join the team.

Without hesitation, Caitriona packed her bag, took a hiatus from her current job as a tour guide at the local historical museum, and informed her parents that she would be gone indefinitely. They weren't too bothered, as they had plans to travel abroad and wouldn't be home for much of the year, as usual. Spontaneity and independence were Cait's strengths, and she never shied away from a challenge or an adventure. Her parents had been absent much of her life, hiring nannies to raise Cait while they traveled, so she'd built a life around her own interests.

Anticipation thrummed through her veins as she tightly clutched her bag in her right hand, her eyes scanning every detail of her environment. Low waves lapped at the rocky shore, and a few quartz rocks glimmered in the sunlight where the water receded. Stratus clouds hovered above, obscuring a cerulean sky, taking turns hiding the sun's stretching rays. The scent of brine wafted in the cold Moray wind, and Caitriona freely breathed it in, allowing it to fill her lungs with its ancient secrets.

The Cave of the Dead stood just to her right, its gaping mouth awaiting her first steps within, almost luring her like a Siren's call. Taking a step closer, Caitriona heard the gravel beneath her boots shift, and she wondered how many ancient people walked this same shoreline or looked into the distance where wild thistles thrived in the rocky soil just at the edge of the cliffs. The purple flowers dotting the horizon with their prickly stems and leaves reminded Caitriona of the thistle tattooed upon her left ankle, a gift to herself on her eighteenth birthday.

As she entered the cave, Caitriona gaped in awe as she looked at its thick walls, a solemn vibration of energy radiating off the cold stone that enveloped her. A heaviness pressed down on her as she walked further into the cave. What secrets did it hold? Why did intense sadness and foreboding hang in the air? Fifteen hundred years earlier, this cave would have been sea level, but rising tides now hid it from the world, erasing it from history's records until the last century. Today, Caitriona became part of its story, and a humbling sensation washed over her as the echo of shovels clacked against the cave's ancient floors.

"Cait," Emilie murmured from behind her GPS camera as she

slowly spun in circles to capture the cave's layout. The images would create a virtual representation of the cave when the team couldn't access it. "What do you make of these?"

Stepping further into the cave where shadows concealed much of the details, Caitriona opened her bag and pulled out a flashlight, shining it on the gray stones. Caitriona scanned the walls up and down, left to right, scrutinizing the images carved into the rock. "Pictish symbols," she muttered in awe as a chill ran up her spine. Cait spent much of her life studying these symbols, yet very little was known about their meaning.

When Caitriona placed a hand against the cool stone, another wave of sharp pain pulsed at her temples. She leaned against the cave's wall to steady herself as obscured images and distant voices overwhelmed her senses.

"Cait?" Emilie gripped her arms, but Caitriona barely recognized her friend's voice through the onslaught of sensations. "You aren't all right."

"Do you hear them?" Caitriona asked, locking eyes with Emilie and wondering why her friend remained so calm. The increasingly loud voices rattled Caitriona's skull, yet Emilie appeared not to hear them.

"What are you saying?" Emilie asked, confusion in her blue gaze. "Cait… you're talking nonsense… like Gaelic mixed with Latin and old Brittonic."

"What? I'm asking if you hear those voices. They all speak at once. I can't understand their words!" Caitriona shouted above the sounds pounding at her eardrums like hammers.

"Cait!" Emilie shook her by the shoulders before dragging her back outside the cave. The voices immediately vanished, and the throbbing pain disappeared. Collapsing into the gravelly sand, Caitriona panted and looked up at her friend. "He's in there."

"Who? You're scaring me, Cait. What language were you speaking?"

Caitriona blinked rapidly and ran a shaky hand through her ponytail. "What are you talking about? I asked if you heard the voices. They were so loud, echoing off the stone!"

Shaking her head, Emilie kneeled beside her, placing the back of her hand on Caitriona's forehead. "You don't feel feverish. Did you eat something bad last night?"

Removing her friend's hand from her head, Caitriona groaned in frustration and shuffled back onto her feet. "From the top, Emilie. What did you witness in there?"

"You spoke an odd language… I had to get you out of there before someone else heard you. It's like you were under a trance." Emilie visibly shivered and stood up. "What the hell was that,rE Cait?"

"I… I touched the wall, and suddenly I felt that pain in my head again—so many voices speaking in tandem. Flashes of light… images of people. Em, they weren't from this time."

"What are you saying, Caitriona Elizabeth Murray?" Emilie scolded her and used her full name for emphasis. "Is this some wild game? It's not funny, and you will get removed from this dig. Do you want that?"

"I'm not playing!" Caitriona huffed. "I heard it. I saw it. He's in there, Emilie!"

"Who is in there?" Emilie shouted with exasperation. "What language were you speaking? Was it… it couldn't be. Nothing of it exists. It was all oral, never written. You couldn't possibly…" her voice trailed off as she frowned at Caitriona.

"Royal bones are buried in that cave, damn it! I know it. The symbols say so."

Emilie looked back at the cave entrance and then back at her friend. "You need to walk away from this dig before losing your mind. Nobody knows what the symbols mean!"

"Well, obviously, I do! The symbols are a bull and a thistle connected with a backward 'Z', representing King Brodyn and his wife! Why else would these be here? You must believe me!"

Swallowing hard, Emilie took a deep breath and grabbed Caitriona's hand. "I do believe you because I have known you long enough to know there is an odd connection between you and this history. I can't explain it, other than that I know that history's mysteries are often inexplicable. But Cait—everyone else will think you've gone insane. You can't be here if this keeps happening. You were speaking Pictish!"

"I… I was?"

Emilie slowly nodded. "I can only assume since, you know, literally none of the language exists today except place names that are a mix of Gaelic, Latin, and other ancient dialects of early language. But yeah, you were speaking it. What the hell, Cait? It's like you were suddenly a Pict."

"Impossible," Caitriona breathed, fisting her hands to keep them from shaking. Her stomach knotted, and her heart pounded. Closing her eyes, Caitriona took a shaky breath and searched her mind for some logical explanation to convince Emilie this wasn't real. She had no answers, no understanding of what had happened to her in that cave, and no answers would come unless she convinced her friend she was well enough to continue with this project. She hated to lie to Emilie, her greatest friend in the world. Still, even Emilie would be obligated to report this to Samuel if she believed Cait unfit for such an important job.

Opening her eyes, Caitriona looked straight at Emilie and said the only thing her jumbled mind could conjure. "April fools!"

"What?" Emilie said with exasperation. "It's February!"

Forcing a grin, Caitriona shrugged. "And we were on opposite sides of the world last April. I never got you! Can't break with tradition, can we?"

"You're full of crap," Emilie growled, gently nudging Caitriona in the shoulder. "No way you were faking that."

"Acting classes, remember? I grew up in L.A. with actor parents and Oscar parties. You've seen the bill for my theater roles. This was just another role," Cait said with another shrug. "Crazy archaeologist travels back in time, possessed by the spirits of the past. It would make a good movie, actually."

Emilie pursed her lips together and glared at Cait. "You're an asshole."

"Admit it. I had you."

"Actually, yeah. You did." Emilie let out a slow release of breath and cracked a hesitant smile. "You've always been good with the pranks, but this one takes the cake. I'd give you a slow clap if I wasn't too pissed off and shaken up to congratulate you just yet. I will get you back, though."

"I look forward to it." Relief washed over Caitriona, but only slightly. What happened in that cave was no prank, and suddenly she wondered if there was more to her dreams than just an obsession. The voices and images felt familiar yet distant, like a tunnel full of memories fighting to reach the light first, flooding Caitriona with fragments of information rather than whole stories. She would piece it all together. More than ever, she was determined.

"Time to get to work. You can plot your revenge while we explore. I'm ready to dig my trowel into some dirt." Wrapping her arm around Emilie's shoulder, Caitriona escorted her shaken-up friend back into the cave, thankful, after all, that her parents had given her acting classes despite her best attempts to escape them.

CHAPTER TWO

T HE CLANK OF tools scraping and digging against the hard-packed floors echoed off the walls as several archaeologists carefully excavated different areas of the double-wide cave where tunnels led to separate chambers. No wonder so much mystery surrounded this place. Mystical energy radiated in the air as Caitriona breathed, feeling light-headed and uncomfortable as she fought to remain lucid. Yet, she was determined to explore despite the bone-searing despair that enveloped her as she moved deeper into the cave.

"Artifacts dating back to 1,000 BC have been found in here," Samuel said from behind Caitriona, making her gasp and spin around. "Sorry, I didn't mean to sneak up on you."

"It's okay," she breathed, trying to lighten the mood with a smile. "The Picts believed caves to be entrances to the fae world, so I can only imagine how many offerings they once left here."

"It appears there are many alcoves and hidden corners. I have other things to oversee and artifacts to prepare for lab delivery this evening. Holler if you need me… the acoustics in this cave are better than any rock concert. Get it… rock concert?"

Caitriona did her best not to roll her eyes at her mentor, who never failed to deliver a cheesy archaeology joke whenever possible.

"Nice one, Sam. If I find anything, I'll shout," she said and grinned. Patting Caitriona on the back, Samuel walked away and left her alone with her tools and ambitions.

Smile slipping from her face, Caitriona tried to control the thrumming in her body. It seemed as if the cave was a living, breathing entity, and she an extension of it, sharing energy and feeding one another in an inexplicable, symbiotic relationship.

Slowly spinning to look at the cave's symbols, she bit back a groan as her temples pulsed once more. Gripping the sides of her head, Caitriona stepped toward the wall, looking closer at the symbols, wondering why she could suddenly interpret them when nobody else could.

"A Pictish king is buried beneath a thistle in this cave," Caitriona murmured as she looked at the oddly familiar symbols. Emilie was right. An odd language flowed from her mouth as if she had spoken it her entire life "What is wrong with me?"

"She says as she speaks to a wall." Squealing, Caitriona spun on her heels and gripped her chest when she saw Rob behind her. How many times could she jump with fright in one day? This cave had her on edge, and one more scare might stop her heart completely.

"Right," she said with a chuckle, pretending her entire world wasn't swaying. "I've just felt a bit off all morning."

"Can I get you anything?" he asked with a worried crinkle on his brow. His brown eyes searched hers. "A coffee?"

Caitriona wasn't sure she could stomach anything right now, not even her favorite beverage in the world. More than anything, she wanted privacy, time to figure out why she felt as if she'd been here before, why she freely spoke an ancient forgotten language—how she understood symbols nobody ever deciphered. If sending Rob on a mission for coffee gave her a chance to think, then so be it. "I don't want to put you out."

"Not at all. It's the dense, stale air in here. Gives everyone headaches, but nothing a strong shot of coffee—or whiskey—won't cure. When in Scotland, right?"

"Right," Caitriona responded wryly. "How about coffee now and whiskey later?"

"It's a deal. I'll be back."

Rob walked off before she could thank him, but she would have her chance when he returned. Looking back at the symbols, she murmured the inscription repeatedly as she contemplated its vague meaning. It felt oddly specific, like it was meant for just one person to understand... like it was meant just for her. That thought gave her chills, and Cait ran her hands over her arms to stave off the sudden chill.

Outside of the cave, hundreds of thistles grew not far from the beach and all-around their campsite. But in here? Looking down, all Caitriona saw was hard-packed gray earth. Without sunlight or water, could thistle possibly grow?

Deciding the message must be mistranslated or referring to a location outside of this cave, Caitriona reluctantly stepped away from the wall and gripped her bag of tools tighter as she began to look for a place to dig. A crack in the cave's floor caught her attention, making her pause mid-step. There was nothing particularly odd about the crack, aside from being the only one in the otherwise solid ground, yet she felt compelled to examine it.

Kneeling, Caitriona ran her gloved finger over the jagged line, following it with her gaze, noticing that it continued around the corner into a dark alcove. Hiding in an area of the cave where the sunlight couldn't reach, the alcove was nearly impossible to see. It reminded her of a small cave she once explored on a beach in LA. There, hidden mysteries also lured her into dark corners, looking for something she couldn't describe. Perhaps her persistent curiosity always led her into the unknown, following the path least traveled. Her mother had frantically dragged her away, scolding her for getting dirty before acting lessons.

However, her mother wasn't here to drag her away this time, and that predilection for discovery pulled her into the darkness. A burst of light blinded her, like fireworks exploding within her skull as she fell backward, dropping her bag of tools as she landed with a thud. Biting back a yelp, Caitriona rolled onto her side and grabbed her bag, frantically feeling inside for her flashlight. Feeling its cool metal against her shaky palm, Caitriona pulled it out and clicked it on, shining light first on the surrounding walls. More symbols covered nearly their entire surface, like archaic tattoos forever marking the cave.

Squinting, Caitriona murmured as she deciphered the symbols, slowly clambering back onto her feet. Many of the symbols were pagan in nature, describing rituals and sacrifices, but some spoke of the newer religion, Christianity, and men arriving from other lands to teach them of one God and his son.

When Caitriona pointed her flashlight at more symbols on her left before shining it toward the ground, she shrieked and stepped away from the wall, her heart pounding against her ribcage as her head grew dizzy and her vision blurred. "Emilie!" she shouted as she collapsed on the floor of the cave. Cait's shout reverberated off the stone walls surrounding her, intensifying her pain, but she was desperate for her best friend's help. "I found something!"

"Cait?" Emilie's voice carried, muffled as she tried to find her way into the alcove. "Where are you?"

Caitlin shined her flashlight in the direction of the small entrance to help guide her friend. "In in a small recess to the left of the main entrance! Look for my light!"

Emilie ran around the corner, flashlight in one hand and GPS camera in another. "Cait!" she cried when she saw her friend on the ground. "What happened?"

"This." She fumbled to move her flashlight, but her hands shook worse than ever before in her life. Pointing the light onto the ground, Caitriona saw the crack that initially captured her interest, yet that wasn't what frightened her. A lone thistle protruded from the depth of the crack, impossibly thriving despite its lack of water and sunshine.

"A... weed?" Emilie asked, shining her light onto the purple flower. "Did you hurt yourself? I know these things are known for their sting."

"No." Caitriona swallowed and felt sweat break out on her brow as the hairs on her nape stood on end. "I've been here before."

"Today?"

Shaking her head, Caitriona looked up at Emilie. "My dream, remember? The cave? This is it. Look at the wall, Em…"

Pointing her flashlight at the wall, Emilie looked at the Pictish symbols and back at Caitriona.

"More symbols neither of us understands, and a weed. Is this more of your joke? I really don't have time for this!"

"I lied to you earlier. I'm so sorry. Emilie, I don't know what's going on with me; I can read those symbols, and I can speak Pictish. The symbols at the cave's entrance said a Pictish king is buried beneath a thistle flower in the cave. I felt compelled to follow this crack in the ground…" Caitriona shined her light onto the floor. "I don't understand why a crack compelled me so much, but it led me to more symbols and this thistle. And those symbols—"

Caitriona directed the light to the cave wall as she stood up and pointed to one particular shape depicting two connected circles with a backward "Z" running through them with attached arrows at its tips. A thistle sat above the top circle and a bull near the bottom circle. "This symbol. I know it… I think I remember it." She let out a wail of agony as a sharp pain struck her head again.

"Cait!" Emilie ran to her side, and Caitriona felt her friend catch her around the waist just as her knees collapsed. "We need to get you out of here. This better not be another joke, or I swear…"

Caitriona groaned and kneeled on the ground, feeling waves of hot and cold washing over her. "I can't… leave! He's here!"

"Who, Caitriona? You're scaring me! I should get help."

"No!" Caitriona shouted, hearing her voice bounce off the cave's walls as she grabbed Emilie's hand. "The king… in my dream. This is where he is!"

Pausing, Emilie stopped trying to drag Caitriona out of the alcove and dropped her flashlight at her feet, kneeling beside her friend.

"The Pictish king from your dream?"

Nodding, Cait swallowed and gritted her teeth against the searing pain in her head. "At the entrance to the cave, there are symbols that represent a cave, a king, and a flower—a thistle specifically, and burial. He is here, I know it. And that symbol, there." Cait pointed at a symbol of a thistle atop a bull. "This is related to the King and his wife."

"How do you know what they mean? No scholar has ever been able to decipher pictographs."

"I don't understand any of it, Emilie. The pain in my head is worsening, and there is a thistle at my feet. It makes no sense, and I'm not leaving this cave until I dig."

"Then I will help you," Emilie spoke softly, knowing her stubborn friend never backed down when she set her mind to a task. "This has plagued you long enough. But you have to allow me and the team to handle this. You are clearly in pain and need to rest. Ask Samuel to take you back to camp. Whether we find bones or not, I promise to keep you in the loop."

Caitriona opened her mouth to protest, but the pounding in her head was nearly unbearable, and she had to recognize that Emilie was right. She had no idea what was happening to her, how she could understand the symbols and speak the language, or why she felt like her brain was bursting. Caitriona admitted defeat—for the moment. If they found bones, nothing would keep her away from the site, not even skull-splitting headaches.

WHEN HER CELLPHONE buzzed from beside the cot where she lay staring at the canvas ceiling, Caitriona was startled out of her wandering thoughts. Five hours had passed, and she'd still heard nothing.

Picking up her phone when it rang a second time, Caitriona

saw Emilie's name on her screen and answered the call. "Hey, Em! What's the news? Did you find bones?"

"Hey, Cait," Emilie whispered. Wind crackled on the other side of the line as she spoke. "They found bones right beneath the thistle... right where you said they would be. We've only uncovered the skull so far. Unfortunately, high tide is coming, so we are clearing out for the day."

Heart in her throat, Caitriona felt chills crawl up her body as she plopped onto the bed. They'd found bones, and she'd missed it because she had lost control. "Great," Caitriona said in a shaky voice, her emotions too intense to conceal.

"I'm worried about you," Emilie said in a breathy tone.

"I'm worried about me, as well." Swallowing hard, Cait felt her heart rate kick up a notch with excitement and fear. What was happening to her? She should jump on a plane and fly as far away from this site as possible, but the visceral pull she felt toward that cave held her interest like a vise, and there was no way she would leave until she had answers.

"Do they think it's the Pictish king from the legend?" she asked, trying not to sound too interested, yet there was no way Emilie, who was well aware of Caitriona's overwhelming fascination with the subject, would fall for feigned calmness.

"It's too early to tell. It's human bones in a cave, just like many others we have found. Most had the heads removed, maybe due to sacrifices or some unknown tradition. Kings or royalty, as you know, usually are found intact. We haven't gotten that far, but finding the skull is already more than we usually find. He also appears to have died violently, based on the skull's condition."

"Are you headed back to camp?"

"Yes, the team wants to celebrate. We all have a good feeling about this." She paused, then asked, "Cait, what happened down there?"

Part of Caitriona wanted to play it down like it was nothing, but Emilie knew better than that, and she deserved the truth.

"I am honestly not sure, Em. Nothing like that has ever happened to me. The closer I got to the cave, the more something took hold of me. It felt like there were bolts of electricity snapping in my brain, and fuzzy images flashed in rapid succession—too fast for me to understand them. When I was in that cave, seeing the carved symbols and kneeling on that ground, it was just like my dream—like I had been there before."

"Right," Emilie said, trying to sound supportive, however Caitriona heard the uncertainty in her friend's tone. "I'll see you soon, okay?"

"Okay, bye." Caitriona ended the call and sighed, plopped onto the cot, and rested her head against her pillow. Until this second, she had been too full of anticipation about discovering an ancient king's remains to realize how exhausted she was. Her short time in the cave had sapped her energy. Why did she feel so protective of whoever had lain in that ground for the past 1,400 years? Were her dreams connected to this cave and this man? Or was it all a coincidence? Closing her eyes, Caitriona let her body rest and her mind shut down, feeling the warmth of sleep take root. The team would arrive soon, and Emilie would wake her to join them, no doubt. For now, sleep was calling to her, luring her away after a physically and emotionally tumultuous day.

"Caitriona." She heard her name drifting in the air, but it was distant, as if floating to her through a tunnel separating her from whoever called her name. Sitting up in her cot, Caitriona rubbed her eyes and looked around. Nothing except blackness surrounded her. A shiver ran through her, and cold snaked across her flesh, making goosebumps erupt on her arms. Cait reached for her tool bag on the nightstand, fumbling through the contents until she felt the cool, round metal of her flashlight's handle. Switching it on, she shone it around her tent, seeing Emilie sound asleep in the cot beside her.

How long had Caitriona slept, and why didn't anyone wake her? "Emilie?" she whispered, but her friend didn't stir.

"Caitriona." She heard her name spoken clearly behind her.

With a gasp, she turned and aimed the light near the opening to the tent, but nobody else was there. Cait slipped on her boots, grabbed her phone off the nightstand, and swiped on her screen, squinting at the clock. Five-thirty in the morning? Phone in one hand and flashlight in the other, Cait walked toward the tent's entrance, shoving aside the flap to peek into the darkness. The campfire was out, and apparently, so was the entire team. Soggy grass crushed beneath her boots as she slowly stepped into the night, the briny air nipping at her nose.

"Anyone here?" Someone had to be awake and calling her name. "Samuel?"

"Caitriona." She yelped when she heard the hoarse whisper from just behind her, but when she saw Sam, she sighed in relief.

"Is your head feeling better? We tried to wake you, but you were in a deep sleep, and we agreed you needed the rest."

"I'm feeling better, thank you," she whispered. "I was exhausted. Usually, the smallest sound wakes me up."

"New time zones will do that to you. I'm glad you feel better. Low tide is approaching soon, and the team will be waking to continue the dig."

"Right. Was there a reason you called my name?"

"Because you called mine," he replied, squinting at me through the glare of his flashlight.

"I awoke to you calling my name," she insisted, frowning when his brow creased in confusion.

"I didn't say your name until you called mine, Cait. Are… are you all right? You've been… on edge."

Warning bells went off in her head, sensing how close she was to being removed from this dig if she didn't pull herself together. "I'm fine. As you said, it's a new time zone. That, mixed with new flora, altitudes, and the excitement, must have gotten to me. Actually, I'm glad to be up a bit early since I missed the action yesterday. I'd like to get a head start and get down to the shore if that's okay with you."

Samuel hesitated and took a deep breath before nodding.

"You are the one who located the k. Emilie told me you had a feeling based on some of the symbols. You do impress me every day, Cait. If you want to head down to see what we've uncovered, I won't begrudge you that opportunity. I know what this project means to you, and I imagine having to leave the cave before we dug up the skull killed you."

"It did!" Caitriona chuckled, glad that her mentor understood her passion since he shared it.

"I still don't understand how you accurately decoded those symbols." Samuel stared, waiting for an explanation that Cait didn't have.

Shrugging, she shook her head. "Lucky guess?" Honestly, that was her best answer. None of it made sense, and she was only glad Emilie kept silent about her speaking the odd language.

"More than lucky, I would say. If you want to head down, go for it, but you'll have to walk. We need all the buggies here to take down the crew and supplies later.

"I prefer the walk, anyway. It's a gorgeous view now that I see the sun peeking over the horizon." Samuel nodded his consent. Quickly, Cait ran into the tent to grab her tools, put on her coat, and head to the shore before he started asking more questions that she couldn't answer.

CHAPTER THREE

GULLS FLEW OVERHEAD, caught between the graying sky and angry sea, seeking their fresh catch of the day. As for Caitriona, she couldn't remember her last meal. With her stomach in knots and her mind blurred, there had been little time for anything else.

"This ends now," she murmured as she traversed the rocky soil, ensuring she didn't twist her ankle on a large boulder. There is no correlation between my dreams and that cave, she repeated to herself with every step. She would help dig up those bones and continue with her job at this site. No more distractions. No more wandering imagination.

When a sharp pain struck her temples the moment the cave came into sight, Caitriona cursed under her breath and kept walking with determination, pushing forward. She'd worked her entire life to get here, and these headaches weren't going to ruin her career or crush her dreams. If she was sent away again, Sam might decide she was ill and send her home or to a hospital, but those weren't options. She would be present when those bones surfaced, and she would be around when the lab results came in.

"Caitriona." She stopped to look around, finding herself alone. The wind whipped her hair into what would be impossible knots to remove, and she pushed it back with her hands, and a few strands of blonde hair tangled in her fingers. She cursed again, this time at herself, for forgetting to tie it back while she rushed to leave the camp.

Maybe she was sick, or worse, insane. As much as she tried to remain calm and brush everything off, hearing voices and speaking in archaic languages weren't normal. Neither was reading Pictish symbols, or at least, believing she could. Though, the symbols did lead her to a thistle. That was harder to explain away. Something was happening to her; either she was insane, or something inexplicable was happening.

Ancient Celts believed this cave to be a gateway to another world, filled with magical energy, things Caitriona outright rejected. Science couldn't explain everything, but magic and fairies were nothing more than creations of people who lacked answers. No, Caitriona preferred the scientific method, discovery, seeking answers to those things that mystify humanity. And she would find those answers.

Approaching the cave, Cait sucked in a deep breath when the pressure in her skull threatened to send her to her knees. Gripping her tools, she entered the cave and shivered when its icy air enveloped her body. Still, silent, cold. The thick stone walls muffled the sound of crashing waves just outside and stifled any sunlight, leaving nothingness and an eerie sense that she was being watched.

Caitriona grabbed her flashlight and shined it on the ground, following the jagged crack into the alcove as she did the day before. She gritted her teeth against the onslaught of throbbing pain, like needle points jabbing into her body's every pore. Tears streamed down her cheeks as she pushed through the agony, desperate to get closer. In the middle of the small space lay a pile of dirt with the single thistle atop, its jagged roots exposed and the flower beginning to wilt. Slowly, Cait bent over to pick up the plant and stick it in her coat pocket as she shined the light on the hole, seeing the flash of bone fragments. Heart in her throat, Caitriona crawled closer, placing a shaky hand on the skull where an apparent injury occurred more than a thousand years ago.

The moment her finger touched the skull's temporal bone, hers began to throb worse than ever, an odd connection forming between her and this ancient man. Lights flashed, and voices shouted through a distant haze of fog. Crying out as both pain and fear clawed at her flesh, Cait backed away until she bumped up against the cave wall. Her body pulsed and broke out in a sweat, making her tear away at her clothes. The searing heat made her nauseous and dizzy, close to fainting. Grief washed over her, the pain and suffering of a thousand years absorbing into her body. A wail escaped her mouth as she frantically wiped away tears and scrambled to her feet, wearing nothing more than her button-down shirt and a pair of socks. She would come back for her clothing later. For now, she had to escape this torment and get as far from this cave as possible.

Gripping her flashlight, she fled the cave, stopping short when the cold ocean water crashed against the entrance, soaking through her socks. Shrieking, Caitriona stumbled and landed in the water. Where had the water come from? Her team should be arriving any minute, and the low tide had only just begun. Caitriona shrieked when she saw the full moon casting its blue glow across the sparkling water, which was impossible. Not only had she entered the cave at sunrise, but only last night, the moon was half-full. Stars winked at her from the inky sky, more brilliant than she ever recalled seeing.

She could sit in the cave and wait until someone came, except Caitriona couldn't bear to approach that alcove again. The water was shallow enough to walk through, unlike the impassable waves that usually crashed against the cave's entrance during high tide. Careful step by careful step, Cait pushed through the freezing water, kicking her socks off when they became another obstacle. She hobbled and winced as sharp rocks dug into the soles of her feet.

The frigid air blew against her soaked cotton shirt, her exposed legs shook as freezing ocean water engulfed her. Caitriona shrieked when a rock slipped beneath her foot, and she nearly tumbled headlong into the water. Something grabbed her shirt and pulled her back, and she found herself restrained as a large arm wrapped around her waist.

Screaming, Caitriona thrashed, dropping her flashlight into the water as she tried to dig her nails into the stranger's arm. "Let me go!"

"Who are ye?" A low growl resounded just beside her ear, warm breath brushing against her neck. The accent was strange—almost Scottish yet with an odd inflection she had never before heard.

"I... I am part of the archaeology team studying these caves! My team leader has the permits!" She knew some locals were angry about Americans poking around in ancient soil, but the work was only done to honor their history and heritage with the utmost care.

"What nonsense do ye speak?" The man growled, giving her a quick shake before spinning her around to face him, never letting his grip loosen.

Even in the darkness of night, with naught but the moon's light to illuminate the world, Cait saw familiar features glaring back at her. Narrowed, light eyes, a strong jaw covered in a short beard, and long dark hair resting upon bared shoulders.

"Taylor?" Caitriona looked up at her ex-fiancé and wasn't sure if she should feel panicked or relieved. "W-what are you doing here?" He was supposed to be in California. Had he flown all the way to Scotland to check on her? He had gone pretty far out of his way to keep tabs on her before, but this was insane. Cait thought ignoring his calls would help, yet it obviously had not. "Why are you talking that way?"

"Ye are the one speaking oddly." His voice softened, but he didn't lose the rough brogue or the low warning in his tone. When she looked up at his giant height, she saw her curiosity mimicked in his own eyes. "Where are ye from? Why are ye wandering my shores?"

"Stop it! Don't play games with me!" Caitriona shouted and tried to jerk away, but he wouldn't release his tight grip on her waist. "Why are you following me? I'll scream even louder if you don't let me go! My colleagues are on their way here now! You've no right to follow me, Taylor!" Never had she feared him, although he'd never done something so extreme.

Her legs shook beneath her, and she craned her neck to see if anyone was nearby to help her escape Taylor's tight grip. And then, in spite of the darkness, Caitriona saw the Pictish-style bull tattoo and the scar just above it on the man's bared chest. She felt herself going limp with terror and struggled not to faint. Taylor had no tattoos, and he disliked even the smallest of them. She recalled the scolding he gave her when she got a small thistle tattooed onto her ankle last summer.

"I dinnae understand what any of that means." The stranger growled. "Did Domnall send ye?"

Where had she heard that name before? As soon as she remembered, she tried to break free once more but he held her in an iron grip as if she was as weak as a child. She didn't stand a chance to escape his grasp.

This man looked and acted so much like Taylor, but he sounded nothing like him. His accent sounded more like that of the man in her dream, the legendary Pictish king. Domnall was King Brodyn's cousin who ruled the Scots of Dal Riata. History was never clear if they were friends or foes, and Caitriona had no idea how to respond. Taylor was a military man with no interest in history. He wouldn't know anything about Domnall. Was this another dream, or had she knocked herself unconscious when she fell in the cave?

"Wake up, Caitriona Murray.... Wake up!" she told herself.

"Caitriona Murray?" the man mumbled and loosened his grip, yet his large, callused hands remained on her forearms. "Are ye the bride sent by my cousin?"

"Your... cousin?"

"Aye. Though, I was expecting a bonnier lass. And one not so disheveled... and mayhap wearing more clothing."

He scrolled her length with his piercing gaze, making her both flustered and insulted simultaneously. The interest glistening in his eyes made her squirm with equal measures discomfort and excitement. *Curse my body for reacting to this ogre's perusal.* She couldn't decide whether she wanted to claw out his eyes or fall into his arms. Gritting her teeth, she shook off the desire to preen for this man and admonished herself for enjoying his obvious approval of her appearance despite his insults. "I am not your bride! You're insane! Let me go!"

"Domnall said ye would be resistant. Ye understand I dinnae want this any more than ye, lass. 'Tis needed to strengthen our people and to end this feud. We have enough enemies surrounding us."

"I don't understand what's happening!"

"I can see that," he grumbled, looking her up and down once more. "I dinnae ken where ye got that ridiculous tunic. And what are these odd…fasteners?" The man tugged at one of her buttons, and Cait gasped when it came undone. His eyes narrowed when the opened shirt flashed a glimpse of her bra and breast before she hastened to close it with numb fingers.

"What is the matter with you? What are you talking about?" she asked with a scowl and pulled away, adjusting her buttons.

"I would ask the same of ye. Why are ye alone? Where is the messenger meant to deliver ye to me?"

Shivering, Caitriona looked around the shore for any sign of her team, suddenly noticing that so many details were similar yet different. More thistles grew along the cave's clifftop than just yesterday. And then, there was the fact that it was night, not morning. None of it made sense. What was going on?

Cait shook her head and looked at the man who so resembled Taylor but spoke like the man from her dream. It couldn't be real… none of this. There was no way Taylor was here in Scotland and no way he had a tattoo or spoke with a new accent. As the clouds parted and allowed beams of moonlight to filter through, Caitriona realized that this man had blue eyes that seemed to glow from within. Caitriona swallowed, accepting the knowledge that he wasn't Taylor, who had dark brown eyes and slightly darker hair.

"This is a dream," she sighed, looking up at the man. "I have confused Taylor with King Brodyn from Burghead and created all of this in my head."

"I am King Brodyn, aye, but this isnae a dream, and I dinnae ken what Burghead is."

"The name of your hillfort, the capital of Fortriu."

"Fortriu is my land, aye. Our hillfort is called Pinnata Castra. Did Domnall tell ye nothing of us?"

"I told you! I was not sent here by your cousin, and I am not your bride!" Caitriona looked down at her bare feet. They were numb. Trying to take a step, she stumbled. It was like walking with frozen ice blocks instead of feet. The chill in her bones was certainly real.

"Ye've had a long journey. I will take ye back to my home where ye can change before my people see more of ye than I prefer." Brodyn examined her legs, and though she saw a flicker of amusement in his eyes, he schooled his features immediately, appearing irritated by the condition of his so-called bride.

Shaking her head, Caitriona stepped back. "I'm returning to the cave. My people will be searching for me."

"I am yer people, now, lass." He reached out and took her arm, jerking her closer. "Ye are a defiant one, but 'tis no use to either of us. Ye are coming with me whether ye want to or nay."

"No!" she shouted, attempting to pull away, and he tightened his grip. There was far too much pain and cold for this to be a dream. "I don't understand any of this!"

"Neither do I, lass. I dinnae wish to harm ye, but ye will come with me one way or another. If I release ye, do ye vow to come willingly?"

"No!" Cait spat, kicking him in the shin as hard as she could, only to wince and hobble as her frozen toes met with the hardest muscle she ever felt. The man did not so much as blink, and his severe expression only darkened to one of anger. "Ye decided yer own fate."

Cait squealed when the man wrapped his large hands around her waist and hoisted her into his arms. "Ye weigh nothing," he murmured as he flashed her a smug grin and headed west of the cave. "I will have to feed ye more, so ye are strong enough to bear my warrior sons."

"What?" Panic overcame Cait as she struggled relentlessly in his arms. "You cannot force me! This is rape! My people will call the police!"

"There ye go, talking nonsense again. I dinnae ken what 'rape' or 'police' are."

"Police enforce the laws, and rape is forcing a woman to lay with you against her will!" Cait shouted, wishing to claw at his beautiful face. Dream or no, all of this felt much too real. There was no denying her attraction or intrigue. He was literally the man of her dreams... but this was turning out to be a living nightmare that she couldn't understand. Clearly, he didn't understand half of the words she spoke, yet he understood her. If this was real, then she was in the year 680-something, and he spoke the lost Pictish language.

Stopping in his tracks, Brodyn looked sharply into her eyes, a glint of rage within his deep blue irises. "I am the po-lice... as ye say, of this land. And I would never force a woman to my bed."

"Only force her to marry you," she scoffed, tightening her grip around his neck for security.

"Ye agreed to this marriage. It makes ye the queen of the Albidosi. The most powerful woman in the land."

Albidosi—the word modern historians supposed the Picts called themselves. But, this was her dream, and she knew this information, so it made sense for Brodyn to know it, as well. He was only a figment of her imagination, after all.

"Right. Queen. I'll go along with this," she murmured. "Once I wake up, it will be nice to have been queen for a night."

Brodyn looked at her as if he questioned her sanity—a look she seemed to receive from everyone as of late.

"So ye agree to this arrangement?"

Caitriona nodded, her stomach doing odd flips when she looked into his eyes. "Then ye cannae say I forced myself on ye," he growled and continued walking. Somehow, his resentment took her aback. She wouldn't expect an ancient king and warlord to have scruples about being called a rapist.

"I have never been to my cousin's lands. Do ye all speak these odd words?"

"I suppose we do," she said with a shrug. If this was a dream, it wasn't worth explaining that she spoke another language and was from a place that Europeans wouldn't discover for over a thousand years.

Cait had so many questions for him, but soon the high walls of the ancient fort modernly known as Burghead came into view. The pitch-black of the night sky and the brightly luminous stars reminded her that this was no modern city with lights flooding the sky and hiding its beauty. Looking up, she noticed the swirls of the Milky Way bolder than ever. "So beautiful," she sighed as he carried her through three tunnel-like areas, each surrounded by towering walls with deep ditches beneath them and long-haired and bearded guards dressed in tunics and cloaks at every turn.

Brodyn carried her past his men as if it was ordinary to find oddly dressed women walking barefoot and alone on their coast at night. She remained silent as she observed the people and the fort. Wooden and stone buildings, some rectangular and others circular, were scattered about the small village within the fort, and smoke rose from the roofs as hearth fires burned. Additional fires burned throughout the town and the smell of smoke wafted on the wind. Flying insects swarmed around the fires, drawn to their flickering flames. People wearing simple tunics, long or short depending on their gender, stood around talking but their voices quieted as they noticed Cait, and she squirmed uncomfortably at their intent stares while Brodyn carried her past them.

"Did ye go fishing, King Brodyn? Looks like ye caught yerself a big one!" Caitriona looked over her shoulder to see a man with bright red hair and a long beard standing by one of the fires with his muscular arms crossed over an expansive chest. Several men and women laughed, including Brodyn. Panic rose in Cait's throat as the wind whipped her hair about her face, and fire warmed her flesh. None of these sensations felt like a dream. These people and this place felt as real as anything else ever had.

"Come with me, Goodwin," Brodyn ordered the man as he stormed past, carrying Cait quickly through the crowd. His stride quickened, and his demeanor hardened, making her quake with apprehension.

"Where are you taking me?" she asked as she clung to his bared shoulders, but he ignored her as he continued with determined steps.

Reaching a large, rectangular building made of stacked stones constructed atop a small hill, Brodyn kicked the door with his large, booted foot, making Caitriona yelp at the unexpected move. Everything was unexpected, and the more he spoke, the more she wondered if she had lost her mind. It seemed as if she had somehow gone back into time, yet that was the height of lunacy even to consider. Yet, here she was, in King Brodyn's arms as he carried her into a well-lit, warm room with candles in sconces along the walls and a raging fire burning in the hearth. An elderly woman silently fed wood into the fire, bowing when she saw the king enter.

With more care than she expected from a man of his stature, Brodyn slowly lowered Caitriona onto her feet before the fire. Murmuring her thanks, she shivered and broke out in goosebumps when the fire's flames warmed her chilled flesh. The floor consisted of smooth pebbled stone and warmed her feet, as well. She sighed as her skin thawed, but nothing could calm the tension coiling in every muscle as she tried to determine her reality.

"Anya, please find a clean, long tunic for my bride," he asked of his serving woman, who nodded and glanced curiously at Caitriona before hobbling off down a lowly lit corridor.

"I'm not your bride," she murmured through clenched teeth,

no longer playing along with what she initially assumed was a fanciful dream. Pinching her wrist, she winced at the pain and took a shaky breath. Okay, so maybe this was, inexplicably, not a dream. And now that she saw this man in full light, there were enough slight differences in his appearance that proved he was not Taylor. Their resemblance was uncanny and not a little distressing, but so was this entire ordeal.

Brodyn shot her a warning glance and looked back at his man, Goodwin. "My bride has arrived from Dal Riata. I found her wandering the shores, and, as ye can see, she has had quite a journey to get here."

"Aye, she is a fortnight late. I worried that Domnall wasnae keeping his end of the alliance. Ye sent him a noble bride in exchange moons ago."

"He isnae in a position to defy the alliance. Too many years of rivalry and war have torn apart this land. With the Angles attacking our people, we have to come together as one. We have to stop our feuding, put aside old wounds, and restore my grandfather's lands."

"You will," Caitriona whispered, eavesdropping on the men speaking about ancient battles that she read about in history books. They'd occurred nearly fourteen hundred years before her time, and many details had been lost. However, monks kept close records of essential information. For example, Cait knew his grandfather was a great Pictish king with much land until the king of the Angles, Ecgfrith, claimed much of it, forcing the tribes to pay tribute in the form of cattle and grain. It was a tale as old as time. King Brodyn would fight for the land back, and he would die but succeed in uniting the Celtic tribes north of Northumbria.

Brodyn looked over his shoulder and quirked a brow, and Cait pursed her lips together, silently reminding herself to watch what she said.

"Beggin' yer pardon, my lady," Anya said as she approached with a neatly folded piece of linen, no doubt the tunic Brodyn requested. "Would ye also care for a bath?"

"No, thank you," Caitriona said softly as she took the dry tunic from the woman.

"Aye. Ye need to bathe to remove the dirt from yer journey. Anya, please have a bath readied," Brodyn commanded. "Goodwin, fetch the priest. This wedding is a fortnight overdue, and I need it done with haste."

"Aye, my king." Goodwin walked toward the door to do his king's bidding, only pausing to look over his shoulder when Caitriona roared in disapproval.

"I am not your bride!" she protested yet again. "I am not the woman you are meant to marry."

Her body quaked as reality slammed into her. This was real. She was here, in King Brodyn's home, and he thought she was the woman meant to unite the Pictish tribes. She wanted to give in to the panic, to collapse on the floor and roll into a ball, close her eyes, and wish herself back to her own time. Instead, she willed herself to remain upright and take deep breaths.

The name of Brodyn's queen was lost to time. Nobody knew who she'd been or where she'd come from, but he was well-documented as being devoted and loyal to her during their short marriage before his death. If he married Cait, history would be forever changed, and she couldn't be responsible for a blip in the timeline.

"Ye will marry me, lass!" He shouted, storming toward her, and stopping only when his face was an inch from hers. With the light in the house illuminating his body, she made out the many tattoos on his arms and shoulders. He was domineering and larger than life.

As she felt the heat radiating off his flesh, she gulped. How had she ended up here? The last thing she recalled was touching the skull in the cave before seeing flashes of light and feeling pain throughout her body. She slipped through time, somehow, and she had to get back. Maybe this explained why ancient people thought the cave to be a portal to the fae world. It was a portal, all right, but instead of another world, it brought her to another time.

"Did Domnall explain to ye how essential this marriage is? How many lives will be saved? How many years of war will be prevented? Ecgfrith, that whore's son, has claimed all of our lands as his own. He enslaves the people and leaves the rivers red with our blood! He stole our grandfather's lands, though my father was the heir, and he takes half of everything we produce! People are dying!" he roared. "I dinnae wish to marry a dirty, angry, defiant hag, but I will because 'tis my duty to unite our people so we may defend ourselves. No more fighting with my neighbors! This ends tonight! And Ecgfrith, my illegitimate and over-reaching cousin, will pay for his sins!"

Cait took a step back, but only barely, as the hearth fire raged just behind her. How could she explain that she wasn't the woman he thought she was? She wasn't sent by Domnall, and she wasn't going to birth his children or bury him in that cave when he died, as his wife was meant to.

"I do understand your situation, Brodyn... Your Majesty," she corrected herself, putting her palms onto his chest to appease him, even though he'd called her a hag. "May I be honest with you?"

Narrowing his eyes, he nodded, almost imperceptively, and his nostrils flared like a bull's. Now, Cait understood the large bull tattooed on his chest. She could see why he'd been notoriously frightening to his enemies. Yet, for some reason, Caitriona wasn't afraid of him. She was more terrified about being trapped in time, and her mind raced with ideas of escape, but this man was not the thing she feared.

"I am not from here. Domnall did not send me. I don't know how I ended up here or why I am here. I do not belong. I'm not the woman you've been expecting. I understand your need to marry a woman from Dal Riata to make an alliance and strength-en your stance against your cousin..." She trailed off and swallowed, knowing he would achieve his goal but die in the process. It was hard to fathom how such a strong and vital man could and would be defeated. Bile burned her throat as emotion welled in her chest. It was one thing to seek the bones of a king long dead. It was quite another to stand before him now, the imposing figure of a viral man who'd soon perish. She didn't want to know him, feel him, speak to him… she didn't want to have a human connection with the warm-blooded man whose remains she'd so emphatically sought. So, why did she feel that connection despite her greatest efforts?

Touching his skull may have been what sent her here in the first place. Out of curiosity, Caitriona slowly raised a hand and placed it on the side of his head, just above his left ear, then closed her eyes, wondering if that would send her back to her time as it had sent her here.

A moment of silence passed, and she opened her eyes to see Brodyn still staring at her, this time with confusion rather than anger. "Why did ye touch my head? Ye are an odd woman, Caitriona Murray."

"You will find me the oddest woman you ever meet, for as I told you—I do not belong here."

"I think ye do."

"Then you are wrong."

"I am never wrong." His tone was cocksure and arrogant.

Caitriona snorted at his patriarchal attitude.

His eyes grew angry again. "We will marry tonight. I'm sorry ye find me so grotesque that ye would rather make up tales than do yer duty, but that willnae work. I dinnae care if ye spit, claw, kick, or bite. Ye will marry me, and we will send word to Domnall that the alliance is made."

Caitriona's heart raced so quickly that she barely could breathe. Think, Cait, think. Reasoning with him wasn't working, and she couldn't tell him she was from the future, or he would have her marked as a witch… or whatever they considered odd women of this time. They were no longer pagans, having converted to Christianity by this time. And Christians notoriously burned women as witches with little hesitation.

She couldn't be his wife, and she had no intention of staying. But perhaps marrying King Brodyn, the most notorious and well-documented king of the Picts, would be a fun tale to share with Emilie when she got back home… if she got home. Or when the dream ended… and, if her friend was inclined to believe any of this. Caitriona barely believed any of this, herself. Yet here he stood before her, rock-solid muscle, beaming blue eyes, demanding she marry him, even if he did consider her a hag.

"I only just arrived. Surely you can spare me a night to rest," she pushed back, hoping to delay the situation so she could come up with a plan or, even better, go back to the cave and retrace her tracks. Mixed feelings warred within her frazzled mind. King Brodyn was the man of her lifelong, repetitive dreams, and he was expecting her to marry him. Still, this wasn't where she belonged, and she couldn't stay.

"Ye will marry me tonight. At dawn, a messenger will leave for Dal Riata to inform Domnall of the marriage alliance. Lives depend on this. I willnae give ye a chance to run again. More than yer happiness is at stake."

Having no other options, Cait resigned, but only temporarily. "I will bathe and change, then I will marry you," she said, straightening her shoulders and feigning cooperation. She knew that she wouldn't be staying here long enough for it to matter. By the time his real bride arrived, Cait would be long gone.

"Good." Stepping aside, Brodyn turned and walked away just as Anya returned.

"My king?" Caitriona dared to ask just before he disappeared around a corner.

Silently, he turned to glare at her, and a warning flashed in his eyes.

"What year is it?"

"Did ye fall and hit yer head on yer journey, lass?" he asked with honest concern. "'Tis the fifth day of February in the year of our Lord, 685. I will meet ye at the chapel in an hour."

Brodyn walked away, and Caitriona leaned against the wall to keep from falling. Maybe she had hit her head, after all.

CHAPTER FOUR

CANDLES FLICKERED AROUND the room as Anya dressed Caitriona in a dark blue silk gown that laced in the back, hugged her bosom, and flared down to her toes. It had flowing sleeves and a bronze chain that cinched around her waist. Caitriona marveled at the smooth fabric. She'd often wondered if Picts had access to silk through trade, and now she knew they did. Still, it must be quite a luxury, and for her to be swathed in it immediately upon arrival spoke to the true wealth and power of King Brodyn and the Kingdom of Fortriu. Her freshly washed, strawberry blonde waves hung loosely about her shoulders and glistened red and gold in the light of the fire as it never did under artificial light.

Surprisingly, the older woman hadn't commented on Caitriona's undergarments, which, in retrospect, she found odd. Bras and thong underwear certainly didn't exist in this time and should have taken Anya aback. Perhaps Anya simply preferred to do her job and not ask questions, but her lack of reaction left Caitriona somehow ill at ease.

Anya brought leather slippers for her feet. They were rather large and clunky but it was better than being barefoot again. Besides, when this madness was finished, Cait would await the dawn and slip out unseen; she'd need something on her feet. King Brodyn's runaway bride. The history books never mentioned such a thing, and Caitriona wondered if it was a detail lost to time or if it never happened because she never escaped. She must.

"Ye are fit to marry our king, my lady. His mother wore this tunic on her wedding day, and she was verra blessed with love and bairns," Anya said as she stepped back and smiled. "Ye have naught to fear. King Brodyn is gentle with his womenfolk. He willnae hurt ye. Still, he is a man of discipline, hardened by a lifetime of war. His entire existence revolves around his people. So do as he bids, for 'tis a matter of life or death for us all, and he will be fair to ye. Ye'll see."

"I don't understand. Why does he need to marry me to secure an alliance with his cousin, Domnall? Surely, they are allies already?"

Anya shook her head and sighed. "Our king will have to explain this to ye another day, but the cousins have always had a strained relationship, and Domnall, though he is a good man, is prideful. They have an uneasy, untrusting relationship. Exchanging honored women from each tribe offers protection. No more battles will occur between the two tribes, for they will be united, bound together by shared blood. Especially when the bairns come."

Bairns? The thought of babies made Cait quiver beneath her gown, itching to escape before this situation worsened. "Anya…" Caitriona stepped closer to the older woman, lowering her voice. "I am not who King Brodyn thinks I am. I am not from Dal Riata, and I do not know how I got here. If he is expecting a bride, he will be angry when he marries me, and she shows up, eventually. It will ruin his alliance with King Domnall. I am not the right woman."

Slowly, Anya nodded her head, seemingly unsurprised. "Ye arenae who he thinks ye are, my lady, but ye are the right woman. I ken this to be true. Follow me out to the chapel."

Ending their conversation, Anya walked out of the room. After a moment's hesitation Cait followed behind her. What choice did she have, really? And she was intrigued by the elderly woman who spoke in riddles. As the lightweight silk dress swished against her legs, reality hit her like an anvil dropping on the coyote's head in those old cartoons she watched as a child. Would she ever see those cartoons again? Would she see Emilie, Samuel, or her parents?

Cait followed the odd woman through the Pictish hillfort on her way to marry a man that she already knew would die in a little over three months if the recorded date of the Battle of Nechtan was accurate. And if her dreams were some omen or premonition, she would be the woman laying him to rest in that cave.

Panic stopped Caitriona in her tracks and heaving breaths escaped her lungs as she clutched her twisting stomach. Bile burned her throat, and she looked up at the stars, so bright—so far away, just like she was. This was no dream. This was no trick of the mind. She was in the year 685, and people long dead now stood all around her, staring at the strange woman about to become their queen.

"My lady. Come," Anya whispered gently, continuing her slow walk through the village as Cait followed, every step weighed down by fear and anxiety. When the villagers slowly fell in line behind her, her nervousness piqued. All eyes were on her, and there wasn't a single familiar face to be seen because nobody she knew even existed yet. That thought didn't help her rising panic.

When they turned a corner, a large fire burned, and through the flames and smoke, Cait saw the chapel and an early medieval priest with shorn hair stood outside its entrance. He wore long, earth-colored robes tied with a simple rope and a severe expression that did nothing to calm her nerves.

Brodyn stood beside the priest, but billowing smoke obscured Caitriona's vision and burned her eyes, ruining her ability to observe him properly. Never had she felt more lost or scared in her entire life. All she could do was follow his commands for now. She would say her vows and become his wife if it meant saving lives, but if she disappeared afterward, would it change history? Would fleeing affect the timeline or result in ruined lives?

When she walked past the fire and saw Brodyn, her heart leaped in her chest. Wearing a white tunic and clean beige trousers, Brodyn wore his dark blond hair down with an intricately carved silver circlet upon his head. His short beard was well-combed, and with his fierce scowl he looked like a dark, brooding demon. Yet, his bright, angelic-blue eyes belied a human side to the man. Caitriona couldn't deny an insane attraction that made this ridiculous situation feel slightly less awful. Reminding herself that he thought her to be a "dirty hag," Cait tamped down her rising interest in the man, knowing he didn't feel the same way about her, the woman he was about to marry.

She stopped before him and looked up to his height, trying not to let her shaky nerves show. The priest began to speak, and she was surprised that many of his words were similar to modern Christian wedding ceremonies. The Picts were once pagan, yet apparently, they stuck closely to their new religion. He read several prayers in Latin before having them repeat vows. Brodyn stared at her mouth the entire time as if daring her to refuse, but Caitriona did her best to remain unaffected by his intense gaze. When the time came to exchange rings, Caitriona looked at Brodyn, surprised when he opened his palm and revealed two matching silver rings with Celtic knot designs engraved into the metal. When Brodyn slid the smaller ring onto her finger without looking her in the eyes, her heart constricted for a reason she couldn't understand. She was nothing more to him than an obligation.

The momentous reality of marrying the most famous Pictish King in history while she was stuck in his time finally caught up with Caitriona. She tamped down the rising panic—and vomit— before making a mess of King Brodyn and embarrassing herself.

Her ears rang, and her head spun as Brodyn placed a plaid around her neck and secured it with a golden brooch. "Upon yer shoulders, I lay the colors of my people, pronouncing ye part of our tribe. Upon yer breast, I clasp a golden brooch that belonged to my mother as yer bride price, pronouncing ye my wife." Next, Brodyn laid a silver circlet upon her head that matched his own. "Upon yer head, I place the silver circlet of Fortriu, pronouncing ye the Queen of the Picts."

Before she knew it, his lips descended onto hers, and she gasped, unprepared for the moment. Kissing the bride was a tradition dating back to Roman times, but she never suspected the Picts followed suit. The kiss was quick and chaste yet stole her breath for several seconds afterward as Brodyn took her hand and faced his people.

"Behold, my new wife and yer queen!" Brodyn shouted to his people, who cheered yet sent her curious looks, nevertheless. She could not blame them. They knew nothing about her, nor she them. Her head swam as suddenly she became a wife and a queen within hours of tumbling through time. "Ye will respect her as ye do me. Her word is mine. Ye will do as she bids, for she symbolizes peace between us and those we once called our enemy!"

The crowd cheered again, and Brodyn led her away from the chapel while curious onlookers whispered about their mysterious new queen. She was more mysterious than any of them could possibly know.

It felt as if she was being dragged along, because her feet nearly refused to move. His indifference was expected, yet it still stung despite her efforts to feel otherwise. He had no connection with her and showed no affection. Why would he? She was nothing more than a political pawn. Suddenly, she understood how women had felt for thousands of years, being forced to marry to save lives while strange men dragged them to their homes to consummate marriages.

Oh, Lord.

Caitriona stumbled and nearly fell to the ground, but Brodyn stopped just in time to catch her by the shoulders, giving her a disapproving look. She scowled back, not approving of his coarse nature, either. He may not know her or even like her, but he treated her like a new addition to his herd and nothing more than a political acquisition. She reminded herself it didn't matter. She wasn't supposed to be here, and any wrong move could upset the timeline. Her only concern had to be getting out of here as soon as possible.

There was a reason she always dreamed of this man and his death; of that, she was certain. However, the connection was lost on her, and certainly, it wasn't because she was meant to fall back in time and marry the man. And the historic love he had for his wife certainly wasn't something occurring between them, based on the way he tossed her about like a used rag. Was he dragging her to his home, expecting her silently to concede to consummate this whirlwind marriage? Brodyn believed that Caitriona was well-prepared for this union, traveling across Scotland for the event, even if reluctantly. He had no way of knowing or even understanding only hours ago, she was a single, modern career woman with a small apartment and an ex-fiancé.

Her heart rate kicked up a notch as he continued to silently escort her across the village with everyone in their wake.

"Where are we going?" she managed to ask through her labored breathing.

"The longhouse. We will feast and celebrate our union with Dal Riata. The people wish to see their new queen."

So, now she was not just cattle; she was a freak on display for all to gawk at—a Pictish queen who would never be named in the history books. Still, Cait took a breath and nodded, relief lightening her heart. They weren't headed straight to his bed.

Truthfully, she wasn't against a night of sex with a handsome king. It would make for a fun memory once she succeeded in returning home. That couldn't possibly harm anything. Still, she wasn't the sort of woman to jump in the sack without at least some conversation and good food. One-night stands weren't her thing, but maybe this would be her first. She was no prude, and short flings were almost all she experienced these days, even if this was entirely different. Brodyn was her husband now, and consummation was required to make the marriage legal.

Caitriona would need a lot of ale or mead in her blood because she'd have no time to emotionally prepare herself for the night ahead.

Awe immediately washed over Cait when she entered the longhouse which was just as she had always imagined. Tall, wooden beams, both vertical and horizontal, supported the thatched roof, and the smell of roasted meat wafted in the warm, smoky air as candles flickered from the wooden tabletops. Brodyn escorted her over to a table and row of chairs at the far end of the room, and Cait silently let him pull out her seat. At least he was a gentleman, even if he barely looked at her.

A crowd of chattering people wearing drab-colored tunics came pouring into the longhouse, ready for food, drink, and celebration. It struck Caitriona just how similar these ancient people were to modern people in a tavern or bar. The clothing and lighting differed, but the people laughed, embraced, and mingled in much the same way.

Meanwhile, the tension in her body made her stiff as a board, unyielding and lifeless as she stared ahead, too nervous to make eye contact with her intimidating husband. He didn't seem to care for her attention either, as he looked straight ahead with the stony features of a man doing his business and nothing more. That's all she was in the end, and truth be told, all he would have been to her had she been the correct queen. She reminded herself of that and of the fact that she could sneak away at night and head back to the cave.

A tankard of frothy ale slammed down onto the table before Cait, making her yelp and jump as she snapped out of her intense thoughts. "'Tis a tradition in Fortriu for the husband and wife to share their meal and beverage on the wedding night. It shows unity and sacrifice... though, Lord kens, I have sacrificed enough marrying ye."

"If you didn't wish to marry me, I would gladly have returned from where I came," she snapped, already tired of being made to feel like a burden to the man quite literally holding her against her will.

"'Tis why I married ye immediately, so ye wouldnae have a chance to run. Drink." Brodyn pushed the tankard closer to her, making some ale spill out of the tankard and run down the table, where it leaked into a wooden crack and soaked her silk dress.

Cait looked down and stared at the tankard, gritting her teeth, and clenching her fist beneath the table. "I don't want to."

"I dinnae care what ye want. Ye vowed to obey me. Drink."

Closing her eyes and taking a fortifying breath, Cait cursed the man sitting before her. Already, he'd caused her immeasurable grief in her nightmares and untold pleasures in many of her better dreams. But now, he sat beside her in physical form, plaguing her waking existence. Opening her eyes, she saw people watching with curiosity.

One night. That's how long she would be here. One. Night. Sucking up her pride and determining to do as he bid, Caitriona forced a smile and wrapped both hands around the large tankard, bringing it to her lips. The ale was bitter and pungent, the unexpected alcohol content burning her throat. A few sips of that would have her under the damned table.

Brodyn took the tankard and did the same, wasting no time downing the remainder as the room cheered for their king and queen. A serving woman came to refill their tankard, and Caitriona wondered how much more she would be expected to drink. Perhaps it was better than a sober reality at this point. Her husband disliked her, and she wasn't his biggest fan, either.

When the food arrived at the table, Caitriona's eyes widened. An array of meats garnished with leeks, garlic, and onions was accompanied by blocks of cheese, fresh bread, and even an assortment of seasonal vegetables. Everything smelled delicious, and her mouth watered at the same time that her stomach growled.

"Ye havenae eaten in a long while?"

Cait shook her head and watched as Brodyn cut large pieces of meat off the platter and plopped them onto another before doing the same with some bread and cheese. "I have many questions for ye, like where yer travel guide disappeared and why ye were a sennight late. But for now, we eat. My people are glad to have ye, for it means we have made peace with our neighbors."

Caitriona had no answers to his questions, so instead, she nodded and followed his lead, using her fingers to pick up the pieces of food he cut up with his knife. The night went on as she sipped the ale and ate the food until her stomach expanded and her vision blurred. Lutes played, and people danced, swinging one another about the room. It was a time of celebration for these people, and though Caitriona felt lost and scared, she was glad to give these people some comfort, even as she knew it was a false sense of security. Whoever was sent to Brodyn to secure the alliance had never arrived, which meant soon enough, Domnall would discover that Brodyn had married the wrong woman. Her presence may very well start a battle that never should have happened. That thought only solidified her desire to flee as soon as possible.

"My queen, ye must dance with us!" A tall, slim woman said as she put out a hand, reaching across the table. Her blue eyes sparkled, and her flaxen hair glittered like spun gold in the flickering candlelight. Her beauty was not only striking; it was intimidating. She wore a finely made green silk tunic and a gold necklace that spoke of wealth and power. Cait didn't know who she was, but she had to be royal to have the authority to approach a queen so brazenly. Cait certainly wouldn't stand on ceremony, for she was no queen in her own right, but this woman wouldn't know such things.

Looking at Brodyn for guidance, she was surprised when he smiled and nodded his approval. Was this woman his mistress? A sharp stab struck her gut, a feeling she didn't like at all. Why should she care if Brodyn had a woman on the side? Cait had no plans to be around for it to matter. Still, his reaction to Cait was disappointment and contempt while this woman got smiles and approval.

"Caitriona, this is my sister, Murielle. Yer new sister."

"Oh…" Was that relief washing over her like a cool wind caressing her flushed skin? "It's nice to make your acquaintance," Cait said as she stood and let Murielle guide her onto the floor. "I'm afraid I'm not much of a dancer." She was pretty certain the Macarena wouldn't get her very far on this dance floor.

"Just follow my lead. What has that cousin of ours been teaching his people all this time if ye cannae even dance?" Murielle said with a lightness in her voice, followed by her charming smile. "I suppose he taught ye to be more a fighter than a dancer. He is always so wary of skirmishes that he never enjoys life, or so I have been told. I have yet to meet the man."

Murielle guided Cait, helping her find a place in the large circle as hands clapped and people stepped back twice, then forward once before clasping hands and moving to the left. The crowd cheered, and Cait found that she was smiling, enjoying herself for the first time all day. She was actually dancing with ancient Pictish people.

As the group spun circles, so did Cait's head from all the ale. When her gaze caught Brodyn's from across the room, he appeared intense as usual but somehow less severe. He and Murielle must have a genuine bond, and how glad Cait was to know that it wasn't the sort of bond she first suspected. As she thought about the night to come, a tingle ran across her flesh, and laughter came easier as she learned the steps to the dance just in time to finish with a twirl before the music ended. Caitriona felt loose and slightly more comfortable than before, thanks to Murielle. Maybe she could enjoy the consummation tonight more than she previously thought.

"Ye are a much better dancer than ye let on, Sister." Murielle looped her arm with Cait's and guided her back to the table with a wry smile.

"Only because I had the right partner," Caitriona said with a chuckle. Murielle laughed and hugged Cait as they approached

Brodyn. "I believe we will get on quite well. Ye have a good woman here, Brodyn. Perhaps 'tis time ye officially made her yer wife." She winked and walked backward toward the crowd, clapping her hands to get everyone's attention.

"I do believe 'tis time for the bedding ceremony to commence!" she hollered loud enough for her words to echo and bounce off the longhouse walls.

Cait's heart slid down to her toes, and the ale soured in her belly. Surely, the Picts didn't practice the same bedding ceremony as the English during the medieval period? This was certainly a detail lost to time, and Caitriona was not anxious to experience it firsthand.

She felt the blood leave her face and rush to her wildly thumping heart. Brodyn's face remained stonelike as he stood up from his chair and came around the table to take her hand. The hall rumbled when feet stomped and hands clapped as the entire village followed them out of the warm longhouse and into the icy night. Rain pelted the earth, leaving puddles at her feet and soaking through her slippers. Her silk dress clung to her skin as she traversed the village with Brodyn silently guiding her, offering no words of comfort to his new wife. She supposed this was a traditional part of life for any royal or noble bride who suffered an arranged marriage, but for Cait, this was pure terror. Being put on display before strangers as every inch of her body was inspected was not on her bucket list.

It was important to make certain one's new wife was free of pox and deformities before consummating the marriage. It wouldn't do to bring a defective woman into the royal house, for she would certainly only bear defective children; at least, that was the reasoning behind this ceremony. Marriages would be annulled and never consummated if a bride was found to be lacking.

Cait wasn't particularly concerned about making the cut. She wasn't at all considered perfect in the modern world. Perhaps her breasts could be a bit higher and rounder, or her hips slightly smaller. This wasn't what Brodyn would be looking for when he unclothed her before his fellow nobles. He would find no deformities on Caitriona. Allowing a man who already considered her a hag to undress her while people watched was new territory. She preferred to keep her clothes on in public.

Arriving at his home, Brodyn silently led Cait inside, where a hearth fire blazed, its dancing flames casting shadows about the simple room. A long wooden table took up most of the space to the left, but her gaze scanned to a set of stone stairs leading up into the darkness. Taking her by the arm, Brodyn guided her to the top step. Slowly, she ascended to the next floor, aware of the small crowd following several paces behind Brodyn. Her knees grew weaker with every step while Brodyn's arm gripped her waist from behind to offer stability.

A narrow corridor with three doors loomed in each direction, and Brodyn guided her to the left, stopping just as they reached the last door. Turning to address the crowd of people, Brodyn stepped in front of Cait and blocked her from their view.

"I can handle this from here," he commanded. The crowd groaned and booed as Brodyn opened the door and gently pushed her forward. More heat and light washed over her as candles flickered around the room.

"Ye dinnae believe I can inspect my wife without yer guidance, aye?" Brodyn responded with the door half shut behind them. "Go inspect yer own wives, ye auld fools!"

Men laughed, and women cackled, but Cait felt like a deer in headlights as her husband slammed the door on the onlookers, something akin to relief washing over her.

That relief quickly turned to trepidation when the large, brooding man towering above her narrowed his beaming blue eyes on her, scanning her body. A shiver ran through her, and Cait became hyperaware that the wet silk dress clung to her like a second skin, her puckered nipples pressing against the thin fabric. She stared back in silence, waiting for him to say something.

"I require ye to remove yer clothing."

Caitriona lowered her brows. That was the least romantic thing she had ever heard. Gently removing the brooch he'd given her, Caitriona placed it on a table beside the bed before removing the tartan cloak around her neck. Reaching around to her back, Cait fumbled with the laces, tugging without progress. "The ties are wet," she whispered.

Brodyn cleared his throat and gently turned her, working at the laces. After a few tugs, the ties loosened, and his fingers turned to her belt next. She shivered when it fell near her feet. His warm hands glided over her skin as he pushed the silk tunic off her shoulders and down her arms. Cait gasped when the fabric dragged over her sensitive nipples before baring them, but she stood still and kept her back to Brodyn. When the material rested on her hips, Brodyn yanked the clinging silk down her legs, allowing it to join her belt on the floor. She stood bared, her heartbeat clogging her throat and crippling her breathing. Several uncomfortable seconds passed as she heard shuffling, and she wondered what Brodyn thought as she stood with her back to him.

"Turn around," he said. Swallowing hard, Cait did as he commanded, turning to face the man she had read about in history books, dreamed of for years, and married hours ago. Her eyes met with his bared chest and his bull tattoo, just as they had earlier that evening by the cave. Her eyes widened as they trailed down his body. Muscle sculpted his abdomen, leading to a tapered waist. When the blood finally rushed to her brain, and she could think again, the reality that he stood naked before her knocked the remaining breath from her lungs. His cock stood proudly at half-mast between his powerful thighs, but she dared not stare and make a fool of herself. Forcing her eyes to meet his, she realized Brodyn's were busy scanning every detail of her body, and she flushed under his scrutiny.

Brodyn's gaze rested on her breasts before he looked into her hazel eyes. "I see no defects upon ye," he said flatly.

He stared at her, awaiting a response, but Caitriona only

stared back, too frazzled to speak. She assumed he would next command her to move to the bed, a command that would not go well in a modern world, yet this was ancient Scotland, and he was her husband. For tonight, Cait steeled herself for what lay ahead, prepared to do as he bid, shamelessly acknowledging that she relished the chance to share a bed with King Brodyn. He was larger, in every way, than Taylor ever was, and his semi-erect manhood proved he at least liked what he saw even if he appeared stoic.

"Have ye found a defect upon me?" he prompted.

Cait shook her head. "No, no defect."

"Verra well. Good night, Wife. I will send a woman to bring ye a fresh, dry tunic and carry away yer sodden one."

Brodyn scooped up his clothing and turned away, prepared to leave the room fully unclothed.

"That's it?" she asked, watching him walk away, admiring the solid roundness of his backside. He was a sight to behold.

"For now, aye."

Brodyn left the room, and Cait stood naked and shivering, feeling both rejected and used. Never had a man stared at her bared body and left the room—and this man was her husband, duty-bound to consummate the marriage. Yet, he left.

Soon, a knock at her door had her scrambling to the bed, snatching up a blanket to wrap around herself. "Enter," she called, and a young woman with black hair walked in carrying a small pile of folded fabric.

"King Brodyn bade me leave ye some clean clothing, my queen." The woman said, placing the clothing on the crude wooden table beside the bed. Before she left the room, the woman turned and gave Cait a reassuring smile. "He is verra gentle lover. Be not afeared of him."

"Thank you," Caitriona belatedly responded just as the servant shut the door, blinking in shock. So, her husband slept with his servants? How many other women had he slept with in this small village, and how many of them lived under this roof?

Perhaps he planned on sleeping with this bonnie young lass tonight, which is why he left Caitriona alone.

Friendless and married to a stranger who thought of her as nothing more than a peace offering, not worthy of his touch, she shivered. He didn't want her here anymore than she wanted to be here. The room still spun as ale flowed through her blood, however her senses were keen enough to remain logical. It was time to find her way home.

Rain pelted the thatched roof, and she had nothing besides the pile of clothes on the bed before her, but she would run naked back to the cave if it meant getting away from this humiliation and back to her own time. Her fear of being stuck warred with her desire to stay and learn more. How many people found themselves thrust into the time period they studied all their lives? Still, her family and friends would be looking for her, worried sick.

With that motivation, Caitriona fumbled with the tunics, putting two layers on before slipping into the provided leather slippers, leaving the cloak and brooch behind. Those belonged to Brodyn, and she would leave them here for his next wife.

Creeping into the corridor, Cait traversed the stairs, running her fingertips along the rough walls to guide herself through the darkness, pausing when a flickering candle moved several yards away. A servant moved through the main room, and Cait held her breath, waiting for her to walk away. Once the candle's light disappeared from her view, Caitriona carefully tiptoed in that direction, seeing the hearth fire still ablaze around the corner, offering a warmth she would desperately miss once she left the house.

Reaching the door, Caitriona looked both ways before pushing it open to face the onslaught of slanting rain. Wet and cold were better than lost and alone, she reminded herself as she took a breath and carefully closed the door behind her. Laughter drifted from the longhouse, but rain had snuffed out the fires around the village, making her escape easy enough. Staying in the shadows, Caitriona walked behind the houses and far from the longhouse.

As she walked, she realized that getting past the guards would be nearly impossible. There was no way in or out of the hillfort without passing them. She needed a plan.

The freezing wind howled, nearly knocked her off her feet. A violent chill swept up her spine as she scrambled to think of a way out. The cave was a mile north, and already her limbs had grown numb from the icy rain. These leather slippers were nothing like her rubber rain boots that offered protection from puddles. Even if she found a way to slip past the guards, how would she manage to make it to the cave in this weather? She had no food, light, or dry clothing. Her heart sank as she understood her predicament. She was stuck here for the night. There was no escaping this place, not with this weather, or with guards in her way. She would have to bide her time, create a plan to get through the gates, and pack food and supplies for the journey. Tonight, she must endure this place.

Her parents had never been the most loving, doting sort, but the thought of them receiving news of her disappearance churned her stomach. They would be frantic, no doubt, spending more money on a search for her than they spent on the numerous activities forced upon her all her life. They loved her, she knew, just in their own way. And Emilie and Samuel would be worried sick by now. Undoubtedly, the excavation was paused while the crew searched for her as news teams fought over the breaking news.

"Ye shouldnae be out here."

Gasping, Cait turned to see Anya frowning at her as she put out a hand. "Ye'll catch yer death. That's all we need is for ye to die before ye consummate this marriage."

"I... I told you. I don't belong here! I need to go home!" she protested over the rushing downpour of rain.

"Ye arenae going anywhere tonight, ye dolt! Get inside before the king realizes ye fled and flogs yer backside."

"He wouldn't!"

"Och, aye, he would! Ye are his property, dinnae ye forget it."

"He doesn't want me! Nor I, him!"

"Rubbish! Now, hie yer arse back inside. Queen or no, I am to keep ye safe. Do ye want me flogged, as well?"

Sighing, Cait swallowed and shook her head, reluctantly following Anya indoors. They were both soaked to the bone, and Anya was right: there was traveling in this storm. Besides, if Anya was punished for Cait's behavior, that would be on her hands and conscience. Though, she prayed her husband wasn't so cruel that he would actually flog a woman who appeared to be pushing ninety.

When they entered the house, Anya prodded Caitriona back to her room with a finger buried into her lower back as if she was herding cattle.

"Ye are fortunate the king is out on business. He would be none too pleased to find ye in this condition or missing altogether when he arrived. Come. Take those clothes off and stand near this fire."

Nodding, Caitriona gladly removed the sodden clothing, her limbs stiff and frozen. "I think Brodyn would be glad to find me missing," she murmured through clattering teeth.

"Ye ken nothing about that man, lass. He wouldnae be glad at all. He would be outright enraged. Ye are his wife, his responsibility."

"His property," Cait reiterated.

"Aye. But, he is a fair man, child. He will be a fair husband."

"He left me here, naked. He just walked away."

Anya clicked her tongue at that news, poking at the fire with a metal rod. "He isnae too good with words. A man of his importance has a line of people awaiting him. A messenger showed up during the feast, requesting his ear. A matter of great importance, the man said. King Brodyn is returning to ye tonight; make no mistake. He willnae be please to return to a drowned rat."

"He already regards me as such," Caitriona scoffed. "Anya... I'm lost. I cannot tell you in a way you will understand. I do not belong here, and I cannot stay." She felt like she was repeating herself, and still, nobody seemed to listen.

Turning from the fire, Anya raised a brow and crossed her arms, amusement gleaming in her eye. "Ye have traveled far to be here. Yer people differ from ours, and we understand this. King Brodyn and I will help ye adjust, but ye cannae let the people see this hesitation. Ye are their queen now, a symbol of a long-sought-after peace. Too much is at stake. Ye cannae leave."

Suddenly thousands of lives were at stake, and it all depended on Cait staying in a time 1,400 years before her own. Her only hope was that the real bride sent from Dal Riata showed up, and Caitriona could go home.

CHAPTER FIVE

P AIN PULSED THROUGH his temples, and Brodyn scowled as he looked at Domnall's messenger. He had fought battles where the metal clanging across the field caused less pain to his head than this news did.

"Ye arrived an hour too late," Brodyn scowled. "I have married the woman I believed to be sent by my cousin." Brodyn stared, refusing to let his headache slow him down.

Domnall's messenger frowned and shook his head. "King Domnall is desperate for peace. The bride he sent ye has fled. Dal Riata is still recovering from our last defeat. With threats coming from Northumbria, our tribes must come together, or we shall all perish."

"So, the woman I married tonight is not the woman Domnall sent? Is this what ye are telling me?"

"I cannae be certain unless I identify her. Either she is here or dead."

Another pulse shot through his temples, and Brodyn relented, pressing his fingers into the fleshy sides of his head to stifle the pain. He had no patience or time for more complications. This alliance with Domnall was already overdue. Sending another woman would take too long.

Worse, Caitriona had been honest, he realized. She was not who he believed her to be, and he had forced her to marry him, thinking she was stubborn and insolent.

"I have no time to wait," Brodyn groused. "The delay in this message has cost us enough time!"

"I apologize, King Brodyn, but we had to search for the lass and return to Dal Riata without her then inform King Domnall of the situation," the messenger puffed with anxiety.

Brodyn popped his knuckles as he listened, understanding the situation yet too irritated to immediately speak. Finally, he said, "The woman I married wandering the shores a mile from here. She was disoriented and alone but insisted she was not the right woman."

"May I see the woman? I can identify her."

"Follow me," Brodyn grunted as he rose to his feet from the stiff, wooden chair within a private chamber just off the side of the longhouse.

Already his wife gave him a headache and pushed his patience. The vision of her fully unclothed before him seared his mind like an image carved in stone, every detail forever engraved in his lusty thoughts. Not only did she have no flaws, but she was also by far, the most beautiful woman he had ever seen, even with her clothes on. Aye, he told her she was uncomely when they first met, trying to keep his distance by pushing her away. He needed the alliance to save his people. War was inevitable and becoming attached to his bride was not a distraction he could allow. When war came, he needed his entire mind focused on battle, not on her safety.

If she proved not to be the bride sent by Domnall, his only options were to send her away and ask for a new bride from Dal Riata or keep her and accept peace with Domnall despite the exchange of blood. He was intent on the latter, and it had nothing to do with the way his blood boiled or his cock stirred when he'd looked upon the lass. Time was a luxury his people didn't have. Dal Riata was a long journey southwest from Brodyn's lands, and he needed unity now.

Brodyn guided the messenger through the village and up the hill. "We will see if my bride is the one sent by Domnall. Either way, ye will have a warm meal and bed for the night before returning home."

"I thank ye for yer hospitality, King Brodyn," the man said as he clutched his cloak closer to his body, clearly unaccustomed to the biting chill of a Highland night. Wind and cold mildly affected Brodyn, for he was merely a flesh and blood man, but his skin was as tough as the land he called home, capable of surviving in any condition. A man had to be if he were to survive at these altitudes at the northernmost part of the large island. "I daresay a lesser man would send me away after the news I have delivered."

"None of this is yer doing. Come." Opening his door, Brodyn knocked his muddy boots against the floor before walking toward the hearth. "Anya!" he called to his serving woman as he walked over to a table and grabbed a jug of ale.

"Aye, my king?" The auld woman looked harried and startled, and Brodyn frowned, wondering what his new wife had done to shake up the hardest-headed women he had ever known.

"Bring Caitriona to me. I wish to speak with her." With a nod, Anya shuffled toward the stairs and began her ascent. He often wondered if traversing the stairs pained Anya, but she refused to slow down, and he knew better than to question her abilities after all the years spent with her. She was like a mother to him and one of the few people unafraid to speak her mind, which he respected.

"Some of our finest ale," Brodyn said as he handed a clay cup to the messenger. "'Tis what we drank to celebrate my marriage tonight."

"Thank ye, yer Majesty," the man said and bowed his head, full of dark curly hair with sparse strands of gray interwoven like fine threads of silver against the blackest silk. His coloring was unique for the area. Few men passed through these parts with dark hair, eyes, and naturally tanned skin. Brodyn wondered if the man was the son of a traveler from somewhere even more distant than Dal Riata.

Pouring himself a mug of ale, Brodyn guzzled it in one gulp, needing to cool his nerves and tame the debilitating ache in his brain. If his wife was the correct woman, she had lied about her identity to avoid marrying him. If she wasn't, he had stolen her away by force. Neither situation sat well with him, but he hoped she lied, for forcing himself on women was not in his nature, and he'd have to let her go… a thought that displeased him more than he cared to admit.

With her hands folded in front of her, Caitriona glided down the stairs with her head high and her hair finely braided; she wore a long, white night tunic with his wool tartan wrapped like an arisaid around her shoulders. Her bared feet and slim ankles conjured dangerous memories of what lay beneath those layers of cloth. Had he not received notice of the Dal Riata messenger awaiting, Brodyn would have consummated the marriage and enjoyed every moment of her smooth skin against his. Even now, he longed to remove her clothing and explore every inch of her tempting body.

You wished to see me?" Caitriona's question snapped him out of his thoughts. Aye, he wished to see her… all of her. Something about this woman was unlike anything he had ever experienced, and he was drawn to her despite his wish to dislike her.

"Aye." Brodyn cleared his throat and stepped closer to his wife, noticing that her hair was damp, as was her tunic beneath the arisaid. He gave her a questioning look that made her flush, and he wondered if his wife had already tried to run away. Something would need to be done with the lass. Fire ran through her stubborn veins, and the flames licked at him, burning him with a need that only intensified with his every breath. But the fire needed to be snuffed out if he was to keep her and his people safe. "Caitriona, I want to introduce ye to the messenger who arrived tonight."

Her eyes, an odd combination of green flecked with gold, widened as she looked from him to the messenger. Staggering back, then plunging forward, Caitriona gasped and tackled the messenger, causing him to nearly fall over before righting himself. "Samuel?" she cried, wrapping her arms around the tall, thin man. A sob tore from his wife, and Brodyn frowned, watching as she clutched to this man as if he was her only anchor in a storm of emotions. "Why? How? I'm… where am I?"

Samuel, the messenger, did not appear shocked by her sudden outburst. Instead, he stroked her head as a father would and made hushing sounds to soothe her. "You are safe here. It's all right." The man's voice suddenly changed, matching Caitriona's odd foreign tone.

"I take it my wife is, indeed, the woman ye meant for me to marry?"

"No!" she cried.

"Aye," the man said, looking at her with sorrow in his brown eyes. He couldn't understand any of this, and between his pounding head and frayed patience, Brodyn clenched his fists to prevent himself from yelling out.

"That is all I needed to know. Come with me, Caitriona." Taking her by the arm, Brodyn tried to drag her away from this man she called Samuel, but she shouted and dug her heels into the floor, refusing to move.

"No! Samuel! Take me home!"

"I cannot, Cait. This is where you must remain." Turning away from Caitriona, Samuel addressed Brodyn. "As you can see, she is very shaken by what's happened on her journey."

"Samuel?" Caitriona stepped forward, but Samuel only stepped away, leaving her to drop her arms at her side in defeat. "Why are you doing this?" she whispered.

"King Brodyn, may I speak with her in private for a moment?"

Brodyn hesitated, wondering why being here with him and doing her duty seemed to pain his wife so greatly. He wanted to protest, but instead, he bit back his pride and nodded.

Putting out a hand to Caitriona, Samuel beckoned her forward, and they whispered near the hearth for a moment, forehead-to-forehead while she grappled at the messenger's sleeve, imploring him to take her away. Their bond was unmistakable, and Brodyn wondered if there was more to their relationship than a messenger bringing a bride to another tribe. Was Caitriona in love with him? Aye, he was mayhap a decade older than her, but Samuel was a fair-faced man with dark features and kind eyes. He wasn't muscular like Brodyn, and it was obvious that he lived a humble existence. Still, there was a connection between his new wife and this man that set Brodyn on edge.

Enough. Pride be damned. He wouldn't allow his wife to whisper words of love to another man in his own home. Storming over, Brodyn grabbed her arm and pulled her to him, pressing her against his side. "That is more than enough private words. Ye have identified her. Please go to the longhouse and tell them I offered ye our best ale, food, and sleeping arrangements. I expect ye to be gone with the rise of the sun. Tell Domnall our alliance is sealed. If battle comes, I will be on the same side of the field as he."

Dragging Caitriona away, Brodyn sucked in a breath when she began to sob. His head pounded as if a thousand drummers wailed on his brain. Cursing under his breath, Brodyn escorted her back up the stairs and into her new chamber. "Did ye run away tonight, lass?" he calmly asked when she walked toward the bed and plopped down, burying her face into the straw mattress.

"What does it matter?" she cried. "I am here now. I cannot leave."

"Ye are my wife, aye. Ye cannae leave. Are ye in love with him?"

Lifting her head, Caitriona looked up at him with her red-rimmed golden eyes. "W-what?" she sniffled, wiping tears from her cheeks. "Of course, not. He is a dear friend of mine. I didn't expect to see him here. Nothing makes sense!"

"I would ask what ye spoke about, except I understand it was private. Ye need to understand that I am yer husband now, and whispering private words to other men in my home won't be a habit, aye?' He spoke softly, not wanting to distress her further, even if nothing but angst and confusion had befallen him since crossing paths with this woman. She pushed his patience to the very edge, yet he found the strength to remain calm for her sake.

She nodded. "I doubt I will ever see him again."

"Messengers from Dal Riata come regularly. Ye will see him again. I only hope that ye are honest with me and never make a cuckold of me."

"I… I would never," she gasped.

"Aye. Good. And I will be faithful, as well. This marriage is an arrangement. Nothing more. I willnae share a bed with ye until ye are amenable to it, and I willnae share another woman's bed. I dinnae expect love, Caitriona, though I do expect honesty and loyalty."

"Do you love her?" Caitriona croaked, wiping away tears.

Brodyn dropped his brow and stared at her with confusion. "Who?"

"The young servant with dark, long hair."

"Did she say something to ye tonight?" Brodyn asked with an edge. The last thing he needed was all the women he'd slept with in the past to share stories with his new wife.

"She said enough," Caitriona replied. "I know you will have bedded women in the village. I just need to know if any of them will be angry at me for marrying you. If I'm stuck here, I do not wish to be made miserable by all of your concubines."

Did he sense jealousy in his new wife? "I'm glad to see ye plan to stay. I wish it didnae take another man to convince my wife not to leave me." Crossing his arms, Brodyn narrowed his eyes, wishing he knew what Samuel whispered in his wife's ear. Was he jealous now? What was happening to him, acting like a young lad who couldn't manage his emotions?

"You didn't answer my question."

Perhaps he liked this jealous side of his wife. However, he didn't want her to believe he cared for another woman. "I dinnae love any woman. It only happened once when I was a younger lad. I havenae concubines, nor shall I ever."

Swallowing, she nodded yet frowned, sniffling again, and pursing her quivering lips. He remembered the feel of those lips, even if the kiss was brief. They were soft, and her breath was sweet. Her teeth were straight and unstained, unlike those of any other woman he knew. Her skin was darkened in some areas as if she worked in the sun while wearing little clothing, which confused him more than her odd accent. Everything about Caitriona confused yet intrigued him. She was a mystery he hoped to solve. But not tonight.

"Get some rest. I will check on ye in the morn. I expect there willnae be any more attempts to escape? Ye willnae make it past the walls."

"I have nowhere to go," she croaked. "I don't belong here, yet according to Samuel, I don't belong there, either."

"I am sorry ye feel that way. I hope ye will eventually feel like a part of our tribe." Brodyn walked away and shut the door, half tempted to find that messenger and learn what he told his wife to distress her so much. However, he would resist. There was too much to be done, too much at stake, and too many lives at risk for him to consider letting her go.

SAMUEL WAS HERE. This wasn't a dream, and she wasn't insane. His words lingered, tormenting her as she stared at a wall and tried to make sense of what she could understand. Her soul was part of a significant time loop. Her past life from the year 685 was entangled with her life from 2023 and always would be. What did it all mean? How could she be stuck in some time loop that sent her here? Suddenly her life had become the things of science fiction and fantasy stories, and it didn't make any sense at all.

Your dreams were memories from this time, Cait, Samuel had whispered. This is why you've always been drawn to the history of King Brodyn. This is why you can read the symbols on the stones.

Losing control of her emotions, Caitriona crumbled into hysterics when she recounted the rest of Samuel's words. The bride sent by Domnall would never arrive because she always died on the journey. Her death was the catalyst that led to Caitriona being pulled back into time—because they were the same woman. Brodyn's bride from 685 and his wife from 2023 shared the same soul, reincarnated from life to life.

Curling into a ball on the bed, she gripped her stomach, trying not to vomit. She'd asked Samuel why he was here and why he'd never told her the truth, but Brodyn dragged her away before she got those answers. Would she ever get home? When Brodyn died during the battle, was she destined to stay here forever or return home afterward?

Her anguish from those dreams—not dreams, she reminded herself: memories—was so intense, so real. She'd loved the man in that cave. Was she destined to fall in love with this brutish man who tossed her around like a rag doll and called her a hag, then spend the rest of her life mourning his loss?

Jumping off the bed, Cait searched the room for a basin. She was going to be sick and had seconds to find something. A copper bowl gleamed beneath the bed, its shiny surface catching the candle's flickering light. Getting on her knees, Cait grabbed the bowl just in time to lose her dinner. Tears streamed down her face, and she cried harder than ever in her life as everything crashed down on her like an avalanche. She might never see her parents or Emilie again. Everyone she knew and loved believed she was missing, or worse, dead. She was dead. Her body and soul no longer remained in her time. There was nothing left of Caitriona Elizabeth Murray in her own time.

"Why?" she cried, feeling the unfinished splinters of wood digging into her knees as she shifted on the uneven floors. She needed Samuel. He was still here, and she had to find him. Right now.

Throwing her arisaid around her shoulders, Cait forgot everything else as she pushed through the rickety door and bolted down the stairs. No force on this earth was going to stop her from finding Samuel. Not the king, or Anya, or any servant. Barefoot and blinded by tears, Caitriona ran through the main door and into the cold night. Seeing flickering lights down the hill and across the village, she ran, feeling cold mud splash against her ankles and slip between her toes with every frantic step.

Something grabbed her arisaid and pulled her back, nearly launching her into the mud. She felt arms wrap around her waist, and she cried out just before a hand covered her mouth from behind.

"Cait. It's me. Stop screaming before they hear you."

Instantly, the familiar lilt of Samuel's modern Scottish accent soothed her nerves, though only enough to push herself to her full height and turn to look into his dark eyes. "Samuel… I need answers. I cannot stay here!"

Gently, he took her arm and guided her toward a dark, secluded area of land where no buildings stood. The biting chill froze her limbs, but nothing mattered until she had answers.

"I am so, so sorry, Cait," Samuel whispered. "I have been here and had this same conversation with you more times than I can remember, and it never gets easier to see you in such pain."

"What? How? I don't understand!" She gripped his tunic, imploring him to help her make sense of the chaos erupting within her mind.

He sighed and stepped even closer. "Do you believe in reincarnation?"

"Do I have a choice at this point?" she responded with exasperation.

"Some of us remember more than others from past lives. Some of us start new lives as different people, different genders, different races, sharing one soul through time and never knowing it. Others return as almost identical versions of themselves, and our souls find each other in every lifetime. You and I are soulbound in that manner. I cannot know why, but we are in some time loop that continues to pull us out of 2023 and bring us back here, to 685 AD."

"I killed my ancient self when I arrived here!" she cried, shaking from both cold and anguish. "By coming through the cave, I somehow destroyed her life, didn't I? The same soul cannot occupy two bodies at one time! I did this!"

Samuel shook his head and took her hands in his. "You did not kill her, Cait. Yes, the Caitriona from this time was sent as Brodyn's bride. However, she dies before you arrive in every time loop. Her marriage to King Brodyn is essential to the timeline. Without it, everything in Scottish history changes. You're brought here when she dies, so you can correct the timeline. She dies with or without your presence here, Cait. That is not on your hands. I've seen this unfold many times over."

"How does she… I… die? And if her family thinks I am her, where is she?" Cait dared to ask. Sadness sat in her belly like a stone when she tried to comprehend this form of grief, a loss she felt so profoundly for someone she never knew because they shared a soul and would never cross paths.

"She died of exhaustion in the highlands, trying to run away to avoid the marriage. That part is true. You cannot imagine how it pains me, in every lifetime, to bury her in the cave before I cross back to 2023, knowing you will disappear next."

Guilt washed over her, crazy as it was. This whole situation was crazy, and even though none of it was her fault, she couldn't help but feel like it was. "I'm sorry, Samuel. This must be so hard for you to bear."

"It's hard for us both, and we are in this together. I do what I must, and you stay here to marry Brodyn, create peace between the warring tribes, and carry on the line."

"The… the line?" Cait tried to jerk away, but Samuel gripped her hands harder and pulled her back.

"I have told you too much already. Just understand that this is your fate, where you need to be. Brodyn is a decent man and will be good to you. You are safe here, Caitriona. However, war is coming, as you well know. Your role isn't insignificant. If you do not stay here, the alliance between the Scots of Dal Riata and the Picts falls through, they don't have the strength to defeat Northumbria on the battlefield, and the tribes die out. Scotland will not exist as we know it. You're correcting history and saving millions of lives, Cait."

Cait swallowed the bile burning her throat. "I can't do this! I'm going to stay here just to watch Brodyn die and bury him!" Collapsing onto the wet earth, Cait covered her eyes and shook her head. "I remember the pain from my dream. Samuel, I fall in love with Brodyn and lose him, don't I? How is this fair?"

"It's not fair to you, Cait. But, you are the savior of millions of lives, even if nobody will ever know it. I cannot tell you about your love for Brodyn. Whether you love him or not, you will be his wife and secure peace between the remaining Celtic tribes of Scotland. The rest is still up to you. You do have free will."

Samuel sighed and squeezed her hands. "I pass between both times. I understand the burden placed on you because of this tangle in time. I'm always born remembering, always knowing I must travel back and forth, never having attachments, except with you."

Caitriona frowned and lowered her head. "I'm sorry, Sam."

"No need. You and I are always together in every life. Know how precious you are to me. I will be passing back and forth, doing what I do. Your family will know you are missing. Beyond that, I cannot say. It's never within my reach to know more or control the actions of those around us. There are always variables in the timeline. Everything will turn out all right as long as the major events occur."

Silence befell them both as rain pelted her brow and rolled down her cheeks, mixing with her tears. So many questions ran through her mind, and already she knew too much and understood too little. There was no time for self-pity. Maybe some other time, but not now. Samuel's existence was wrapped around hers, serving her soul and guiding her here so she could fill the void in the timeline.

She would pity Samuel if she didn't know him better. Samuel would reject any pity, any victimization of his character. He found great joy in teaching history at the university and forming archaeological digs, especially in Scotland. Now she understood why he'd insisted she come to this site, why he'd stayed calm and understanding during her dreams, accepted her obsession with the Picts, and even shared it.

"When will you be back?" she asked, knowing she ran out of time. If Brodyn found her outside again, he would tie her to the bedposts… and not in the way she imagined he would in her fantasies. Besides, he'd showed no interest in her at all. Perhaps that was for the best if he was destined to die. Keeping her emotions in line was the best thing she could do.

"I must return to our time now. Everyone's looking for you."

Caitriona felt a wave of grief wash over her like the sea pounding the shore in California, a place she would never see again. The faces she would never see again. Perhaps the unknown was the hardest part. If she knew she was stuck here, she would reconcile, eventually. But Samuel wouldn't answer if she could leave, and that unknown would eat at her for as long as it remained elusive.

"I will return when next I can. Be careful returning to your home. You cannot be seen in dark corners with another man. This time is not like our own. You are a married woman now and queen of the Picts. Do not forget the position you now hold. King Brodyn is a fair man, but he will not abide by disloyalty in a wife."

Nodding, Caitriona held back the urge to hug Samuel tightly, his warning fresh in her mind. "I will miss you. Please tell my family and Emilie how much I love… loved them." She was past tense now in their world, and that thought pained her like an arrow through the heart.

"I will, but they already know this. You wear your heart on your sleeve, Cait. Everyone knows how well you love. Until we meet again." He began to turn away but paused and said one

more thing. "Oh, one last thing. Anya is one of us, a traveler."
Then he nodded and stepped back a few paces into the darkness,
a specter fading into the night.

"Bye," she whispered weakly, feeling her entire life slipping
away. A new life started here, at this moment, in this time… and
she'd never felt so lost in all of her life.

CHAPTER SIX

HIS EYES FELT like they had been rinsed with sand. Between his headache and frustration with his new wife, Brodyn had slept very little, and his eyes burned. He assumed they looked like they burned, as well.

The messenger left their stronghold at dawn, as he promised, but the connection between Samuel and Caitriona sat like a stone in Brodyn's gut. He shouldn't care if his wife was attached to another man. This was an alliance, and nothing more. Yet, her rejection of him stung once he saw her show affection for another. The woman was capable of feeling, she just didn't feel anything for him. That's what he wanted, right? No complications. He had an army threatening him from the south and a legacy of Celtic peoples to defend in the north. Stuck between the old pagan traditions and the new Christian faith, Brodyn had to tread lightly.

His grandfather had accepted the Christian religion for his own reasons. It offered protection, advancement, and a written language even if the Picts, as they were called by those outside Fortriu, didn't comprehend the language just yet.

Brodyn wanted nothing to do with the new religion, but in a land surrounded by power-hungry men, the church offered strength in numbers and existing alliances throughout the world—in places Brodyn never even knew existed. The world was vast, and new opportunities for his people beckoned daily as travelers arrived with new goods to trade and advancements in medicine. Still, his people were an ancient one whose beliefs ran deeper than the roots of the tallest trees on their island. Older than the new religion were the pagan traditions of his people, who never wrote a word in their time, instead sharing their history through tales and ballads spanning back thousands of years.

To be king now meant navigating new waters, respecting the old religion, and melding it with the new religion, never insulting either, for both meant trouble. He allowed his people to practice their beliefs as they saw fit, never condemning one neighbor for praying to multiple gods while the other prayed to one almighty God. It was not his place, nor did he care. He had bigger issues to deal with, like growing threats on all sides from those who would see his kind wiped off the face of the earth and forgotten forever.

So, why was his stubborn, feckless, infuriating, beautiful wife consuming his every thought, keeping him awake as he wished to share a bed with her rather than sleeping on separate floors of his home? Why did jealousy punch him in the gut when he recalled his wife's forehead pressed against Samuel's while they whispered secrets with such familiarity? Something was off about his wife, but he couldn't place it. If she was so close to Samuel, why had she run away from him? Why had she run away from her duty if she was raised to understand the need for marriage alliances? It seemed this whole world was new to her, but why? Was she addled in the brain? It was something he wondered on during the night until he remembered the intelligence alight behind those golden-green eyes of hers.

There was much to be done, though he couldn't move forward before speaking with Caitriona. Standing from the bed, Brodyn stretched before slipping on his trousers and tying them loosely around his waist. This wasn't his usual chamber, and Anya's auld bones didn't do well climbing the winding, stone stairs to the top floor. He would need to get into his chamber, where Cait stayed, to find clean garments in his trunks.

Traversing the stairs two steps at a time, Brodyn knocked on the door leading to his chamber, never thinking he would have to ask permission to enter his own room. Already, his wife had him acting more like a child and less like a king. When nobody responded, Brodyn opened the door to find Caitriona sound asleep in the bed, curled up in a ball beneath the woolen sheets.

Taking a moment to observe his wife, Brodyn stood by the edge of the bed, memorizing her soft jawline and flawless skin, unlike anything he had ever seen. Her hair shone copper and gold in the rays of sun streaming in from the small rectangular slits high above her head on the stone walls.

Losing his restraint, Brodyn reached out to run his fingers through her silky strands of hair, unbound and flowing about her angelic face. Never had he believed in angels until this moment. Mayhap that's what his wife was. His people would call her fae, a creature with allure and mystical powers. He believed in neither fae nor angels, but he knew his wife was a rare beauty who held tightly to secrets he longed to know.

Small freckles dotted Caitriona's nose, and her lips parted slightly as her breathing came soft and rhythmic. Brodyn longed to stare at her uninterrupted, to read her thoughts and know her mind. Unfortunately, he could never know her mind if he did not try to know her first. Marriage for alliance or not, he wished to understand his wife.

"Caitriona." Brodyn touched her cheek with the back of his knuckles, wondering how skin could be so soft compared to his rough, callused hands.

Her long, dark lashes fluttered when her eyes opened, slowly first, then widening as she focused on him standing above her. With a startled screech, Caitriona sat up, grappling at the sheets to cover herself. Her bare shoulders and arms were all he saw, and again, her odd tan lines caught his attention. Two thin straps on each shoulder were lighter than the rest of her flesh, and he wondered what sort of garment she'd worn and why she would be out in the sun long enough to become tan, especially during the cold, winter months.

"I dinnae mean to startle ye," he said. "I wanted to see how ye fair after last night. Ye were verra unnerved." Looking down, he noticed her night tunic on the floor, its hem caked in dried mud. "Did ye run out again?"

When she didn't respond, only looked away from him and down at the dirty tunic, he bit back a curse and resisted raising his voice. "I dinnae ken why ye wish to be away from me, but I am afraid that is not possible. Ye are my wife now, Queen of the Picts. Ye understand the responsibility of this, aye?"

"I did not ask for any of this," she said between gritted teeth, raising her chin proudly and staring him in the eye. "I was forced to be here."

"As was I, lass," he responded dangerously. "If ye think I wanted a shrew for a wife, a woman who runs away rather than doing her duty for her people, a woman who keeps secrets and whispers in corners with other men, ye had better think again. I am a patient man, but ye wear on me. I dinnae have time to manage yer outbursts like ye are a wee bairn. I have duties, and I expect ye to do yers while I do mine. Ye can try to leave a hundred times, and ye will be dragged back to me a hundred times. Do ye understand?"

"Did you come here to check on me because you care or because you don't trust me?" Caitriona asked, defiance lacing her tone.

Brodyn narrowed his eyes at his maddening wife. "I came because I cared, but now I stay because I dinnae trust ye. Anya!" he shouted for the servant, who shuffled into the room slowly. The woman was older than the cursed mountains jutting out across the lands. She wished to remain in his service, and he saw no reason for that to change. She did her work well and never seemed to tire. She also wasn't afraid of him, which he appreciated. It wore on a man to have people cowering around him for no reason. Never had he raised his hand to a servant or a woman.

"It seems my wife made a mess of herself yet again. She requires a bath and clean clothing. Mayhap she has confused herself with the animals in the byre. If I find any more mud on her clothing or bared feet, I will set the cot up outside so she may sleep with the boars since she insists on living like one."

Caitriona glowered at him and hastened to hide her muddy feet beneath the blankets. Too late. Nothing passed his notice. Anya said nothing, only shuffled out of the room to do his bidding.

"You made your point. I did not try to escape last night. You dragged me away from Samuel before I was finished speaking with him, so I sought him out."

"Ye left yer husband's home to seek another man outside in the rain? Do ye wish to find yerself the talk of the village? I dinnae ken what yer relationship is with that man, but ye are making a fool of yerself over him. Act like the queen that ye are."

"I don't want to be a queen! And Samuel is my friend, more like a father than anything! He is the only family I have in this place!" she yelled, balling her fists into the sheets until her knuckles turned white.

Coming closer, Brodyn stood above her and lowered his face, so his nose almost touched hers. "I am yer husband… Murielle is yer sister. We are yer family. I willnae deny ye the family ye ken from Dal Riata. They are mine, and mine is yers, Caitriona. But I willnae have ye treat me like I am not yer husband. Mayhap I should remind ye that we are married and will create a family once I put a bairn in yer belly."

Her eyes widened, connecting with his before he saw her visibly swallow and trail her gaze across his bared chest. Her breathing quickened, and she went silent. Perhaps he had done neither of them a favor by leaving after the wedding night. Not only had she been far too distressed after her travels and seeing Samuel, but his headache had threatened to tear his skull in two. He'd decided they both required a night of rest before making this marriage valid, yet their tension only grew with the delayed consummation.

Servants dragged a wooden bathtub into the room, filling it

with hot water from a cauldron, perhaps from another room she'd yet seen. These items looked incredibly heavy, and Caitriona hoped both the tub and cauldron had already been above stairs. Being fussed over was not something Cait was accustomed to, nor did she enjoy watching others work for her.

One woman tossed dried flower petals into the water, and another poured some floral oil fragrance out of a vial, immediately perfuming the very air in the room. When Deidre, the servant he'd once bedded, entered the room carrying a bucket of water, Brodyn looked at Caitriona, noticing how her back stiffened and her eyes shifted away, avoiding contact with either of them.

When the servants finished, Anya came back into the room with a small linen cloth for scrubbing, a bar of soap, and a larger linen cloth to dry Caitriona. Brodyn nodded and took the supplies from Anya, signaling her to leave the room. With a slight shrug, the old woman left and shut the door behind her.

"W-what are you doing?"

"Making sure my wife gets a bath."

"I can bathe myself."

"Can ye? I dinnae ken if that's true. Ye seem to run away every time ye are left alone. If ye wish to be trusted, mayhap ye should quit behaving like a child."

"Excuse me for being upset! I left everyone and everything I knew, was forced to marry a stranger, and my new husband took one look at me naked last night and left! I know you think I'm a 'hag' and I don't meet your expectations, but you are the one who left me unattended last night without a word!"

"Ye think I left because I dinnae find ye appealing?" Brodyn asked, stepping closer to her.

"Why else would you leave me standing naked and alone in the room? I didn't think you wanted me any more than I wanted you, so I ran!"

Brodyn observed his wife for a silent moment. Her reddish-golden hair mussed about her face, her cheeks enflamed with frustration, her chest heaving as she struggled to breathe through her anger… Damn, if she didn't excite his loins simply by existing.

Gently, Brodyn reached and pushed her hair behind her ear before grazing her smooth, flushed cheek with the back of his fingers. "Ye dinnae want me?"

"No," she croaked, pulling away from his touch.

"What if I told ye that I want ye?"

"You do not. You left me. I wasn't good enough for you." Caitriona crossed her arms, which pushed her breasts together beneath the sheet wrapped around her body, and Brodyn didn't need to try hard to recall how perfect, full, and plump her breasts were. He had seen enough last night to know she was built like a goddess.

"That is where ye are wrong, Wife." Brodyn felt his desire rising, sitting so close to her. He knew so little about his wife, but she intrigued him in a way nobody else ever had. She was frightened yet never submissive, and he respected that about her. She didn't fear him, though she was wary. "I left because Samuel arrived during the celebration, demanding we speak before the consummation to verify ye were the right woman. I am mighty grateful that ye are because I liked what I saw… quite a bit."

"You did?" Her voice trembled a bit, letting him know she wasn't unaffected by him. She wasn't fearful, he knew that for a fact. Maybe she was as aroused by him as he was by her.

"Aye…" Brodyn slid his hands down her arms, wanting to touch her, walking a fine line. As her husband, he had a right to her body, to take his pleasure as he saw fit. But that sort of coupling never suited him. If the lass wasn't willing, he wasn't either. "Ye are a beautiful woman, Caitriona Mac Cuill. That is yer name now, my father's name, and his before. Ye are my family."

Gooseflesh prickled her skin, and she shivered despite the rush of blood to her head, making her cheeks glow brighter. Aye. He felt her want, her need radiating off her warm, soft flesh. Still, he didn't want to push his advantage too quickly. He wanted her to want him as badly as he wanted her.

"I liked what I saw last night, also," she murmured, almost hesitantly. Her eyes locked with his, and her pupils dilated. She was shy yet bold, and that combination drove him mad.

"Have ye seen a man fully unclothed before?" he asked. It was customary for a Christian bride to be chaste upon her marriage, but many of his people still believed in the pagan ways, and women often took lovers. Secretly, he hoped she wasn't so innocent. A woman with knowledge of a man's body separated her from the tittering lassies who only spoke about such things behind closed doors with their wee friends. He wanted a woman educated in more ways than one, someone who understood the world and could lead his people. Aside from showing her strong will, Caitriona hadn't shared anything about herself, and that was his fault for leaving her alone last night after Samuel left.

"Yes, I have. Does that bother you?"

"Not in the least. It pleases me. You understand the ways we can pleasure one another," Brodyn whispered against her ear, making her shiver again and squirm on the bed. He hoped she was as aroused as he was. He wanted to tear the blanket away from her body and feast on her flesh, to watch her bathe, or better yet, drag the cloth along her skin and lick the drops of water off her wet skin. Damn, if he wasn't pained with his desire. However, until she was more than willing, he would wait. Whether she wanted him or not, she claimed not to, so he must control himself.

"But…" Brodyn abruptly stood and backed away, leaving her to sway with half-masted eyes, just as he hoped. "Ye dinnae want me, as ye say, and I will respect yer wishes. There is much to be done today. Bathe quickly. Murielle will be awaiting ye in the longhouse to show ye around the village, introduce ye to the people, and explain the duties. I expect they willnae be much different than at Dal Riata, except ye are a queen now. And not just any queen. Queen to the strongest, stubbornest, proudest people in the land. They will expect ye to show equal strength, stubbornness, and pride. So far, I dinnae see that to be a problem."

Stepping closer one more time, Brodyn planted a chaste kiss on her lips then turned and walked toward the door before he couldn't stop himself from wrapping his arms around her and pulling her close enough to feel his arousal. "Enjoy yer bath and yer day, Wife. I shall see ye again at the evening meal in the hall. Ye are in fine hands with my sister."

Brodyn shut the door behind him, curious what sort of a woman she would prove to be. So many questions still plagued him, but he couldn't expect to know more about her until she trusted him enough to open up. He hoped that wouldn't take long, for he knew that Ecgfrith, king of Northumbria, would be upon him soon enough, and he wanted to know the feel of his wife before leaving for battle. He might never make it back alive, and what a shame it would be to never lay naked atop his bonnie wife or know her mind.

THE HOT BATH soothed her sore muscles and warmed her chilled bones, but her flesh continued to burn after that encounter with Brodyn. She would have preferred a cold shower after all he'd said. His hot breath fanning her neck, his roughened fingers gliding down her flesh… The thought made her ache and throb as she got dressed for the day, pretending to seem unaffected.

Never had she seen a man built like King Brodyn Mac Cuill. Sure, men in her time, including Taylor, hit the gym, and had six-pack-abs, but Brodyn's form was built through arduous work and training for battles, not just for personal gains and self-esteem like the men she'd known before. He was the leader of his people, a warlord of sorts. He was strong because he had to be, to survive. He was intimidating, yet she felt no fear around him. After all those years of dreaming about him, she was his wife, thanks to an unexpected twist of fate. Her eyes still stung from shedding so many tears the night before, and her mourning for the life she left behind may never go away. If she had to be stuck here, being Brodyn's wife was a satisfactory compromise... but no handsome Pictish king could replace the life she left behind and the career she'd worked hard to achieve.

Knowing his fate made everything feel tainted with sadness. She would be a widow within months. The thought made her stop in her tracks. Should she tell him? Would it even matter? Changing the course of fate was out of the question. If he didn't die and get buried in that cave, then she wouldn't end up in Scotland on that dig, and the time loop would be destroyed, as would the fate of Scotland.

Four tribes of people shared this land. The Scots of Dal Riata, Picts of Fortriu, and Britons of Alt Clut shared the land with the Angles in Northumbria, who demanded tribute. She knew those tribes would come together to fight Ecgfrith and win the battle that secured Scotland's future as a county, keeping them from becoming part of what would later become England.

That's why she was here, to unite the Scots with the Picts and secure that alliance, and thus victory. She couldn't leave, not now. But in a little over three months, she would be widowed and have no reason to stay here. Until then, she had to play her part in history. How could she be with a man she knew would die in battle?

Grabbing her arisaid, Cait left her room, hoping to find Anya and ask her some questions, only she was not home. Leaving quickly to meet Murielle at the longhouse, Cait traversed the hilly landscape leading away from home, offering smiles to the curious onlookers as she passed. To her surprise, everyone seemed pleased to see her and smiled or shouted greetings in return. Perhaps the people embraced this marriage, for it solidified a sorely needed peace, especially since the last feud between the tribes had occurred less than two years ago. Reaching the hall, Caitriona found Murielle standing in front of the hearth just inside.

"Greetings, Sister," Murielle said with a genuine smile. "I didnae wish to wake ye at dawn. I assume my brother kept ye up all night." A sly grin slid up Murielle's face, and she chuckled when Cait flushed at the insinuation. "Och, 'tis nothing to be meek about. 'Tis the natural order of things."

"Do you reside in the village?" Cait asked, changing the subject to avoid the reminder that Brodyn had left her alone last night.

"I live where ye live, of course! Until I am married, my brother is my ward. My chamber is up the stairs from yers."

"Of course," Caitriona murmured. Already, she appeared to be an outsider. No amount of studying the Picts could teach her the smaller details of daily life, for no direct written documents existed. Still, families stayed together until marriages occurred, and she knew this.

"I wish to show ye around the village today so ye may better ken the people ye now rule over."

Rule over. That was not something Caitriona would ever get used to hearing. "I appreciate you showing me around," Cait said as they left the hall and started walking through the village. Murielle pointed out people and what role they played in the tribe. Everyone had their place, but farming seemed to be the focus. Sheep bleated from the fields as the shepherd stood by, and cattle and pigs rustled in the byres attached to the sides of homes. Livestock and agriculture consumed much of this land, and now that spring was approaching, men and women worked beside their older children while the younger ones ran through the village chasing chickens. Caitriona laughed, noting how familiar a scene it was. Some human behaviors never changed.

"Tell me about yerself, Caitriona. Was life in Dal Riata verra different from here?"

Cait paused and thought about what to say. Her life was vastly different than anything these people could ever understand. Though, as far as Murielle knew, Cait was a noble-born Scots woman. "Much the same, I suspect," she replied.

"Ye have seen my cousin, Domnall, many times, then? I have yet to meet him. Unfortunately, Brodyn has met him but only from opposite sides of the battlefield. Tell me about him."

This was becoming more difficult by the second. Cait had no real answers to these questions, aside from what she had read in books. "If Brodyn, Domnall, and Ecgfrith are all cousins, how did this feud start?" Cait asked to deflect the question.

"There is a long-standing feud between cousins in this family." Murielle sighed. "Our grandfather was King of the Picts and ruled much of the land on the island. After he died with only female heirs, the lands of Northumbria, Fortriu, and Dal Riata were split, each going to one male cousin. Domnall attempted to take over Fortriu, which led to the battle two years ago. Our brother, Talorc, turned traitor during that battle and tried to kill Brodyn. I think he was angry to be the only male cousin without a piece of land."

Murielle took a deep, shaky breath. Caitriona could see that speaking of her brother's betrayal of Brodyn upset her, yet Murielle continued. "Brodyn retaliated and attacked a fort near Dal Riata, weakening Domnall's position. This is why ye were sent here, to reinstate the peace between the cousins, especially as Ecgfrith threatens war daily because we refuse to pay tribute. He believes he is owed more than the other cousins, being the eldest. Men. They demand so much more than they already receive yet deny women basic rights. I am of the same blood, yet have I inherited land? Do I start wars over it?" Murielle asked as they walked past a thatch-roofed home with smoke billowing out of the top. The smell of fresh bread wafted in the air, and a woman washed clothes outside her home as her children fed the animals in the byre.

"I am sorry to hear bout Talorc," Cait said. Murielle was not wrong about the ambitions of men. How many must die for one man to become more powerful? Sadly, this reality never changed throughout history. "Is that how Brodyn got the scar above his tattoo?"

"Aye. He never discusses it, though. I confess I am frightened for my brother. He has fought too many battles on all sides. Our cousin Ecgfrith is none too pleased with Brodyn convincing other tribes to stop paying him tribute. 'Tis said that he gathers an army as we speak to march on us all. My brother risks his life to keep us all safe and uphold our family honor."

"I cannot blame you for being concerned…" Cait felt sweat form on her brow despite the frigid morning wind. Murielle would lose another brother. Brodyn was more than an ancient king whose bones were found in a cave. He was flesh and blood, and he would soon perish. The burden of this knowledge was enough to make Caitriona stop in her tracks to catch her breath.

"Are ye all right?" Murielle placed a hand on Cait's shoulder and furrowed her brow.

"Yes. I am also quite concerned."

"Are ye?" she asked with a quirked brow. "The way ye hollered when ye arrived, I was worried ye'd slit his throat in his sleep." Murielle cracked a smile, the only indication that she jested.

"I was not a willing bride. However, I understand the importance of this alliance and what's at stake. I may not know your brother yet, but of course, I'm concerned. I do not wish for him to…" Caitriona couldn't bring herself to finish the sentence.

"We women dinnae have much say in our lives," Murielle sighed. "I ken that more than I ought. My brother will be good to ye. He's boorish and stubborn, but from what I see, so are ye." Murielle chuckled; as she did so Cait realized that she enjoyed her sister-in-law's company.

"Women will have several centuries to wait before things get better." Cait laughed before realizing what she had said. Thankfully, her new sister simply tilted her head with confusion and nodded.

"I wish that werenae true, though it likely is. I ken…" she stopped and grabbed Cait's sleeve. "Women should revolt against the men and demand more rights! We have equal numbers!"

Cait laughed it off for the joke it was meant to be, but Murielle had the right idea. Unfortunately, history repeatedly proved that change didn't come without revolts and violence.

A shrill cry from behind made Caitriona and Murielle stop and look over their shoulders. A young woman ran out of the round-shaped house behind them, waving her hands and storming toward Caitriona like a fox running from a wolf.

"Sorcha! What is it?" Murielle asked, grabbing the woman by the arm when she came within reach. Wild waves of ginger-colored hair floated about her round, reddened face as the lass heaved for breath, gripping her chest.

"'Tis Pa! He came back last night from his journey south for trade. He seemed all right until he just awoke. Something is wrong!"

Murielle began to run toward the house, but Sorcha pulled her back. "Nay! I dinnae ken what is wrong with him, and he bid me stay away and seek help. We need one of the healers!"

"What exactly is wrong with him?" Cait asked.

"He is burning up, has the sweats, is vomiting, and has small bumps all over his body and face! I have never seen the like!"

"I will go find Anya! She will ken what to do!" Murielle said and hurried off.

Caitriona nodded and decided to stay back to ask Sorcha more questions. If Anya, indeed, were a traveler, she would likely suspect the illness to be smallpox, as did Cait. "Where did your Pa travel to, Sorcha? Did you touch him at all?"

The young lass shook her head. "Nay, he slipped in under the darkness of night after over a moon of traveling. I dinnae ken where he went. He often leaves for trade and is gone for many days. He told me to seek help as soon as I saw him this morn, and wouldnae allow me near him."

"Good. May I see him?"

"Nay, my queen! King Brodyn would have our heads if ye fell ill!" she tittered, rubbing her hands together nervously.

"Sorcha, I am not a healer, but I know more than most. If this illness is what I believe it to be, I cannot become ill with it."

Sorcha frowned and shook her head again, hesitating to believe such nonsense, and Cait couldn't blame her. For the woman's peace of mind, Cait decided to stay by her side until Murielle arrived back with Anya. Then, they could discuss a plan. If this was smallpox, the entire village could fall ill if it wasn't contained. Caitriona was immunized, though these people could never understand such a concept.

"I cannae find her!" Cait turned to see Murielle running toward them. "My brother is on his way, but Anya is nowhere to be found," Murielle huffed.

"She was not home this morning, either," Cait noted. "I believe I can help. I'm going in."

"Caitriona..." Murielle whispered. "'Tis not safe to do so. We cannae lose our queen."

"I have been queen for less than a day, Murielle. Nobody here would miss me. Aside from that, I am quite sure I know what this illness is, and I am immune."

"Immune?" Sorcha questioned, dropping her brows.

"I have been exposed to this once before. Once someone is exposed and recovers, they cannot catch it again." That was the best she could explain without discussing modern medicine or appearing insane.

Taking a deep breath, Cait steeled her nerves for what she was about to witness. Seeing photos of smallpox was very different from experiencing it firsthand. But, with Anya missing, Caitriona was the only person who could be safely exposed and stop the spread before it was too late. Stepping into the house, Caitriona coughed as heavy smoke lay thick in the air from the raging hearth fire. Covering her nose and mouth with one arm, she waved away the smoke and squinted into the dim room.

"Who is there?" an old, deep voice called from the corner. "Dinnae come any closer! I am ill!"

"My name is Caitriona, and I am here to help," she replied, following the voice toward the back of the home.

"I dinnae think ye can help me, lass. Help yerself and hie yer arse out of here before ye catch yer death, too!"

"I believe I have seen this illness before, and I know how to manage it."

"Are ye a healer?"

"Of sorts…" It wasn't exactly the truth, but she was confident she understood this illness better than any healer at this time. However, herbs weren't something she understood. She would require help from an herbalist to create tonics for the fever.

Once the man was in sight, Caitriona stopped a few feet away and took in the situation. Small boils covered his face and exposed arms, and his skin flushed red from the fever. "How long have you had these symptoms?"

"I awoke with them. Never would have come home had they shown up before I arrived," the man explained before eyeing her warily. "Who are ye? Never seen ye before."

"My name is Caitriona. I just arrived from Dal Riata to marry King Brodyn."

"Ye are our queen?" The man's eyes widened. "Ye shouldnae be in here. Yer life is worth far more than mine."

"That is absurd," Caitriona said with genuine disapproval. "I cannot catch what you have. Trust me. I will tend to you the best I can, but we need to keep Sorcha away for a while and burn these sheets before she comes home. Everything will need to be cleaned. Where are your wash linens?"

"Sorcha keeps them in the wicker basket near the cauldron," the man said weakly.

Cait nodded and walked over to the cauldron, pleased to see water simmering away within it. Taking an iron hook from the wooden slab table beside the hanging iron cauldron, Cait dropped a linen cloth inside the boiling water and used the hook to submerge it for a moment before removing it and allowing it to cool. Now, it would be sterile.

While it cooled, she walked to the door, surprised to see Brodyn on the other side, just about to barge in. "Ye cannae go in there!" she demanded, placing a hand against his chest to push him back a step.

"Neither can ye! Ye run away from Samuel on the way here, try to escape after our wedding, and now ye walk into a sick man's home? Would ye rather die than remain my wife?"

"Not everything is about you!" she retorted. "I cannot catch this illness."

"I wish to ken how ye decided that."

Pushing past him, Cait approached Sorcha. "I require a bucket of cold water and some herbs for fever. Can you get me those items?"

"Aye, I will fetch water from the well. I have herbs in pouches on the shelves against the wall. The herbs within the dark blue pouch are for fever. Mix it with hot water and have Pa drink it."

Caitriona nodded her understanding, and Sorcha hurried off to get water. "Ye allowed my wife to go into a dying man's home?" Brodyn scolded his sister, his features more severe than Caitriona had ever seen them. Now she understood why many feared him, for he looked ready to tear Murielle limb from limb.

"He is not dying just yet and won't if I can help it! And Murielle is not my keeper. I went into the house of my own free will." Caitriona narrowed her eyes, ready to fight him on this if she had to. He wanted to save his people from the Angles in Northumbria, but nobody would be left to fight for him if smallpox swept through their village.

"Brodyn..." Caitriona placed a placating hand on his large forearm and looked up at him, craning her neck. This was her first time seeing her husband in the light of day. Strands of copper glittered in his dark blond, loose hair. His blue-gray eyes matched the sky above, a stark contrast against his golden-tan skin.

So much had happened since she arrived. From being carried away by Brodyn to becoming his wife, finding Samuel here, standing before Brodyn naked, and their conversation this morning, her brain scurried to keep up with every passing moment. Now, they faced a greater threat than any of these people understood.

"Please, trust me, Brodyn. I've seen this illness before. I know how to handle it, and if it's not handled properly, many will die."

"Including ye," he pressed, placing a hand on top of hers and sending a warm wave through her body.

"I won't get sick. Trust me, please. I know I haven't given you any reason to trust me since my arrival, but I can do this."

"Ye are a mystery to me." Brodyn locked eyes with Cait. "I will remain here. Call if ye require any help."

Nodding, Caitriona saw Sorcha arriving with the bucket of water, took it from her, and went back inside the home, hoping she could save this man and stop the spread of a disease she knew would kill many lives over the next fifteen hundred years. But today, she hoped to protect those that she could.

CHAPTER SEVEN

"H E DEMANDS TRIBUTE from you and your rebellious Celtic tribes by the new moon, or he will come and collect it himself... he and an army."

Brodyn sat back and glared at Ecgfrith's messenger. His cousin had no right to force others to swear loyalty to him, and yet he continued to demand goods and payment from the northern tribes, threatening war if they should resist. He knew it was no idle threat, but his people would fight for their freedom if they must. Although Pict-born, his cousin was king of the Angles from the south, influenced by the Romans who'd always believed themselves better than the northern Celtic tribes. The Romans had been gone for over two centuries, yet the mentality had remained; the southern tribes always attempted to subdue the north... and had always failed.

What they lacked was not only the ancient pride the Celts carried for their traditions and culture but the knowledge of the rough, wild, and often brutal lands that surrounded Fortriu and many other territories. Ecgfrith could bring his men through the Highlands, though the treacherous journey would weaken them, making them easy targets for the born-and-bred northerners who could survive in the harshest conditions.

Like the thistles that thrived in the rockiest soil and coldest winds, the Celts managed to thrive under harsh conditions. The Picts, Scots, and Britons may have quarreled in the past, despite Brodyn's tireless work to bring these groups together and unite against Northumbria. His marriage to Caitriona was a strategic move ensuring peace with the Scots, but already the lass drove him mad with both frustration and desire. He wanted to shake sense into her and fill her with his seed, not necessarily in that order.

"Tell my cousin that tribute willnae be coming from the Picts. I willnae speak for the other Celtic tribes, but I can assure ye that we are all tired of toiling over our lands just to have his greedy paws outstretched, expecting payment. Our grandfather ruled these lands, and I will protect them even if Ecgfrith wishes to take more than he deserves."

Goodwin, Brodyn's trusted companion and finest warrior, stood beside him in silence, arms crossed as he glared at the messenger.

"I will relay the message." The man bowed and turned away, leaving the hall. With tension straining his muscles, Brodyn sat from his seat and left the longhouse with Goodwin. He needed fresh air and time to think before being surrounded by people during the evening meal.

"We will have a battle on our hands before the summer months," Goodwin said as they walked through the village.

"We will. However, with the northern tribes now all allied, I believe we can fend for ourselves. If Ecgfrith wishes to be greedy and march his men into the Highlands because we refuse to send him our hard-earned goods, he will be sending them to their deaths."

"Aye," Goodwin said distantly, obviously something else on his mind. "What think ye of yer new wife? She is a comely lass, no?"

"Aye, she is."

"That's all ye have to say about her? How did the bedding go last night? Ye chased us all away. Now the entire village wonders if ye've plowed her."

Brodyn stopped and shoved his companion back. "Dinnae speak of yer queen with disrespect, Goodwin."

"All right, all right." Goodwin raised his hands in mock defeat, but a small smile played across his lips. "I've never seen ye like this about a woman."

"Like what? I've not said more than three words about her."

"Ye dinnae need to. 'Tis written all over yer face. Ye are smitten with the lass, and I cannae say I blame ye. And I mean that respectfully. She is a beautiful woman. Ye will make handsome bairns."

"I cannae be smitten with a woman I met only last night. She has been a thorn in my arse since the moment I found her on the coast, refusing to do her duty."

"Aye, she seems a spirited one, I confess. But ye never did like the simple lassies. They bore ye. I doubt our new queen will bore ye."

Brodyn grunted. That was true enough. She tried his patience at every turn, and her insistence on caring for the old merchant, Cadwyth Mac Bielich, was both warming and worrisome. He appreciated her will to help his people and understood the impact an illness could have on his village. He had seen many people wiped out by a single cough. Still, risking her life to save others sat uneasily in his stomach. But the woman had insisted she was safe and begged for his trust. So, he gave it. Though he hadn't seen her in hours, and he prayed all was well.

"Speaking of the queen, is that not your bonnie bride over there by the well… bathing herself?" Goodwin tilted his head and quirked a brow. Brodyn turned toward the well and found his wife stripped down to her undertunic with her red hair unbound as she leaned over the well, her arse sticking out as she bent over.

"What, by the new God, is yer wife doing?" As a gust of wind blew past, her tunic clung to her curvy rear, and Brodyn growled when he caught Goodwin staring at his wife's backside.

"Keep staring at my wife, and ye will find yer bollocks at the bottom of that well."

"I kenned ye liked her." Goodwin chuckled and elbowed Brodyn in the arm. "Yer a fortunate man, my king. I will leave ye with yer new bonnie wife. I must inform the other men about Ecgfrith's threats. I've been preparing them for many moons. They will be ready."

Brodyn nodded, and Goodwin smacked him on the shoulder before turning to walk toward the training fields where the men awaited news. Before approaching Caitriona, Brodyn observed her from a distance for a moment. Nobody else was around, and his wife had rolled up her tunic sleeves and scrubbed her arms with well water and a cloth. Gathering her skirt, Caitriona bent over and washed her legs. Dunking the rag once more into the bucket, Cait squeezed the water over her face and neck.

When Brodyn moved closer, gravel crunched beneath his feet, startling Caitriona. With a gasp, she clutched her chest and leaned against the well's side, nearly falling backward. Without a second's hesitation, Brodyn ran toward Caitriona and clutched her to him, his heart beating frantically.

Instinctively, Cait wrapped her arms around his waist to steady herself. As they embraced, Brodyn enjoyed the feel of her in his arms. She was small but not fragile. She owned a slim strength that spoke to a woman used to hard work—not something one often saw in noblewomen. However, she was not your average noble. No other noble-born woman he knew would risk herself to save a lowly merchant from an illness. He knew he should loosen his grip, but she fit so perfectly in his arms.

"Thank you," she whispered and slowly released her grip on his waist.

Reluctantly, he let her slip from his arms, already missing the sensations her touch pulled from deep within him. "Ye wouldnae have stumbled if I hadnae startled ye. I apologize. I was walking through the village and found ye washing at the well. Ye ken, we have a washbasin at home."

"Yes, but I cannot return home just yet. Cadwyth still needs constant care, and Sorcha cannot return home until the worst of this passes... Or he passes." She said with a frown. He saw genuine concern in her eyes, and something fluttered inside his stomach. He'd heard of this fluttering before yet had never experienced it until now. It was more than lust, more than affection. Though he barely knew his wife, Brodyn felt a bone-deep connection with her, as if she was always meant to be his.

"Do ye believe he will survive?" Brodyn asked and gently took her hand in his. He was unable to be so near her and not feel her softness. If her hand was all he could hold, he would hold it as long as she allowed. Fortunately, she did not pull away.

"It's hard to say. His fever rages, and the blisters have covered most of his body. I cannot heal him. All I can do is keep his fever down and offer him liquids and herbs for strength. Whether he survives or not depends on many factors, and I will not leave his side until I know his outcome."

"Why do ye care so much for a man ye have never met?" Brodyn asked, tilting his head, and running his thumb across the inside of her wrist, feeling her pulse quicken.

"He is a fellow human in need. Is it not the very meaning of humanity to help those in need? Besides, as I said, I cannot become ill with the pox. So, I risk nothing being by his side."

"The 'pox'? Ye have seen this before then, in Dal Riata?"

Caitriona paused and hesitated to answer, and more and more, he knew his beautiful wife held closely guarded secrets. "Where I come from, it is well known, yes." Her answer was cryptic, but so was everything else she said.

"Yer certain ye cannae become ill?"

"I am certain."

Brodyn nodded, frowning at her wet tunic as the sun disappeared behind her. Night approached, and the wind intensified, carrying that icy chill from the sea. She was so busy saving someone else that she forgot she was capable of falling ill herself. He wanted her to come home with him, not only to consummate the marriage but to share more time with her.

He made it known that he wanted her, yet she didn't seem to share his desire. Aye, she was attracted to him, for certain. However, that need, that pull he felt toward her, was not reciprocated, and Brodyn would never beg for a woman's affections. At some point, the marriage needed to be consecrated by their coupling, but she had only been here two days and had spent much of it tending to one of his people, something he couldn't fault her for.

"The sun is waning. Ye should get back inside before 'tis dark outside. Do ye require anything?"

"Have ye seen Anya?" she asked, wrapping her arms around herself as a gust of wind swept past.

"Nay. She comes and goes. Always has. Not the finest of servants. Still, she is our family and our wise woman if ye believe in such things. She kens that which none of us do. Where she goes, I may never ken. She always comes back."

Cait nodded, not nearly as shocked by anything he said as he had expected. "I see." She took a step away from him, and he knew that whatever moment they shared was over. "I must return now that I've bathed. His fever will require more cool cloths."

"Thank ye for yer care of my people, Caitriona."

"They are my people too, are they not?" she said with a wee smile that made him chuckle despite himself.

"Indeed, they are. Dinnae forget that ye are also my wife, and I would care for some time with ye if we are to ken one another."

"I shall not forget. I will return as soon as I am able."

Nodding, Brodyn tore himself away from the woman who captured his interest more than he wished she did. But there were important matters to discuss with his men, particularly the impending war that would lead to the continuation or destruction of the remaining Celtic tribes on this island. It was more than keeping his land or expanding. It was about keeping thousands of years of tradition alive, about showing the spirit of the Celts, pride, and loyalty. It was all at risk, and it was up to Brodyn to achieve it.

THREE DAYS PASSED, and Caitriona was pleased to see the healthy color returning to her patient's cheeks. She had grown quite fond of Cadwyth as he improved and spoke more. He was a well-traveled man who sought new supplies for the tribe, opening new trade opportunities. His last journey brought him to mainland Europe, where he ran into smallpox. It had not yet found its way up to the Highlands, and Caitriona very well may have prevented many deaths, including Cadwyth's.

His fever had broken the day before, and the sores began to scab over and heal. He drank broth and tea without issue and seemed to be on the mend. Caitriona wanted to believe she stayed the extra day to ensure he was well enough for Sorcha to return, but part of her dreaded returning to Brodyn.

It wasn't that he was unpleasant or unattractive. The problem was that he was those things and so much more. For a Pictish king on the brink of war, he was quite kind and attentive—more than she deserved after avoiding him this long. Worse, he was going to die. How could she become attached to a man whose bones she would one day discover in a cave? She couldn't allow it. Instead, she decided that she would see this through without becoming emotionally involved, and then return home to California in 2023. And really, for now, she was stuck in a time fraught with danger; falling in love with her husband was the least of her worries.

When Sorcha arrived on one of her daily visits, she was pleased to see her father, who smiled and waved at her in for the first time in three days, sitting up and chatting with Caitriona. No longer did Sorcha have to stay elsewhere. Caitriona gathered the used linens, tossed them into the boiling water to sterilize them, and told Sorcha she would come by tomorrow to check on Cadwyth.

"Thank ye for all ye have done for us. I cannae say what it

means. We are all fortunate that ye came to us, my queen."

Being addressed as royalty still sat uneasily with Caitriona. "I am happy to have helped. Your father is a wonderful man."

"Aye, he is. Speaking of wonderful men, King Brodyn has been asking about ye. He seems anxious to see his wife," Sorcha said as she dragged a stool over to her father's bedside.

"Is he now?" Cait said with equal parts excitement and trepidation. The bottom line was that there was no more avoiding the man. And she found that she did not want to. With nothing but time on her hands, Caitriona had thought of Brodyn often, and though she wished to shield her heart, she wondered if Brodyn didn't deserve a loving wife while he yet lived. The pain of becoming attached would destroy her, but so would treating him poorly and avoiding him when he so clearly wished to be a proper husband to her.

Leaving their home, Caitriona slowly walked through the village, weary, sore, and tired. Dusk approached, and the evening meal would begin shortly. She should be present to show solidarity for her people and support her husband. She may never adjust to being a queen, but she was stuck here for now, and her resolve to remain isolated waned. These people welcomed her, and they deserved better than an elusive queen.

And what Cait needed most was a hot bath to soothe her muscles and warm her bones. Stiffness slowed her movements as she walked the graveled path up the hill to her home. People looked at her as she walked, some smiling, others offering only side glances. Cait couldn't blame them, for she hadn't been seen around the village much since arriving. That had to change.

Reaching Brodyn's stone house at the top of the hill, she walked inside and looked around. "Anya?" Caitriona desperately wished to speak with the woman, but she was not in the house.

Alone, Caitriona could concentrate on her own thoughts for the first time in days. The wooden tub sat near the hearth's fire, and Caitriona didn't want to risk running into the pretty, young servant who once slept with her husband, so she decided to fill the tub herself using hot water from the nearby cauldron. She stoked the fire in the hearth before undressing and sliding into the hot bath with a sigh of relief. Never had a bath felt so wonderful. The inside of Cadwyth's home had had a permanent chill despite the hearth fire that blazed all day. The roof leaked, and the door allowed the freezing wind to seep through. After three days inside that home, Caitriona was frozen stiff and she had made a mental note to help weather-proof their home later.

The fire crackled beside the bath, calming her thoughts as the heat soothed her skin, and slowly, her eyes slid closed.

When she opened her eyes again, Caitriona furrowed her brow and looked around, realizing she was in her bed beneath a pile of covers. Scrambling to sit up, she looked around the dimly lit room. A fire crackled in the corner just as one had while she bathed, but somehow she was now in another room. Looking beneath the covers, she noticed that she was still unclothed. She must have fallen into a deep sleep while bathing, and only one person could have carried her up the stairs and into bed.

Feeling flustered, Cait stood up and looked for her tunic, unable to find it. She had nothing except the worn tunic Anya gave her when she arrived, but it was filthy after days of caring for a sick man. Remembering that she undressed in the main room, Caitriona wrapped a woolen plaid blanket around her body and stepped out of her room.

Splashing water sounds caught Caitriona's ears as she crept into the otherwise silent room. Tiptoeing closer, Caitriona stopped in her tracks when she saw Brodyn sitting in a chair with a bucket of water between his legs, scrubbing something with a bar of lye soap.

Clutching the blanket tightly against her, Cait silently watched Brodyn, wondering about a king who washed clothing rather than having a servant do it for him. Surely, he had more important matters on his mind.

He looked up and saw her standing near the corridor. "Yer awake," he said, wringing out the wad of fabric.

"I must have fallen asleep in the tub," she explained. "It was an exhausting few days, but Cadwyth is on the mend, and Sorcha has returned home to continue his care. I believe he will be all right."

"That is great news, indeed. I cannae thank ye enough for what ye sacrificed to help him."

"Has Anya arrived?"

Brodyn continued to wring out the fabric before standing up from his seat. "She is not back yet. I suspect she will return soon. The auld woman always disappears at her whim, but she doesn't stay away long."

Caitriona looked at Brodyn and cocked her head. "Did you move me into the bed?"

"Aye. I came home to wash up for the evening meal when I found ye asleep in the bathtub, and the fire was dying out. I tried to wake ye but ye slept like the dead. So, I moved ye to the bed and have washed yer tunic."

Caitriona looked at the fabric in his hand, recognizing it as her only two garments balled together, the undertunic and overtunic. Guilt niggled at Cait as she realized how unfair she had been to Brodyn. She took care of Cadwyth and possibly saved him and the tribe from a smallpox outbreak, though it hadn't been entirely selfless. She'd also hid away from her imposing husband, doing all she could to avoid him when she left the home to wash up or seek supplies.

He hadn't wanted this union any more than she had, but he was trying to make this work. Knowledge of the future prompted her to remain distant, yet Brodyn prepared for a battle, trying to unite separate tribes of prideful Celts to save their culture, land, and lives. Yet, Brodyn still found time to care for her and show his softer side. He deserved more than he'd received from her, and Caitriona knew she needed to stop avoiding him.

His tunic sleeves were rolled up past his elbows, his clothing covered in water from scrubbing her clothing while she slept in the warm bed he placed her in. The thought of him carrying her naked into the room made her tingle all over, and her nipples hardened. Damn, if she didn't want this man. He was strength incarnate, bold, and by all accounts unrefined. Still, he was passionate and selfless, living his life to serve others—including the wife he hadn't wanted. But he wanted her now. He said as much the day after their wedding celebration. She had been married four days and had yet to have an in-depth conversation or share more than a kiss sealing their vows.

"Thank you, Brodyn, for everything," she said as she stepped closer to him. Caitriona put out a hand to touch his arm, and he stiffened. Frowning, Cait looked him in the eyes, her stomach sinking when he shifted his gaze toward the fire before turning to lay her tunics onto the table to dry.

"I… I'm sorry if I haven't been the best wife."

Her words must have touched on whatever he was battling inside, for his head snapped toward her, and he shook his head. "'Tis I who should apologize. I have been so concerned with Ecgfrith and allying with other tribes that I paid no attention to who paid the price for the peace I sought. Ye were an unwilling bride. Ye didnae want to be here. I dragged ye away kicking and screaming, forcing ye to marry me, forcing ye to live among strange faces without a thought. Ye were a symbol of peace between my people and the Scots, another step toward securing our victory. But I never considered how ye felt about being forced to marry a man ye didnae ken. Our new religion forces marriage bonds for certain purposes, yet our old religion, the religion of my ancestors, allowed women to choose their mates. I still believe this is the way. I never thought I would be a man to force a woman to wed for the greater good."

"You had no choice. I see this now. I do not blame you," Cait insisted, feeling her stomach twist and dive with every sullen word he spoke.

"I had other choices. Marriage wasnae something I wanted, but Domnall offered a bride as a peace offering after our last skirmish. I was desperate for peace, so I agreed when he said he had a bonnie woman who would offer me strapping lads and a blood bond between our people. Nothing is stronger than marriage bonds resulting in bairns. Ye didnae want this. And the way ye looked at Samuel…"

Brodyn swallowed and turned away to stare at the fire. "Ye do not want to be here. Ye wished to leave with him, and I denied ye. And ye repaid my selfishness by being the most selfless person I have ever kenned, giving days of yer life to care for a man ye dinnae ken without concern for yerself. So now, I am prepared to do the same."

"What do you mean, Brodyn?"

"I'm letting you go." Brodyn kept his back to her, crossing his muscular arms over his chest as he watched the fire burn.

"I can't leave. We are married…" she said slowly, taking a tentative step closer to him.

"The marriage was never consummated."

"But, this marriage is necessary for the alliance," she insisted, taking yet another step closer.

"I can either have a more willing bride sent over or simply accept a peace offering from Domnall, mayhap foster a child from your tribe to show peace. There are other ways. Ye may go home."

Silence fell over the room for several moments as Cait stood behind Brodyn, staring at his strong frame silhouetted by the fire. So much of her longed to accept his offer, walk away, and return home—if she could. What if she could not return home and became stuck here without protection? Samuel had made it very clear that she was to remain here, that she was the key to preventing a disaster that would destroy Scotland's path toward autonomy. History was one long chain of events, both big and small, and some events profoundly impacted the world for centuries and millennia. This battle was one of those events.

She could tell herself all the reasons she should stay, but one thing was so clear to Cait that it rose above all the other reasons, and it surprised her: She wanted to be here. She wanted to be

Brodyn's wife, even if she hadn't only days before. More lay between them than mutual attraction. Their connection spanned thousands of years, and she had been in love with him through countless lifetimes. He was her soul's mate, and no amount of denial would change that. Whatever reason she was stuck in this time loop, she was here to be his wife and his support. That's what she wanted beyond anything else. Now that the dust had settled and Cait had had time to process her reality, she wanted to stay… and now, he wanted her to go.

Memories of her many reoccurring dreams about Brodyn flashed through her mind, especially the sensual ones. Many nights she had dreamed of making love to him. She knew now that they were memories of a past life. And she remembered the powerful emotions she felt, the connection she'd shared with the man caressing her body and kissing her so tenderly. That man now sat before Caitriona with his back turned, ready to send her away.

"You think I am selfless, but you are the most selfless person I have ever known," she murmured, taking another step, and gently placing a hand on his shoulder. "I want to stay."

Finally turning to face her, Brodyn looked at her with stone-cold features that would have frightened her if she didn't know this man in a way that nobody else could. "Why do ye wish to stay, Caitriona? Why this change of heart?"

Heart had more to do with it than she was willing to admit. "I want to stay to honor the alliance and to show that peace between our people is essential, to show your people that the Scots are with them against Ecgfrith." Caitriona sighed and stepped closer. "I wish to stay because I want to be with you. I want to be a proper wife. I was scared and lost when you found me. I've had time to adjust."

"Ye arenae frightened of me?" he asked, shadows from the flames dancing ominously across his face.

"No. Should I be?"

"Nay. I would never hurt ye."

"I want to stay," she reiterated.

"If ye choose to stay, ye choose to remain here as my wife. Ye will be my equal in all things, Caitriona. I will consult ye when needed, and I hope to have a true marriage," he added, looking her over with that burning gaze of his. "I willnae force ye to ever lie with me."

"I am not the one who left the night of our wedding," Caitriona reminded him with a raised brow.

"Ye werenae exactly a willing bride. I may be a warlord, but I dinnae force myself on women… though I did force ye to wed with me, and it's eating me alive with regret and guilt," he growled through clenched teeth, clearly angry with himself.

"Brodyn." Caitriona placed a hand on his chest, feeling his heart racing against her palm through his thin white tunic and the warmth of him against her skin. "I'm sorry I've avoided you. You're right that I was lost, confused, and unwilling. I still feel lost and confused, however I want to stay and be your wife, in all ways. I cannot begin to feel like this is my home if I do not know my husband."

"Ye are far away from home, lass. 'Tis normal to feel this way."

"I'm much further away than anyone understands," she murmured. When Brodyn lowered his brow, she shook her head. "I want to stay. I…" She paused and looked up at him, staring into his blue eyes as her heart quickened, stomach fluttered, and blood heated. "I want you, too, Brodyn."

Standing on her tiptoes, Caitriona placed her lips against his, slowly, tentatively, unsure how he would react. With a groan, Brodyn responded by taking her face in his hands, parting his lips, and deepening the kiss.

Heat engulfed Cait's entire body as if his mere touch could set her aflame. His kiss felt familiar… like home. His tongue slid against hers with passion and need, and Caitriona placed her hands on his hips, feeling the heavy blanket around her body slide to the floor. Completely nude, Cait continued to kiss him, her body aching for more, remembering the feel of his touch from every previous lifetime.

Brodyn's hands slid down her back and across her waist before settling at her hips just as he broke the kiss, leaving them both breathless. Her knees quaked as his eyes fixed on hers before scanning down her naked body. "Ye are breathtaking, Caitriona. I am having a hard time keeping my hands off of ye."

"Then don't keep your hands off of me," she whispered, taking one of his hands off her hip and moving it to her breast. "I want you to touch me."

With another low groan, Brodyn brought both hands to her breasts and gently caressed them, kneading them in his roughened hands. When his thumb slid across her nipple, Caitriona closed her eyes and sighed, tilting her head back as waves of sensation washed over her.

Would he find her too forward if she tried to undress him? She was a modern woman, used to taking the lead with men, but would a woman of his time be so brazen? Slowly, she slid her hands beneath his tunic, feeling the ridges of muscle and coarse hairs against her fingertip. Though he was but flesh and blood, he was her soulmate, a man beyond her reach all her life... until now. Now, he was here—solid, warm, consuming her every sense.

Firelight flickered behind him, illuminating the room with a magical glow, casting dancing shadows across the walls. Brodyn's hands roamed down her abdomen, delicately running his fingers over her skin. She matched his movements, sliding her palms down his stomach to where his trousers rested on his hips.

When her fingers touched the unfinished leather string, she took a fortifying breath and tugged on it, rewarded by Brodyn sliding his tongue out of her mouth, down her throat and chest, before gliding it over her taut nipple. Cait moaned and instinctively reacted by wrapping her hands around his hardened cock, pleased with his responsive groans of pleasure.

To Caitriona's delight, Brodyn swept her up and cradled her in his strong arms as he walked toward the stairs, loosening his trousers' strings as he went.

CHAPTER EIGHT

THE WOMAN WAS a temptress, a siren, a fae… mayhap even a witch, for she had weaved a spell over him that he could not resist, nor did he want to. For as little as he understood the woman, their connection felt like an inferno melding them into one being. It was like he had waited his entire life for this woman to show up on his shores. Flashes of old dreams long forgotten seemed to cloud his mind, and she felt so familiar in his arms as he carried her into the room.

"Where are you taking me?" she asked, lacing her arms around his neck.

"The first time I make love to my wife willnae be on the cold, rough floors in the main room. Ye deserve to be pleasured among the furs and blankets on the bed."

"Pleasured, hmm?" she murmured, and he saw the desire in her eyes, reflecting his own. He throbbed for her and had since the first time he saw her, but he wanted to make this moment last, draw it out into exquisite torture before he plunged deep inside her warmth. "You seem pretty confident."

"If 'tis not pleasurable for ye, then I am doing it wrong," he grunted. Entering the room, Brodyn laid her on the bed and felt his heart rate kick up several notches. This woman was his wife, something he never thought to have. A man like him did not expect to live a full enough life to include a family. He had spent years securing his land, keeping his people safe, and preparing for war. He'd known if ever he took a wife, it would be for political reasons, but never did he expect such an attraction, let alone this connection that drove him mad when she came near. It somehow only intensified when they were apart.

Caitriona looked at him with lust glazing her golden eyes, her pert breasts heaving as her breathing quickened. Unlacing his boots, Brodyn kicked them off, removed his trousers, and tore his tunic over his head. He stood before her as bared for her as she was for him. Her gaze moved over his body with appreciation.

"Are ye certain this is what ye want, Caitriona? Ye will be my wife in truth for the rest of our lives."

Something he said made her face turn pale, and she sat up on the bed, staring at him with horror-stricken eyes. Was the thought of being his forever truly so terrible? His blood boiled, and he clenched his fists at his side. This woman changed her mind more than a Highland summer's day changed temperatures. Without saying a word, Brodyn gathered his clothing and turned to leave the room before saying something he would later regret.

"Brodyn, wait!" she cried, scrambling out of bed, and rushing over to him. He kept his back to her, more hurt than he was angry, but he refused to let her see the pain in his eyes. No woman ever affected him so profoundly, yet he knew next to nothing about her. "Please! I wish you understood! I wish I could tell you!"

"Tell me what?" he snarled, turning to face her. When she didn't jump back with fright, he was pleased to know she didn't fear him. "What is it, Caitriona, that eats away at ye, that keeps ye distant? What secrets do ye harbor that are so dangerous, ye cannae tell yer husband?"

Caitriona put a hand on his chest, and he wondered if she felt the wild beating of his heart against her palm. "I... I want to tell you, but I don't know how. You will only believe I am insane."

"Ye cannae ken this until ye try," he insisted. "Whatever it is, it prevents ye from embracing me as yer husband. Tell me now, or I will have ye delivered back to Domnall on the morrow. I have many troubles, Caitriona. Many people keeping secrets, many battles to fight. I willnae suffer it from my wife!"

"I am not from this time!" she cried, stumbling back as the words rolled out. She shook and stepped back until she sat on the edge of the bed, looking down at her worrying hands. "I told you… I am a long way from home."

"Ye dinnae speak of Dal Riata."

She shook her head. "No."

Brodyn regarded his wife sitting on the bed, naked and vulnerable, distressed and confused. She had much less body hair than any woman he'd ever seen, as if she'd shaved and it had begun to grow back. As far as he knew, that wasn't common in Dal Riata. A tattoo depicting a bright purple thistle adorned her ankle, and the colors were more vibrant than any other tattoo he'd ever seen, including his own. Then, he remembered her strange tan lines, clearly caused by clothing unlike anything he could imagine. He'd known she was different, but the more time he spent in her presence, the more mysterious she became.

He did not believe her to be mad. A madwoman wouldn't have her wits about her, nor would she have been able to save Cadwyth and their village. How had she been so sure she was immune to this illness? Aye, she held secrets, but Brodyn knew she was not mad. "Tell me."

"I… know things," she said. "I know what will come to pass."

"How?" Brodyn narrowed his eyes and stepped closer, somehow believing her, though uncertain why. "Ye are like Anya?" he asked carefully. Her head popped up, and her eyes widened.

"You know about Anya?" Caitriona asked, somehow appearing more relieved and at ease.

"I ken she comes and goes between this world and another. I am not a man of much faith. I dinnae care for the new religion or its rules, but I have also lost touch with the old pagan ways. I am too busy trying to keep my people alive to allow gods or deities or unseen nonsense to cloud my judgment. However, I realize there are things in this world nobody can explain. If ye were another woman, I might think ye mad. But ye are different. I've sensed it from the first."

"May I show you? It's the only way to make you understand."

"Show me what, exactly?" Brodyn crossed his arms and looked at her with bated breath. Was she going to snap her fingers and disappear? He knew the thought was ridiculous, but he had no idea what to expect. Pagans would call her a woman with the sight, or a seer. Mayhap even a fae woman. Christians would call her a witch and have her locked away or worse. She was taking a risk speaking this way to him, and he knew she was aware of the dangers. Her faith in him softened his heart.

"If I tell you, I do not think you will believe me. I wish to show you. I vow I will not try to run away. I am determined to stay here with you. But before I can truly be your wife, I must be honest about who I am and where I come from. If you think me insane and unfit to be your wife after tonight, I will leave."

"Is that what ye hope for? That I will turn away from ye and let ye leave?"

Caitriona shook her head and frowned. "Of course not. You gave me the option to leave already, and I did not. If I am going to be a proper wife, I need you to know the truth. You cannot know me without knowing this truth. I need you to take me back to the cave."

"The cave? Tonight?"

"Yes. We can take a horse and be there and back by the night's end. Once you know my truth, you can decide to return with or without me."

Knots formed in his gut. This was not how he saw this night going, but he was pleased she wished to be honest. He was certain his wife wasn't insane. Beyond that, he was certain of nothing else.

WEARING A TUNIC and undertunic that Murielle had kindly

allowed her to borrow, Caitriona held tightly to the horse's saddle as they galloped through the rocky terrain with the sun's rays disappearing on the horizon. A waxing moon hung sullenly in the sky, a grayish-blue light leading the way. With Brodyn's plaid wrapped around her shoulders and his strong arms around her waist, Cait felt free as the wind blew through her tangled hair.

She told her husband she was from another time, and he hadn't rejected her. Cait wasn't sure if telling him had been wise, but if she was to stay with him, he had to know the truth. How she would fully explain this, she did not know. Samuel had said she had free will, and she exercised it by telling Brodyn the truth. Would she live to regret it?

When he'd spoken of being married until their death, all the desire drained from Caitriona, replaced by icy dread. His death approached, and she couldn't tell him, yet she could tell him about the cave.

It was a risk; however, it was worth taking. Caitriona had to follow her instincts, and her gut told her he would listen. Whether he believed her was another matter entirely. Cait wasn't sure how much he knew about Anya and where she came from or disappeared to, but his acceptance of that situation only fueled Cait's belief that he would listen to what she had to say. If only she had proof of her story.

Arriving at the cave's entrance, Brodyn brought Tatha, his bay mare, to a stop and hopped down before helping Cait onto her feet. "Ye are not much of a rider," he said with no amount of judgment.

"Horses aren't too common where I come from." Taking his hand, Caitriona led him closer to the cave entrance, surprised that her head didn't throb as it had before. Perhaps that was a sign that she wasn't meant to leave. "I don't know how much I should tell you. Samuel didn't guide me on this part..."

"The messenger kens about... whatever this is?"

Cait nodded. "He is like Anya and me."

"How many more of ye are there?" he asked, looking at the

cave before staring out to sea as waves lapped against the shore.

"I don't know. I thought I was alone until Samuel showed up, then he told me Anya was the same."

"What exactly… are ye then, Caitriona? My people say this cave leads to the fae folk. I never believed such things."

Taking his hand, Cait walked toward the cave entrance and turned to look at the sea, just as Brodyn had done a moment before. "This cave entrance is usually inaccessible due to the high tide, where I come from. When I come from," she sighed. "We had to wait for low tide before entering it again every day. When I arrived here, I knew something was not right. The water is much lower, and thistles grow everywhere. Time does change all things."

"Are ye telling me ye are from another time?" Brodyn asked her with disbelief lacing his tone. She didn't blame him, but she didn't have it in her to pretend any longer. There was too much about her that was different, too much to conceal. He would either accept her truth or not.

"Yes. Do you believe in time travel? I didn't until I found you on this beach. Even then, I thought I was having another dream. It wasn't until later that night when I realized I was truly in this time."

"What time are ye from, and what dreams do ye speak of?"

Caitriona took a deep breath and braced herself. "I'm from the future. My entire life, I have dreamed about you, Brodyn. I dreamed about a king of the Picts and this cave…" She trailed off, not yet willing to discuss everything. "These dreams led me to study your people in great detail. It became my greatest passion, learning all I could about you and Fortriu, the Picts—everything. Unfortunately, in my time, there is very little known about your people. Nobody knows the language or what the symbols on stones mean. Somehow, I always knew things I couldn't possibly know. Now, I understand why."

Brodyn listened and did not speak, which was for the best, she decided. If he thought she was insane now, just wait until she finished explaining her life to him. "Samuel is from my time. Or maybe, he is from yours. Honestly, I do not even know. In my time, he is my mentor… a teacher. He taught history and archaeology at the University. He came and went often, and I thought he was just away on a dig… but now I'm not so sure."

Caitriona dared not look at Brodyn as she spoke. Instead, she turned to enter the cave and looked at its walls. Some carvings already existed, though the symbol with a thistle and bull was not there. Otherwise, the cave looked exactly the same. She ran her fingers along the cold stone walls, noticing the symbols describing a king's burial did not yet exist. A chill raced up her spine, and a tear slid down her cheek.

"What is… 'archaeology'… and this word, 'university'?" Brodyn tried to follow along, but she should have known that many words did not yet exist at this time.

"University is where young men and women go after finishing several years of education. We can decide what we wish to study and take several classes for many years. I studied anthropology and archaeology, which is the study of ancient people and learning how to properly uncover and study ancient civilizations by locating the sites where they lived and died and digging into the ground. We find old jewelry, clay pots or plates, weapons… bones," she added before clearing her throat. "Anything that can survive in the soil. Clothing is much harder to find since organic—I mean, natural, not manmade—materials dissolve. I studied your people, Brodyn. I studied you."

She turned to look at him then, so many mixed emotions pulling her in all directions. She was relieved to tell her husband the truth. Yet, telling him about her dreams made her feel exposed and vulnerable. She knew how insane she sounded. It was hard to believe any of it herself.

"Ye studied me? What time are ye from, lass?" His eyes bore into hers, and he hadn't outright rejected her claims so far. His questions were encouraging.

"I am from the year 2023."

"Ye arnae. 'Tis impossible." He shook his head and ran flus-tered fingers through his hair, clearly ill at ease with all she thrust upon him. She couldn't blame him, even if it devastated her.

Caitriona frowned and blinked, feeling her stomach sink to her toes. He didn't believe her. She turned from him before he saw the tears glittering in her eyes. "I didn't think you'd believe me. I don't blame you for that. It's hard to believe," she forced through quivering lips, doing her best not to show her pain or disappointment.

"Caitriona. Look at me."

"I would rather not."

"Why not?"

"It hurts too much," she answered honestly. "To open up to you and have you reject me."

She felt his strong hands grab her shoulders and turn her to face him. Tears tracked down her cheeks, and Brodyn swiped them away with his thumb. "'Tis a lot to take in. Tell me about these dreams."

"It started when I was a young girl, glimpses of something I couldn't understand. As I grew up, they became more vivid, like memories. I always saw your face. I knew who you were when I saw you on this shore because I had seen your face a hundred times before, but only ever in my mind. When Samuel spoke with me, he said I am stuck in what's known as 'a time loop', that my soul is connected to yours, and we find each other in every life. Only, in my time, I am sent back here because the Caitriona of this time dies on her way to you.

"Domnall did send you a bride. She was me, my soul, any-way, just in a body from this time. Samuel said the same soul cannot exist in two bodies at once. She dies before reaching you, leaving the peace alliance unfulfilled between the Scots of Dal Riata and the Picts of Fortriu. I believe the timeline corrects this by pulling me into the year 685, to marry you and fulfill the alliance."

Brodyn nodded. "How did ye end up here?"

"I traveled to Scotland… that's the name of this land in my time. I traveled here to explore this cave. For a long time, the cave was mentioned in oral stories, yet its whereabouts were unknown, as the tides are higher in my time, blocking the cave from view. But we found it and knew it was connected to you… your people," she stuttered, not wanting to discuss his bones. Her stomach churned to think about him dying in her arms in only a few months.

Deciding to skip over the bones they found, Caitriona continued. "We found the carvings on the cave walls. These are still visible 1,400 years from now, and there are more than there are now." Caitriona pointed to the cave walls, running a hand over the area where her symbol would one day be.

"My friend, Emilie, said I spoke an odd language while looking at the symbols. I could somehow read the symbols that nobody else understood and speak a language forgotten well over a thousand years ago. Your language. The one we're speaking now.

"I was exploring the cave alone when a bright light flashed and propelled me backward. When I stood up and left the cave, the shoreline was lower, the stars were bigger and brighter, and you appeared. I know it sounds crazy, Brodyn. It is crazy. I am telling you the truth! I risk making myself sound insane by telling you this! But I cannot live beside you and hide all of this."

"Lass…" Brodyn pulled her into his arms and rubbed her back. "I believe ye. I dinnae ken if there is one God or many gods, but one of them sent ye to me. I kenned this the moment I saw ye. I dreamed of ye, as well, only they were not as frequent or vivid as yer dreams, and I couldnae see yer face, though I ken it was ye. We are bound, Caitriona."

Her angst, fear, and doubt melted away as his words soothed her soul. "You cannot know what it means to me to hear you say that," she sighed as her tears soaked through his tunic as his heart pounded against her ear. All of those dreams and years spent studying him had been preparing for her to enter this world and be Brodyn's wife and Queen of the Picts.

Brodyn kissed the top of her head and placed his hands on her hips. "I thought it was impossible, aye, but ye have shown me already in so short a time that many things I believed impossible do exist."

"Like what?" she asked?

"A loyal, honest woman, for one," he scoffed. "Ye dared to tell me yer truth rather than live in the shadow of secrets. Ye gave of yerself to save my people from a disease that has wiped out entire villages in Europe. And ye have shown me that I may, indeed, enjoy the company of my wife… something I never expected."

"Since you value honesty, I must confess that we have healing methods beyond anything you can imagine in my time. One poke of a needle into the arm can prevent us from becoming ill with certain diseases. Cadwyth had smallpox. I knew I could not catch it because I received a smallpox vaccine… it's hard to explain how it works, but I knew I could not become sick. I am not the selfless heroine you believe me to be," Caitriona urged. "I also used those three days to consider my place here, in this time, as your wife. I hope you can forgive me for avoiding you."

"Ye gave up yer own time to care for a man ye never met. I saw how tirelessly ye worked. When I came home and found ye in the tub, ye wouldnae awaken, tired as ye were. That is selflessness, Caitriona."

She thought about being carried in Brodyn's arms, her naked, wet skin against him as he laid her in his bed. Did he look upon her nakedness when he laid her down, or did he turn away while covering her? Either way, heat rushed through her body at the thought of being naked in his arms. After years of dreaming about his naked body covering hers, every moment without consummating this marriage felt like an eternity.

"This cave is feared by the locals and has been for many centuries. 'Tis thought to be home to the fae. People disappear here and never return. Those who dare to enter on solstice days are believed to pass into the underworld. Mayhap this is what happened to ye, only ye passed into another time, not another world," Brodyn added, pointing to the back of the cave. "I never believed in such things, but if this cave brought ye to me, I am grateful for its miracles."

His voice echoed off the cave walls, filling her heart with joy because he believed her. Her confession could have gone terribly wrong. Still, she'd taken a chance and now truly felt connected with Brodyn. This was her fate. He was her fate. Nothing either of them could do would prevent time from joining them together. And suddenly, the resentment she felt for him, for this cave, and for time as she knew it melted away.

Walking up to Brodyn, Caitriona placed a hand on his chest and looked up to his great height. "You make me the happiest woman because you believe my truth, though it is even impossible for me to understand."

"Ye make me the happiest man by offering me the truth, though ye kenned I could not understand it. My only fear now is that one day ye will leave me. I see now, more than ever, that I forced ye into this union. Ye have been honest from the beginning, and I believed ye to be an unruly bride full of falsehoods and deceit. Ye are here, now, Caitriona, and if ye should wish to leave, I willnae stop ye. I dinnae wish for aught but yer happiness. I will handle my cousins another way, even if it means freeing ye from this forced marriage."

Caitriona's stomach fluttered, and her heart squeezed, stealing her breath away. He would sacrifice all of his hard work to create alliances just to let her go. She was not sure if he loved her, nor was she sure she loved him, for Caitriona truly did not wish to fall in love with a man who would leave her a widow soon. All she knew was he was a good, caring man.

Suddenly, her desire to return home was replaced with the desire to stay here beside Brodyn and be the wife he deserved for as long as she could. Their days together were numbered. It was the only truth she could not bring herself to speak. No man wished to know the moment of his death, nor should any woman know the moment her husband would perish. It was her burden alone to bear.

A sob caught in her throat as she thought about the vivid grief in her dreams. The pain she felt as she stood over him, desperate to staunch his wounds as his life slipped away. She couldn't allow herself to fall in love with this man. They were destined to come together and just as destined to be ripped apart.

"I want to stay here, in this time, as your wife. I was scared when you found me on that shore. I wasn't sure if I was dreaming or insane. But you've helped me just by listening, and I'm proud to stay here by your side."

The intensity in Brodyn's eyes, more gray than blue by the light of the moon filtering through the cave's entrance, sent a tingle up her neck. The wind howled, and rain pelted the world just outside, but the cave enveloped them like a cocoon as Brodyn laced his fingers through hers before bringing them to his lips.

Caitriona quivered, desperate to feel his mouth on hers. When he stepped closer, pinning her back against the cave wall, its glacial stone soothed her inflamed skin as his lips lowered to hers.

Slipping her arms around his neck and balancing on her tip-toes, Caitriona opened her mouth to him. Their tongues entwined in a rhythm of passion and desire, hope and need. Gripping her hips, Brodyn moved closer, crushing her between his muscular body and the cave's wall. Cait moaned as his hands wandered her body, desperately seeking access to her bared flesh.

Caitriona pressed her hips against his, rubbing her needy core against his stiff manhood, and they both groaned with pleasure and frustration. Dizzy with desire, Caitriona lifted one leg and wrapped it around his hips, pushing herself against him like one of the wanton debutantes she read about in her historical romances. She lived inside the pages of a romance story now, one written by the stars just for her and Brodyn to experience.

Brodyn groaned and broke away from her lips to nibble on her earlobe, making waves of ecstasy rush down her entire body. "I want ye more than I have ever wanted anything," he whispered into her ear. "I would give up my kingdom to have ye right here, but ye deserve to be bedded properly." His breath hitched, and his mouth trailed tiny kisses down the column of her neck.

"I cannot wait any longer, Brodyn… I want you here and now," she sighed, tilting her head back. "This cave brought me to you, and this is where I wish to become yours." Slightly pulling back, Caitriona unclipped her golden brooch and gently allowed the tartan to slide off her shoulders and onto the cave's floor before unlacing the top of her tunic with shaky fingers. "I've waited my entire life for you, Brodyn. I want you, now."

For all of his gentleness and respectful demeanor, Brodyn became a caged animal released into the wild, ripping the top of her tunic down her shoulders. Her exposed breasts heaved, and her nipples hardened in response to both the cold and desire. Growling lowly, Brodyn took one nipple into his mouth, sucking until the sensation went straight to her throbbing core, intensifying her need.

"Ye are perfection, Caitriona Mac Cuill, my wife… my queen." Unlacing his trousers with one hand, Brodyn lifted her skirts with his other. Before Caitriona took another breath, he drove himself into her with a feral growl that made her dig her claws into his back as she tore off his tunic, yanking it over his head.

With her breasts pinned against his chest, Cait wrapped her other leg around his waist, crying out when he deepened his thrusts. His mouth crashed down onto hers, and she pushed back, thrusting her tongue against his while they took their pleasure with abandon.

"My… husband," she whispered into his mouth, making him groan his satisfaction in response.

Pulling his mouth away, Brodyn pressed his forehead against hers and stared into her eyes while his thrusts slowed to a caressing pace. "I want to pleasure ye…" he whispered, and Caitriona's heart beat wildly, her breathing labored.

"You are," she sighed, gripping his hips, and thrusting against him.

"I want more…"

Caitriona frowned in confusion as Brodyn pulled away, untied his boots, removed his trousers, and spread her tartan out on the hard, flat cave floor. "Lie down, my love."

He spoke softly and without any hesitation. She knew they were only words, that he couldn't truly love her yet, but warmth blossomed within her chest, nonetheless. Doing as he asked, Cait removed her tunics, slid them down her hips, and laid upon his tartan.

Slowly, Brodyn lowered himself, giving her a soft kiss before moving his lips down her body, laving her breasts with soft, suckling kisses that made her head spin and mind hazy. As his mouth slowly trailed down her stomach, she quivered, anticipation building to nearly exploding.

"I have wanted to do this since the night of our wedding." Caitriona cried out, her voice echoing off the stone walls as she flexed her hips. Then the tip of his tongue caressed her sensitive flesh, focusing on the one spot that drove her wild, making her clench his hair in her fists as the wet heat of his tongue moved in rhythmic circles, drawing out her pleasure until she nearly screamed.

Explosions lit behind her eyelids as waves of ecstasy washed over, making her arch and cry out just as Brodyn pushed inside her again, his rhythm frantic and rough but precisely what she needed.

Wrapping her legs around his back, Caitriona dug her fingers into his shoulders, bracing herself as their bodies came together, thrusting and writhing until they both cried out without inhibition. Brodyn twisted her nipples between his thumbs and forefingers, making Caitriona buck her hips and take him inside even deeper, heightening every sensation.

Never had she experienced a connection this meaningful, this powerful. This wasn't simply the consummation of a marriage. This was the reunion of two souls starving for one another, parted by nearly1,400 years. As he'd done in her dreams, Brodyn hovered above her, thrusting, gazing into her eyes, and searing her soul with the possession of a long-lost lover. She wanted to cry out, to shout her love for him until the cave walls shook, but instead she bit her lip and felt a lone tear slide down her cheek, something that had never happened to her before while lying with a man.

He pulled from her every raw emotion, every dream, every fantasy until their sweat-slicked skin melded. With a final cry of euphoria, their bodies went limp, and they lay together on the cave floor, a tangle of limbs.

"I wish to ken everything about ye, Caitriona. Tell me," Brodyn panted into her ear as he lay beside her.

"And I, you," she replied with a satisfied smile. "This was a good start, but we must return to the stronghold, should we not? I am famished, and we should be seen together before our people."

"Our people," Brodyn responded, kissing her temple before jumping to his feet like a nimble feral cat. "I am pleased to hear ye accept yer place in the tribe. And I wouldnae wish to deprive my wife of a hearty meal after such exertion." Putting out a hand, Brodyn helped Caitriona to her feet, and she held on for a moment to gain her balance, weak and disoriented after such a powerful experience. Somehow she felt zapped of all her strength yet stronger than ever.

Reluctantly, Cait dressed, wishing she could lie in that cave forever with Brodyn, wondering if the next time they would lie beneath its stones was the day she buried him.

CHAPTER NINE

BRODYN SIPPED HIS ale as he watched every motion within the longhouse. His people had taken to his command to respect his new wife and their new queen, but did they truly accept her? The odd glances they gave her made him question their intentions. He understood that his people needed time to trust her fully. Since the wedding, Caitriona had been tucked away at Cadwyn's home, and rumors buzzed that she was already unfaithful, which was not something Brodyn would tolerate.

His pride wasn't in question, but his wife's dignity was. Putting his clay mug down, Brodyn honed onto words floating through the hall, watching lips move and eyes narrow. Murielle commanded a group of men, as always, in the middle of the hall where she laughed and flirted, though Brodyn never worried overmuch about his wayward sister. She could hold her own among their tribe, and everyone had a healthy respect for her, as they should.

Nay, his concern was making certain nobody demeaned Caitriona. Still, he struggled to comprehend much of what Caitriona had explained within the cave. If any other woman had said such things, he would believe her insane and send her back to Domnall, wondering if his cousin had intentionally betrayed him with an unstable bride. However, from the moment he laid eyes on Caitriona, he knew she was different, special. She spoke their language yet used odd words and curious inflections. When she'd arrived, she wore strange clothing with fastenings he had never seen, made of strange materials. He knew very little about her or the world she came from, but he knew enough to believe every word she spoke.

Anya was a wise woman who came and went with the changing of the seasons, often arriving with odd objects and medicines. There was more to this world than war, but he had been too embroiled in tribal raids to pay attention to anything beyond the battlefield.

Never had Brodyn thought to have time for a wife, but political alliances often went hand in hand with kingship, which meant taking a bride to secure peace. His connection with Caitriona was unexpected, especially since she was not from this time. He was as foreign to her as she was to him, yet somehow, they had mutual respect, and Brodyn feared he would lose himself to her if he wasn't careful.

Already, his need to defend her honor threatened to upend him as he sat with a stiff back and watched his people for signs of scrutiny. Making love to her in the cave had been unexpected yet enthralling. Caitriona was a lioness with no qualms about baring herself to him and seeking her pleasure. Just the thought of it made him hard again, and he placed his hand on her thigh beneath the table.

When she gave him a satisfied smirk and a raised brow before taking a sip of her mead, Brodyn bit back a groan, desperate for this meal to end so he could properly make love to his wife in their bed.

Goodwin stalked over with a look in his eyes that Brodyn knew all too well. The man attempted to keep his notorious temper in line but was losing the battle. "Ye had better set the people straight about where yer wife has been since the wedding, lest they cast her out."

"What nonsense is this?" Brodyn growled through clenched teeth. It wasn't unexpected, but he was furious and disappointed in his people for speaking ill about his wife behind his back.

"Many say yer wife spent the last three nights at Cadwyth's

home, displacing Sorcha, who sought an extra bed elsewhere. The only time she left the man's side was to wash herself at the well." When a dangerous look flashed in Brodyn's eyes, Goodwin glowered back and held his stance. "Dinnae take yer temper out on me, Brodyn. I am on yer side. The tribe doesnae trust yer wife's intentions. They believe she is Domnall's spy, gathering information to bring back to him."

Pounding his fist on the table, Brodyn stood from his chair, nearly toppling it over. Caitriona jumped and shrieked beside him, and the entire room went silent, all eyes on him. Fire blazed in his chest as he glared at his people. "Yer queen has been absent these many days because she nursed an ill man back to health, risking herself to save yer husbands, wives, and children from succumbing to the same illness! Few survive, and Cadwyth is cursed fortunate my wife arrived from Dal Riata when she did and kenned how to help because she was once exposed to the disease! If ye speak ill of her, then ye are unworthy of her sacrifice!"

His voice bellowed, echoing off the walls. Brodyn clenched his fists at his side to prevent his hands from shaking. "If any of ye have anything to say, say it now, for I willnae tolerate whispers behind her back. Say it to our faces right now, without fear of retribution. This is yer only chance to speak yer concerns."

He crossed his arms and looked around the room. The guilty stared at their feet or avoided his gaze, as they damned well should for judging her. Caitriona's face blanched, and his blood boiled that his wife should be so humiliated by those who would defame her behind closed doors.

"She dinnae come willingly. We all saw ye carrying her across the village when she arrived like a squalling pig going to slaughter. How do we ken she willnae betray us or kill ye in yer sleep for Domnall? He has planned many a raid against us. Now he wants peace. Can we trust him? Can we trust her?" The room nodded and murmured when the smithy, Dunbar, bravely spoke his concerns, his gray bushy brows raised in question.

Brodyn began to speak, but he felt Caitriona's hand touch his arm as she stood from her seat. "I would like to speak for myself, if I may."

Looking at his wife, pride washed over him. She was a strong woman who would speak for herself, not some flower ready to wilt in the sun's heat. She'd mentioned women were educated in her time. That meant that women would obtain a sense of freedom and equality at some point in history, and he damned well wished it was within his lifetime.

Nodding, Brodyn sat down in his seat, giving full speaking power to his wife, who cleared her throat, straightened her back, and calmly folded her hands before her. "I appreciate and understand your concerns, all of you. I, indeed, did not willfully become King Brodyn's wife. Such is the fate of many women. I suppose I've always had a problem taking commands." She shrugged, and Brodyn was pleased to see many women smile and nod, understanding the truth in her words.

"However, I have not only accepted this marriage; I happily embrace it, for your king, my husband, is a good man who only wants what is best for his people, as do I. I am the bridge between you and the Scots, and I understand the importance of this alliance. We are all Celts, no matter the tribe, and it is time we all came together. I come to you with peace in my heart and a will to fight beside you as your queen."

The crowd listened intently, and many faces softened to her, though some remained unreadable. Brodyn couldn't expect everyone to be overly trusting too soon. Too much blood had been spilled between the tribes, and the Pictish elders had witnessed it firsthand.

"As for my time at Cadwyth's, I consider myself a fair healer, but I apologize if I displaced another healer. When Sorcha ran out of her home seeking help, Murielle and I were nearby. We couldn't find Anya, and as soon as she explained what ailed her father, I knew what it was. It's very easily spread and deadly. I have been exposed to it and knew how to support him. There is no cure. He was in God's hands, and God was merciful. I simply helped keep his fever down and fed him. This is why I sent Sorcha away, so she and the rest of you did not fall ill. There was no untoward purpose. I simply wanted to help."

"She saved my father." A voice called from the entrance of the longhouse. Brodyn and Cait looked over to see Sorcha pushing through the crowd. "I'm sorry to interrupt ye, my queen." She bowed her head and turned to the people. "I came in just as I heard King Brodyn speak. I am appalled at the wagging tongues of my kin. Without ever having met my father, our queen left the comfort of her marriage bed to sleep on my hard, cold, earthen floor so she might help my father recover from the illness he caught abroad. She saved him. She saved me, and she saved all of ye. She did not kick me from my home. She kept me alive. Queen Caitriona has my undying loyalty, as well as my father's, who still lies abed this night, peacefully asleep, regaining his strength thanks to our fine queen."

Brodyn popped his knuckles, waiting for anyone else to naysay his wife. Candles flickered, smoke wafted, and feet shuffled, but otherwise, there was no sound or movement across the hall.

"Anyone else wish to speak?" Brodyn asked calmly, looking around. When he met with silence, he nodded. "Good. I trust we have no further concerns. Let us continue the feasting and music, for we have much to be grateful for this evening."

The voices picked up at once as the men in the back started playing the lute and harp. Brodyn leaned toward Caitriona and kissed her cheek, making her blush before she took a sip of her mead. Her straight, white teeth and perfectly smooth skin mesmerized him. Many women in his time were missing teeth, and their skin was marred with scars, pox, bumps, or lines—but not hers. Did the future have some odd potion for perfect skin and teeth? He had so many questions for his wife.

She was an enigma, and the more he knew about her, the deeper he felt for her. It was fast—too fast. He never expected to love a woman, however when he looked at her, his heart pounded like a drum, his breath hitched, his stomach fluttered, and his cursed cock stood proud like an untried lad's, with no control of his lusty thoughts. Damn, if he didn't half wonder if his wife had bewitched him.

"Thank you for standing up for me," Caitriona said with a genuine smile as she touched his leg beneath the table.

"I will always defend yer honor," he said before kissing her cheek.

"By God, ye are a lost man," Goodwin chuckled from beside Brodyn as he finally settled into his seat to enjoy his food and ale now that his concerns about Caitriona's safety had been addressed. Brodyn was fortunate to have Goodwin on his side. The man wasn't loyal out of obligation. He was as good as family, and Brodyn knew he could always trust his word—even if his words were currently being used to point out Brodyn's newfound affection for his wife.

"Excuse us, my queen." Brodyn and Caitriona looked up to see three women varying in age and size standing before their table. "King Brodyn." The women bowed their heads to address them properly.

"Caitriona, this is Fiona and her two daughters, Maeve and Lorna."

"It's nice to meet you," Caitriona said, smiling at the three women.

"We wish to thank ye for what ye did for Cadwyth and offer our services in any way. We ken ye arrived with naught but the tunic ye wore from Dal Riada. We are the weavers in the village and would like ye to stop by for some fresh clothing. Do ye work the loom?"

Caitriona frowned and shook her head. "I am afraid I don't, though I would love to learn. I wish to make myself of use."

"Ye saved our village from disease, and ye clearly make our king happier than he has ever been, if ye dinnae mind me saying so," Fiona said with a cheeky grin as she looked at Brodyn. "I have kenned him since he was a lad. His mother was one of my greatest companions. Ye have been here less than a sennight, and already, ye have helped a great deal. Still, if ye wish to learn, I'd be honored to teach ye. Come in the morn, and we will fit ye with new tunics and teach ye the basics."

Caitriona lit up with flushed cheeks and a wide grin, making Brodyn lighter than he had felt in a long time. Fiona was correct; Brodyn hadn't felt this content since his mother passed away a decade ago.

"I would be honored," Caitriona said, and the three women bowed their heads once more and left the table.

Cait turned to Brodyn and wrinkled her brow. "Is it odd for a woman in this time not to know how to use a loom?"

"Not for a noble-born woman, worry not." He patted her leg reassuringly. "They willnae think anything of it."

She nodded and relaxed, taking another sip of her mead. Brodyn was grateful that Caitriona shared her secret with him, for it made all of her oddities more understandable.

The longhouse door swung open, and a gust of wind trailed in, making the candles flicker. Murielle, like the storm she was, dragged leaves in with her trailing black cloak and removed her hood as she approached her brother.

"Greetings, brother and sister."

"Where have ye been?" Brodyn groused at his mysterious sister. She came and went at her leisure, which didn't generally bother him, but she was absent frequently as of late.

"Here and there," she shrugged. "Did I miss anything of great import?"

"Just the village uprising against my wife. She could have used an ally, Murielle."

"Oh, everything is fine." Caitriona waved off his concern. "Murielle doesn't need to worry over me."

Arching one brow, Murielle looked at Brodyn and flashed him a smug smile. "Ye ken, I will gladly run through any man or woman who dishonors my kin; however, it appears Caitriona has it all in hand," she said and signaled about the room as men and women danced and chattered, guzzling their daily dose of ale.

"Ye havenae been sneaking off to meet a man in the village, have ye? If ye get with child before ye are wed, I will have to run a perfectly good man through, and I dinnae wish to do so."

"Not a single man in this village is worth a moment of my time," she retorted, wrinkling her nose.

"Thanks…" Goodwin said from the head table, rolling his eyes before chugging his ale.

"Ye ken I dinnae speak of ye, Goodwin."

"Care to dance?" he asked, perking up with useless hope.

"Nay, but thank ye." Winking, Murielle swished her cloak as she turned to move through the crowd and disappear into the darkness like always.

"Dinnae take her to heart, Goodwin. She doesnae see a good man when he is standing before her." Brodyn sighed and shook his head. Goodwin was the only man in this entire village worth Murielle's time, but he needed his sister to wed outside the tribe for alliances, much like he had. Too bad the lass was unwieldy and flighty.

"I dinnae take anything to heart lest it is a sword or arrow in the name of my king. I have plenty of other skirts to raise, and none would be hers, for I dinnae wish the sword that pierces my heart to be yers."

"Wise man," Brodyn grunted.

Nodding, Goodwin walked away to flirt with a small gaggle of lassies in the corner, all of whom appeared to be most interested in his finest warrior.

THE NEXT MORNING, Caitriona excitedly dressed in her faded tunics, knowing she would soon have new clothing, and better yet, she would learn the real art of weaving from genuine Pictish women. After last night's accusations, the village warmed up to Caitriona, waving and offering easy smiles as she walked past. Today was a new start. She would meet more people from the tribe and make herself useful as long as she was here.

After last night's evening meal, she and Brodyn had made love again, taking their time, exploring every inch of one another, memorizing every detail of each other's bodies. She ached in the sweetest way after their night of lovemaking. He was by far the best lover she ever had, and his size was nothing to scoff at, either. If she closed her eyes and imagined the man of her dreams from every romance novel she ever read, Brodyn would check all the boxes and then some.

After, they'd talked, cuddled in his bed until the fire turned to embers and the sky had begun to lighten with the coming dawn. She shared stories of her childhood, her parents, Emilie, and her career and of her childhood, filled with dance lessons, theater, and vacations, all things she'd needed to explain but which he seemed to understand. He'd shared his youth with her, telling her of how he'd trained for war, was involved in political intrigue, and learned to be a king by watching his father. Somehow, despite experiencing opposite upbringings in different historical times, they found common ground.

Her face hurt from smiling, and though she still dreaded how this fairy tale would end, Cait tried to focus on today, willing herself to enjoy every moment with her husband and the Pictish people.

"Ye seem mightily pleased this morn, Sister." Murielle glanced sideways at Caitriona as they walked toward Fiona's home.

"Should I not be?"

"Ye and my brother are getting on well, then?"

"We are," Cait replied. "For a man who dragged me to the altar, he's quite good to me."

Murielle laughed and nodded. "Aye, he is a good man, as I told ye. I wouldnae wish to face him on the battlefield, though we've had our share of wars between us. I miss Talorc at times. He was good to me, but he deserved his fate for turning on his brother and his king. I still havenae visited his grave. Is that wrong?"

"We all grieve in our own ways, Murielle." Caitriona touched her new sister's arm to offer comfort.

Nodding, Murielle looked ahead. "Here we are." Arriving in front of a large, round home built of wood and with a thatched roof, Murielle knocked on the door, and Maeve answered, her dark brown curls tied back with a leather string. She held a pile of folded fabrics in her other hand and stepped aside with a smile.

"Welcome. We are honored to have ye here." Fiona and Lorna waved from within the home, and Cait entered with Murielle by her side. Large, woven baskets lined the walls with piles of fabrics protruding from the top, and three looms sat in a line near the hearth. Colorful threads laced through long rows of thin, vertical ropes, creating plaid patterns reminiscent of the tartan cloak Brodyn offered her during their wedding ceremony.

"Did you make all the fabric in those baskets?" Cait asked, walking around the room to admire their work.

"Indeed, we did," Fiona said as she rummaged through another pile. "Aha." Walking over to Caitriona, Fiona handed her a large pile of tunics ranging from simple to intricate in color and pattern. "I hand-selected these for ye last night, my queen. I stitched the hem based on your height. I do believe they will serve ye well. There are simple tunics for daily wear and a few for festivals or ceremonies."

"This… this is too much," Cait whispered as she looked through the clothing. "Ye worked so hard on these."

"'Tis what we do, my queen. We all have our craft, and this is ours. We come from a long line of weavers, and ye would be surprised at how quickly we work the loom. There is no limit to what I can offer ye, so please ask any time."

Caitriona swallowed the ball of emotion welling in her throat. These people were so talented and giving. In a society where there were no grocery stores or malls, every item had to be created using local resources or imported through trade. Every gold torc or pair of earrings were handmade works of art. Every spear, sword, shield, or metal item was created skillfully by the smith. Animals were owned and cared for by each family for their own use, and the more cattle you owned, the more prominent you were. But, crops were grown by farmers, and Fiona's family created the garments. It was a perfectly oiled machine, and Caitriona wondered how life had become so complex in her time. Man's pursuit of convenience and mass production had led to a society that disconnected people from one another and from the land. These wonderous skills were now only practiced by the few who attempted to keep the art alive.

"I cannot thank you enough," she mumbled humbly.

"Nonsense, my queen. No thanks are necessary. We cannae have our queen wearing used, worn tunics... no offense. Ye represent our tribe, after all."

"No offense taken," she chuckled. "Had I not been so stubborn about the marriage, I would have arrived with finer things. It's my own doing," she lied. There was no point in admitting that she wore jeans and tank tops most of the time. "Oh, and please call my Caitriona. I prefer being referred to by my Christian name."

"Verra well, Caitriona," Fiona said with a proud grin. "Shall I have Lorna take ye out back to see how we first dye the threads? I willnae have a fine lady like ye dying anything, mind ye. 'Tis a stinky, messy business. But ye seemed mighty interested in the learning."

"I would love to see!" Caitriona said with pure excitement.

Murielle wrinkled her nose. "I have seen it plenty of times and dinnae wish to smell it any more than necessary. I will leave ye in their capable hands, Sister. Try not to bring the stink home with ye."

Murielle left the house, and Caitriona rolled up her sleeves, ready to spend the day bonding with women from her new tribe and learning from the people she'd spent her life studying.

CHAPTER TEN

ROLLING OVER IN bed, Caitriona wrapped her arms around Brodyn and squealed with delight. "I cannot believe it! You have no idea how much I've studied Beltane festivals, and today I get to experience one firsthand!"

Brodyn grunted and pulled her closer, pressing his face against her neck and deeply inhaling her scent as he so often did. His bedhead made Cait laugh; seeing this man, whose legend persisted fourteen centuries after he'd lived, with ridiculous hair in the morning only made her love him more. Nearly two months had passed, and Caitriona had adjusted well to the Pictish way of life, helping around the village, and participating in their customs. She'd learned more than she ever expected, and though she would never get to tell her contemporaries all that she'd learned, the thrill of experiencing it delighted Caitriona.

"Does Beltane not exist in yer time?" he asked, nuzzling her neck. Their bared bodies remained tangled after a long night of lovemaking, and Caitriona traced his bull tattoo with her finger, saddened by the scar left as a symbol of his brother's betrayal.

"It exists, but it's certainly not the same. We call it May Day, and many of the traditions are recreated. This is the real deal!"

"I am starting to understand yer odd sayings," Brodyn said, groaning as he stretched and detangled himself from Caitriona before climbing out of bed. "Sadly, my love, I must get started with the day. We have much to oversee. Be aware that Beltane is the celebration of the longer days, warmer weather, growing harvest, and rebirth, which means people will be disappearing into the forest throughout the day. In nine months, we will see many bairns born." Brodyn chuckled. "Mayhap one of them will be ours?"

Clutching her stomach, Caitriona frowned. She had been enjoying her time with Brodyn and doing all she could to avoid discussing anything beyond the impending war that she hadn't even considered what would happen if she became pregnant. Her cycle ended two weeks ago, so she knew she wasn't pregnant yet, but was it her destiny to have his child or not? She wasn't sure and decided it was best not to know.

"Does it distress ye to think about bairns?" Brodyn asked, sadness glittering in his blue eyes. Waves of grief washed over her, a feeling she avoided as often as possible. It wasn't having his child that upset her—it was the knowledge that he would be dead before the child was ever born.

Choking back the desire to tell him the truth about his death as she did about everything else, Caitriona shook her head. "Of course not. I just wondered how dangerous labor would be here. In 2023, we have pain medications, special equipment, and clean places called hospitals. The death rate for women and babies is significantly lower than it is here."

"Ye give up too much to remain here with me. These things ye call toilets, showers, hospitals, and cars...and cellphones! 'Tis beyond me why ye stay."

Getting up, Caitriona wrapped her arms around her husband, enjoying the heat they created when their nude bodies embraced. His manhood twitched between her legs, and she bit back the desire to continue last night's activities. "Nothing I gave up compares to being here with you. I..." Cait paused, flushing when she caught herself before speaking those three words she longed to say. She loved him, and she had the entire time.

She'd never stood a chance.

Still, he had yet to speak those words, and she refused to say them first. It wasn't a point of pride so much as self-preservation.

She knew he loved her, and the words never felt necessary to speak, but confessing her love would make her more vulnerable, and she wondered if it was better never to tell him the truth.

"You… what?" Brodyn asked, looking down at her curiously.

"I forgot what I meant to say." Caitriona placed a quick kiss on his lips, desperate to end this awkward conversation. "We both have busy days ahead. Anya has been a wonderful ally to me these past two months. It's helpful to have someone else who knows my truth. She's been teaching me what to do for today's festival so the villagers don't think I'm insane."

Quickly, they both dressed, and Caitriona put on a lovely purple tunic with gold Celtic designs embroidered around the hem and seams. Fiona had made it for Cait to wear during the festival, and it fit like a glove with flowing sleeves and a beautiful train. It was perfect for a Pictish queen and finished nicely with a gold belt around her hips, her simple bronze circlet upon her head, and the gold brooch from Brodyn pinned to her cloak.

Stepping out of her house, Caitriona was immediately greeted by half a dozen young lassies, all chatting excitedly in their finest clothing and with floral wreaths adorning their long, loose hair. "Queen Caitriona! We made something verra special for ye!" Wee Adalaide said, bouncing on her tiptoes.

"Oh! Did you, now? Whatever could it be?" she replied, feigning ignorance. As excited as they were, the lassies hadn't been very quiet about gathering wildflowers from the nearby fields.

"It's a floral wreath!" One shouted.

"Just like ours!" another lass replied.

"Ye gooses! Ye arnae supposed to blurt it out before ye show it to her!" the eldest lass scolded them.

Caitriona laughed and smiled at the girls as Adelaide presented her with a beautiful wreath of multicolored, fragrant flowers.

"Oh, my! It's lovely!" Caitriona took it in her hands and gently placed it upon her head, making sure to fit it around her bronze circlet. "It's a perfect fit. I shall treasure it always!"

"Yay!" The lassies jumped up and down as they cheered before running off to beg treats from the baker.

"The lassies sure do look up to ye," Anya said, shuffling over to her side.

"I look up to them, as well. They are so innocent, having never experienced danger, thanks to their king. I pray it is always this way for them." Cait sighed as she looked around the village. Music played, and people danced, swinging around with mugs of mead in their hands. Laughter rang out from every direction as the people celebrated the beginning of Spring. Lazy clouds obscured the cerulean sky, but the rain had taken mercy on them thus far, though puddles still lined the graveled road from rain the night before.

Silk ribbons adorned a nearby wooden pole that stood upright, secured into a deep hole that was dug into the ground specifically for the day. Happy maidens danced around the Maypole, giggling at the lads watching them from a distance. Now and again, Caitriona noticed a young lass bend over to capture morning dew in her palm, patting it into her face. Anya had already explained to Cait that morning dew on Beltane was considered an elixir of youth. Interestingly, only the young women partook in this ceremony, while the older women seemed content to avoid the tradition.

"My dear, I am off to the cave," Anya said, shifting the leather bag slung over her hunched shoulder. "As much as I enjoy the festivities in the village, the veil between worlds is thinnest on this day, and passing through the cave is much easier on me auld bones. Beltane brings an ambush of bairns, and I will need supplies aplenty to help birth them all come winter."

"I do not mean to insult you, Anya, but I cannot understand how you travel so easily."

"Ye mean because I'm ancient?" The old woman chuckled, putting up a hand when Caitriona began to protest. "Och, dinnae fret. 'Tis impossible to insult me these days. I ken I'm old, however my legs serve me well enough, and I find the exercise renewing."

Caitriona nodded. "I will leave you to your business. You are a mystery to me, and we've never truly spoken of how you ended up here and why you stayed. I hope to learn more about you. It helps me greatly to have your guidance, Anya." Cait squeezed her hand, and Anya nodded her understanding.

"I dinnae speak of it much, for I dearly miss my Edwin, but for ye, I will find the time to share my story when I return." Anya smiled and walked toward the stronghold's gates.

Caitriona continued to observe the festivities. As the day wore on and the Beltane fires were lit throughout the village, she watched as men and women jumped over the lower flames to purify themselves. Later, all hearth fires in the homes would be extinguished and relit using the central Beltane fire, a tradition meant to cleanse the house. Young couples lined up to become handfast, and as Brodyn had predicted other couples disappeared into the forest, not to return until some time later.

Sipping on her mead with Brodyn's arms wrapped around her waist from behind, Caitriona delighted in being present for this event. No amount of reading could replace this experience. She was a Pict now, fully accepted by the villagers who flashed her warm smiles, handed her food and drink, and made her bouquets of wildflowers. Her heart was near to bursting with love for Brodyn and these people.

When Brodyn's hot breath fanned her neck, Cait shivered, feeling dizzy with longing. How she could be so easily turned on by his merest touch, especially since it had been less than a full day since their last coupling, she couldn't explain. She was putty in his hands, freer than ever before.

"Care to take a walk with me in the forest?" Brodyn whispered into her ear.

She cocked a brow and turned in his arms, staring into his mesmerizing eyes. "I would be delighted," she responded, allowing him to drag her away. Fortunately, most of the village was busy celebrating, too deep in their cups to notice them slip away.

The night breeze caressed her heated flesh, and critters scurried into the brush as she and Brodyn dodged low-hanging branches. Stars glittered overhead, and owls called into the night, while crickets chirped their nightly lullabies. Holding hands with Brodyn while they walked felt natural, and though she spoke very little while they soaked in their surroundings, everything felt perfect. She knew this happiness had an expiration date, but she forced dark thoughts out of her mind. It was too late to change her fate, and impossible to change his. She was deeply in love with this man, and she valued every second she shared with him.

When they came to an area where the tree branches overlapped, creating an umbrella, Brodyn stopped and pulled her to him, giving her a soft, lingering kiss that made goosebumps cover her arms. The smoke from fires couldn't be seen from here, nor could the sounds of the festival be heard. They were completely alone, surrounded by nature's beauty.

A large stump protruded from the ground, surrounded by remnants of fall leaves, and Brodyn removed Cait's tartan cloak, placing it over the stump before taking a seat and pulling her down onto his lap.

"I have something to say to ye," he murmured, wrapping his arms around her waist.

Cait froze, unsure what he had to say at a moment like this that would turn his expression so severe. "You can say anything to me."

"Can I?"

Cait frowned and nodded. "Of course. If I can tell you I'm a time-traveler from 1,400 years in the future, I think we can say anything to one another."

"Caitriona," Brodyn whispered before clearing his throat and sliding his fingers through her hair. "I am in love with ye."

Waves of heat washed over her body like she suddenly stood within a raging fire, and her heart began pounding. "Why was that so hard to say?" she laughed, kissing his cheek.

"I have never said such words. They arenae spoken lightly. If ye dinnae return my love, I verra well may perish here in the forest."

Cait turned her body, straddling his legs so she could fully face him, running a finger across his short beard. "There is no need to perish. I am very much in love with you, Brodyn. I have been all along. I've loved you my entire life."

"Ye've haunted my dreams so many years. Now that ye are here, I cannae fathom being without ye."

"Ye don't need to worry about that. I'm not going anywhere. This is where I belong."

Sliding her hands beneath his tunic, Cait felt the heat of his chest and the pounding of his heart. Leaning in, she pressed her lips against his, gently at first, squirming as need crept up her core. Brodyn groaned and pulled her tunic down her shoulders until her breasts sprang free, her nipples puckering in the cold night air. The faster their tongues entwined, the more Cait moved her hips against Brodyn's rising desire. She needed him like she needed air. Brodyn's hands roamed her body and gripped her backside as his mouth moved to her breast, capturing one of her nipples in his mouth.

Caitriona arched and sighed, sliding her hands down to the string of his trousers, and tugged until it loosened. Slipping her hand inside, Caitriona wrapped her hand around his rigid flesh, satisfied when he shifted and moaned, reaching under her dress to slide one of his fingers inside her. A torturous minute passed as they caressed one another, dragging out the pleasure, both needing more yet savoring the sweet temptation. When Brodyn's thumb worked small circles over her most sensitive flesh, Cait arched and cried out, ready to explode. Her body demanded more.

Lifting her hips, Cait slid herself onto his manhood, sheathing him entirely, feeling him deep within her as she rocked rhythmically. His hands cupped her backside, and he stared into her eyes, watching as she took her pleasure.

"That's it, Love," he groaned, eyes locked on hers as he let her take control. One of his hands came up to caress her breast, and she felt the tension building with every thrust. He filled her, physically and emotionally. Brodyn was everything she ever wanted in a husband, and never had she felt so free and safe while giving herself to a man.

"I love you, Brodyn," she panted as her pleasure peaked.

"I love ye, Cait. Yer everything to me." Brodyn groaned and dug his hands into her backside as he pulled her down faster and harder. She knew he was ready, and so was she.

Together, they floated on waves of ecstasy, finding sweet release, panting as pleasure washed over them. Heart pounding wildly, Caitriona gulped for breath and rested her forehead on his shoulder. "You are beyond any expectation I ever had," she whispered, overcome by a raw vulnerability. She was loved, and she was safe in his arms.

"I never kenned a love like this existed." Brodyn kissed her damp forehead, and together they sat on the tree stump for several minutes before deciding to head back to the festival. The king and queen would be missed soon, and Cait didn't wish for the entire village to see them creeping out of the forest.

Arriving back, they carefully slipped in with the crowd, somehow unseen, and Cait bit back a satisfied grin before anyone suspected what they had been up to. She was a grown, married woman, and this was a festival built around fertility, love, and renewed life, but she wasn't keen on everyone knowing her private business.

For the first time since arriving, Caitriona felt fully contented, capable of enjoying herself without worrying over the future. No amount of trepidation would change history, nor could she try without affecting the timeline. She would fret again on the morrow, for tonight, Caitriona relished her time with Brodyn, determined to enjoy the rest of this night with her husband.

Just as Brodyn and Cait settled near the central fire, a guard walked over with a serious expression, alerting him to trouble outside his walls. Brodyn groaned. He had just lain with his wife and confessed his love. Was it too much to ask that a man enjoy one night without trouble?

Ronan, one of his most trusted warriors, leaned close to his ear. "My king. We have a situation."

The nape of his neck prickled, but Brodyn kept a cool head, knowing that his warriors would be calling for backup and riling up the tribe if an immediate threat loomed. He also knew Ronan was being discreet for some reason. "Is this about Ecgfrith?"

"I dinnae ken. A man was wandering close to our land. He wears odd clothing and speaking an odd language. He shouted at us and wielded a strange object. We restrained him and brought him into the stronghold. He keeps saying the queen's name. 'Tis all we can understand."

Brodyn took a deep breath and rubbed his forehead, looking at Caitriona. His wife smiled as she watched men and women dance around the fire, enjoying herself as she sipped on mead, completely unaware of trouble.

"There is one more thing, my king," Ronan whispered and lowered his brows. "The man looks like yer brother. Only, he cannae be because…"

"Talorc has been dead for two years," Brodyn said, finishing Ronan's thoughts. His brother was younger by thirty minutes and always envied Brodyn. Talorc, full of jealousy and pride, was determined to best Brodyn, to prove himself the better man. He was angry, violent, and prideful, losing control over himself when he felt threatened by an imaginary enemy… and much of the time, Brodyn was that enemy.

Two years past, a raiding party of Scots had attacked their stronghold. Brodyn and Talorc led the troops out of Pinnata Castra and down the hill, keeping the danger away from the women, children, and elderly. Domnall led the raid, hoping to kill both brothers to claim their land and extend his power. During the battle, Talorc had turned on Brodyn, attempting to murder him. With his life seconds away from ending, Brodyn had no choice but to defend himself, but he lost his brother that day.

Brodyn still wasn't sure why Talorc had turned on him. Was he involved with Domnall? Had they plotted against him and planned that raid? Many good men were lost that day, and many more lives would have been lost had Brodyn and Domnall not agreed to exchange brides and make peace. Caitriona was a reminder of why this marriage was essential. Why did this wandering man look like his brother yet call Caitriona's name?

Ronan grimaced. "Aye, we all saw Talorc turn against ye that day," he said, shaking his head. "Yet he appears to have arisen from the grave, or mayhap he was never dead. He speaks the language of the fae! He is cursed, I vow, and he wants our queen."

Brodyn scowled and looked at Caitriona again. Sensing his gaze, Caitriona turned to look at him, her smile fading when she saw the look in his eyes.

He knew distrust laced his every feature. He never believed in tales of fae traveling through the veil between their world and the human world that was said to exist within that cave. But, it was Beltane, and the veil between the living and dead was wide open. And Caitriona herself had traveled through that veil. So was this man also a traveler, or fae, or the walking spirit of his deceased brother? Worse, was he Talorc in flesh and blood, coming to seek his revenge? Brodyn had never seen his brother's body, nor had he ever been to his grave. But he knew he'd run his blade through his brother in self-defense after the betrayal, and then walked away, too heartbroken to face reality. There was a chance that he'd sought protection from Domnall and had been plotting revenge these past two years.

Was Caitriona part of the ploy? Perhaps his bride was sent to lure him into a false sense of peace. It felt wrong to suspect Cait of treachery, for she had appeared honest in all ways. Yet tales of kings being taken down by beautiful women and cunning men littered history's graveyard. Was he to join those kings in their downfall? Had he been tricked by a bonnie face the same way he had been tricked by his brother's false loyalty?

Brodyn knew painfully well that no bond was unbreakable when power was at stake. The scar he bore on his chest served as evidence of betrayal from someone he'd trusted with his life. He refused to make that mistake again.

"Is something wrong?" Caitriona asked, placing her hand on top of his. Suddenly suspicious of everyone and everything, Brodyn moved his hand away from hers and did his best to still his features. "Come with me," he ordered and swiftly walked away with Ronan in his wake.

When they were far from prying ears, Brodyn turned to face her. "Where is he?"

"Who?" Caitriona asked, but he didn't respond.

"He is with Anya in your home, my king. She spotted him first while traveling to the cave. She understands the words he speaks," Ronan asked.

"Anya came back? Who did she find?" Cait asked.

Taking Caitriona by the arm, Brodyn stormed across the village and up the hill to his house, not responding to his wife's questions or pleas to slow down as Ronan followed. Instead, he continued to drag Caitriona behind him until he got to his house and kicked open the door.

"Show me this man ye found," he snapped at Ronan.

Caitriona's eyes narrowed on him, and she crossed her arms, clearly angry as she awaited answers, but Brodyn was too aggravated to consider her feelings.

"He is locked in the room below the floors," Ronan replied.

"Who is locked in the holding cell?" Brodyn heard Goodwin's voice from behind, though he was not surprised that his best friend had followed them from the festival to the house when he saw the commotion. In fact, he was glad of it. Mayhap Goodwin would help to calm Brodyn's suspicious thoughts.

When he turned around and saw Murielle standing behind

Goodwin, Brodyn shook his head and pointed to the corridor. "Nay, this may be dangerous, Murielle. Go to your chamber until I tell ye otherwise." She opened her mouth to protest but must have changed her mind when she felt his visceral rage. Turning on her heels, Murielle stomped down the hall, acquiescing to his demand begrudgingly.

"Will you tell me what is going on?" Caitriona huffed.

Turning toward his wife, Brodyn finally spoke to her. "A man was found wandering near Pinnata Castra."

"So?"

"So, he wears odd clothing and speaks an odd language… like ye."

"And you are angry with me because of this?" she questioned with matching fire in her golden-green eyes.

Anya stepped forward and placed a hand on Caitriona's shoulder. "He was calling your name, lass."

Caitriona's eyes widened, and her gaze turned back to Brodyn. "Who… who is he?"

"Ye tell me, wife." Grabbing her wrist, Brodyn walked toward a hatch hidden beneath a bench in the corner that led to a flight of stairs leading down to a dank holding cell.

"Be easy on her, Brodyn," Anya whispered, but he only glared at the old woman, mistrust now pinned on her. He'd never questioned the woman's loyalties or why she disappeared for days on end, though it was too convenient that she was nearby when this man arrived. Mayhap she'd been a spy for Domnall all of this time. He knew his paranoia toward Anya was misdirected, but right now, everyone was suspect until he had answers. He hadn't gotten this far without seeing the worst in those around him. Even his father had perished before his time at the hand of his own brother. If Brodyn had learned anything from his past, it was that trust had to be earned.

When they descended the stairs, Brodyn grabbed a lit torch from the wall and slowly approached the single stall. His eyes met the man's gaze from between the iron bars, and memories of his brother flooded his mind like a torrent. The scar across his chest throbbed as a painful reminder that even those closest to you could prove to be your enemy.

"'Tis impossible," he whispered, looking at his brother, or a man who looked just like him. Talorc's face had always been nearly identical to his own. The only difference between them had been the way his brother's hair had been lighter, and his eyes the darkest brown, like their father's.

The man began shouting in an odd language, shaking the bars. His short-sleeved tunic was a bizarre color between red and brown with strange symbols scrolling across its front. The man looked at him and continued to yell, but only one word made any sense to Brodyn—his wife's name.

Turning, he scowled at Caitriona again. Had Talorc survived the battle and been nursed back to health by Domnall? Had he resided on their cousin's lands this entire time and had she known all about it? About him? Brodyn didn't doubt that she had played him a fool. Curse her for her lies and curse him for believing in anything as ridiculous as time travel. Had she not spoken of her "acting skills," as she'd called them?

"Come here, Caitriona," he said through clenched teeth. "Do ye ken this man? He seems to ken ye quite well."

Slowly, she stepped forward with her brows drawn together, stopping in her tracks when Brodyn lifted the flames high enough for her to see the man's face.

"Taylor?" she whispered, taking a step back and turning white as a specter.

STARING THROUGH THE rough iron bars, Cait gasped as her stomach roiled and blood rushed to her toes. Dizzy, she gripped the bars to steady herself. When Taylor placed his hand atop hers, Brodyn roared and pulled her away, knocking her off-kilter before grasping her by the waist and yanking her upright.

"What are you doing here? You… you should not be here!" She couldn't recognize the choked screech as her own voice, even though she knew it was. What she was seeing was incomprehensible.

Meanwhile, Taylor seethed. "You went missing! What did you think I would do? Leave the manhunt to a bunch of dirt diggers?"

She flinched at the familiar insult he'd always used when referring to her colleagues. He'd never agreed with her career path. She was supposed to stay in LA and audition for all the pilot episodes that would never make it on the air while he saved their country, fighting one bad guy at a time like the true hero he thought himself to be. Much like her parents, Taylor could never understand her fascination with history, with Scotland, or with the man holding her by the waist, digging his fingers into her flesh so hard that she was sure to bruise.

"Who are these people? What is this place? I know Scots take their history seriously, but is this some phony village, like a Ren fair or something? And who is this guy with his hands all over you? I'll kill him!" He shook the bars in his rage.

"Stop!" she told him, holding her hands over her ears, swallowing the bitter bile in her throat. "Taylor… you've put yourself in great danger by being here… how did you get here?"

"I went to the cave where you disappeared, but when I got a massive headache, I left. I searched the shore for clues, and these crazy dudes in ancient clothes with swords and spears took my gun and tied me up! I'm not afraid of this… this… actor… is that what this is? Are you part of some elaborate festival or play? And why does he look like me? You found a Scottish version of me and decided to shack up? What the hell, Cait!"

"What is this man saying?" Brodyn startled her out of the conversation.

"What is he saying?" Taylor asked immediately after Brodyn. "What language are you speaking?"

"He is asking what you are saying!" Cait wished she could run away from everyone in this room and disappear forever.

Anya stepped closer and touched Caitriona's hand reassuringly. "King Brodyn… they are from the same place. A place verra far away. There is much ye dinnae ken."

"Och, I ken what she told me! Fool that I am, I believed my wife could be honest and faithful! This is a trap set by Domnall!"

"Domnall set you up?" Goodwin asked from near the door. "That bastard will pay with his life!"

"No, you have it all wrong, Brodyn!" Cait urged him to listen, touching his arm to soothe him, but his face remained stonelike, his body as rigid as a statue. "I told you the truth!"

"Then who is this man? What is it he says to ye in this odd language? This is not the language of the Scots of Dal Riata! Have ye created a secret language?"

Caitriona threw her hands in the air. "You are both more alike than you think! Both of you accuse me of things I have not done, treating me like I'm yours to command, believing the worst of me! I was wrong about him, and apparently, I was wrong about you!" She got on her tiptoes to meet Brodyn's gaze, poking him in the chest with a pointed finger. "Neither of you deserve me! Let me leave this place. I do not belong here, after all! Not with a mistrusting ogre of a husband!"

She had opened up to Brodyn and told him truths even when she was certain he would call her insane. Instead, he claimed to trust her, had sex with her all over the damned village, and confessed his love. But just like all men, his love was conditional, fleeting, fickle. "You claim I've tricked you, yet you tricked me into trusting you!"

"Is he Talorc? Ye call him Tyler, but he is my brother." Brodyn was so focused on Taylor that he seemed not to hear anything else she said. Her heart shattered, and tears slid down her face.

"That's impossible! He is from my time. I was being honest with you! When I went missing, he flew to Scotland to look for me!"

"Flew? Now I ken ye are making a fool of me! I willnae believe he is fae any more than I believe ye are! Ye are both spies sent by Domnall to lure me into peace. Then, ye plan to slit my throat in my sleep and allow Domnall's army to enter this village! I willnae allow it!"

Brodyn grabbed her shoulders and pushed her against the iron bars. Though the sudden move scared her, she knew that he wasn't a man who would harm a woman, even in his rage. Pressing his lips against her ear, he whispered, "I trusted ye, and ye betrayed me with my own brother."

"Get your hands off her!" Taylor roared from the other side of the cell. "I'll kill you if you hurt her!"

"I dinnae ken what yer lover is saying but tell him that if he speaks one more word, I will cut out his tongue, shove it down his throat and watch him choke on it."

"Brodyn," Caitriona whispered back. "He is not my lover, and he is not your brother. I am not from Dal Riata! You know this! I told you who I was! Ask Anya! She knows!"

"What are ye saying?" Goodwin called from behind Brodyn. "Ye cannae be serious. Ye expect us to believe this madness? Does Domnall mean to insult us by infiltrating our land and feeding us ridiculous lies? He failed once, and he will never get a chance to try again. I will kill him myself if I get the chance!"

"Will ye ninnies stop yer blathering?" Anya shouted, her commanding voice echoing throughout the dark and dank room. "Ye men have nay idea what is possible in this world. Did ye not see his clothing or the weapon he carried with him? Ronan seized the weapon and is mighty fortunate it didnae go off! 'Twould have blown a hole the size of a bairn through his chest! What sort of weapon do ye ken could cause that sort of injury? Nothing from this time, I assure ye!"

Something Anya said broke through to Brodyn, though only slightly. He looked at Caitriona with uncertainty gleaming in his eyes, and she held her breath, wondering what he was thinking.

Cait knew he was confused and hurt, but so was she. She'd entrusted him with the truth, and though she didn't blame him for questioning it, this visceral reaction scared her, as did Taylor's sudden and most unwelcome appearance. He was going to get them both killed, and if Brodyn believed she and Taylor were part of a scheme contrived by Domnall, their tribes wouldn't unite against Northumbria, and the future of Scotland was in jeopardy.

She needed Samuel but had no way of finding him. Thank goodness Anya was a traveler who could talk sense into Brodyn, though right now, he was much too angry to see reason.

"Brodyn, I—"

"Dinnae say my name," he whispered with a dangerous edge. "I will find out the truth, and ye had better hope ye havenae betrayed me. Ye saw that scar on my chest, evidence that my brother cannae be trusted, nor anyone who conspires with him. I thought him long dead. Now ye show up with him not far behind. It doesnae add up, and I am no fool, lass. Tell me now. Why is he calling yer name?"

"If you would only let me explain…"

"Have ye lain with this man?"

"Brodyn… I told ye I've lain with other men, and—"

"Have ye lain with this man?" he repeated, banging his fist on the iron rod behind her, making her jump when rattling metal echoed around the stone-walled room.

"Yes. But he—"

"Take her away, Goodwin. Keep her securely in her chamber until I can decide what to do with her. Make sure a man is on guard until I decide what threat she poses to our people."

"Brodyn!" Cait looked around the room for an ally but found none. Brodyn looked at her like she was his enemy, not the wife he had made love to just hours before. Goodwin made no hesitation in grabbing her arm and dragging her away. Anya had already slipped out of the small room, and betrayal and fear clouded Caitriona's ability to think.

"Mayhap ye were bedding Cadwyn all along, aye, lass?" Brodyn shot at her as Goodwin dragged her away.

"You're a bastard!" she shouted, never feeling so insulted in all her life. How could he take every kind act she had made, every honest word she had shared, and turn it against her so effortlessly?

"Cait!" Taylor shouted. "I don't know what's going on, but I will get us out of here!"

Caitriona locked eyes with Taylor, a man she'd once thought she loved when she was young and foolish until he'd become overly controlling, wanting her to be something she wasn't and never would be. He thought he loved her still, but what he loved was the idea of her and what he hoped she could be for him. Now, he was here, in the past, threatening a peace treaty he knew nothing about. She shouldn't be angry at him. He'd flown across the world to find her. Would Brodyn, the man having her carried away, do the same?

Brodyn slammed his fist on the iron rods once more and snarled at Taylor. "I will deal with this one later!" Pushing past Caitriona, Brodyn stormed toward the stairs, leaving her in Goodwin's care.

"Brodyn!" she called, but he didn't look back. How had everything gone so terribly wrong? Where was Samuel? This wasn't the great love of the ages she'd read about. King Brodyn from the legends would never have had his beloved wife locked away.

Maybe she hadn't saved the peace; instead, she'd destroyed it. Somehow, she needed to get out of here and bring Taylor back to that cave before he was killed or destroyed everything.

Panic seized her limbs, making her stumble as Goodwin pulled her along, and her breath froze in her chest. "Goodwin... please... you have this all wrong. Someone has to listen to me!"

Turning to look at her from over his shoulder, Goodwin said, "Save it for the king. Only he can decide yer fate. I do his bidding, not yers." His jaw set into a stubborn line, and his eyes narrowed before he turned away to ascend the stairs, entering the main room before dragging her up yet another set of stairs to her chamber.

When the door slammed behind her, Caitriona spun on her heels and banged her fists into the wood, kicking and thrashing until she thought she would break a toe and bruise her hands. "Let me out! I never wanted to be here! I stayed for your people, for peace, and you do this to me!"

Caitriona was met with silence. Tears slid down her face as she gave up hope of being let out or even gaining a response from the other side. "I hate you, Brodyn…" she whispered as she looked around her ancient room with its rudimentary wooden walls and roughly built furniture. It had just begun to feel like home. Now, it was her prison, and her husband was her jailor.

"No, I love you," she whispered again. "Damn you, King Brodyn Mac Cuill, for making me love you."

CHAPTER ELEVEN

"SEND FOR THE messenger named Samuel in Dal Riata. I would speak with him. If Domnall refuses to comply, tell him our army will be at his gates by the new moon."

"Aye, my king." Owen, his fastest messenger, nodded and immediately left the room.

"I should have seen this coming," Brodyn grumbled as he stood from his seat in the back of the longhouse and began to pace.

"We will get answers," Goodwin said reassuringly. "And we will do what we must, once we have them."

"I willnae harm the lass," Brodyn said, turning to shoot daggers at Goodwin from over his shoulder. "If she betrayed me, she will be sent back to Domnall in shame, but I shall not harm her."

"I didnae mean to imply that, my king. Only Talorc… he is another matter."

"Aye," Brodyn agreed. He wanted to rip the man limb from limb for calling out his wife's name and defending her honor as if Brodyn was the one whose morals were in question. No other man had a right to defend her. Yet, Brodyn had imprisoned her, not protected her. Too much was at stake for him to fall prey to a bonnie lass with deceit in her heart.

He recalled how he'd slid into her wet heat just hours before, their bodies joined in ecstasy as she clawed at his back, nipping on his ear until shudders ran through his body. She'd responded to him like no other woman ever had. It felt real, like she genuinely cared for him. Had everything been a ploy? The ache in his heart rivaled the twisting in his gut.

"Brother… you locked up your wife?" Murielle stormed into the room with her green eyes ablaze. "Have ye lost yer mind accusing her of treachery?"

"Ye ken nothing about it, Murielle!" he responded, not wanting his cursed sister's opinions on matters she couldn't understand.

"I ken she gave three days of her time here to care for a dying man and stop the spread of a deadly illness! That is not the action of a woman sent here to destroy us. She could have sat back and watched us all die by sickness, never having to lift a finger! Ye have lost yer senses, Brodyn, and I ken why!"

"Och, and why is that, Murielle, if ye ken so much?" Balling his fists, he turned to face his sister, and Goodwin stood beside him with his arms crossed.

"Because ye love her! Ye are vexed because another man who loves her came after her, but instead of defending her, ye locked her away for yer own selfishness and bruised ego! Ye ken as well as I that Talorc is dead, and yer wife has no treachery in her heart, yet ye are angry at her for inspiring love in another man willing to go the distance for her. Well, brother… are ye willing to go the distance for her? Nay! Ye lock her away as if she is naught but an intruder. What will this say to the rest of our tribe? How will they ever trust her now?"

"Mayhap they shouldnae trust her at all," Goodwin shot back, always ready to fight with Murielle as if they were still young children tugging on one another's plaits and tunics.

Rubbing his temples, Brodyn closed his eyes and took a deep, steadying breath. "Ye ken nothing about what ye speak. Love has nothing to do with this. I have to protect my people. There is too much at stake, too many oddities surrounding her."

"She claims to be from the future, Murielle!" Goodwin interjected. "She speaks the odd language of this man who looks like Talorc, and she speaks of things we cannae understand. Can ye not admit that Domnall has been a threat long enough to warrant us being careful?"

"If Domnall meant to trick us by sending a deceitful bride who would lure Brodyn into a false peace alliance, why would he send Talorc—who is dead—to our lands? That would only trigger suspicion," Murielle argued. "Mayhap she is from elsewhere. Ye've never believed in the tales of the cave, but they exist for a reason. Folk have told the tales for generations."

"He wasnae sent here!" Brodyn shouted. "He came to retrieve her because they are lovers! She admitted to bedding him!"

Murielle shook her head. "Let me speak to Caitriona and look upon Talorc's ghost. I am not in love with either of them. I have not been nearly killed by either of them. I can think more clearly than ye."

"Ronan stands guard, but ye are free to enter so long as he stays near," Brodyn said, too strained to argue. "However, she cannae be set free until I have more answers. Anya has disappeared once again, cursed woman! I cannae tell if she is on my side or not at this point!"

"Of course, she is, ye ninny! Yer mind is addled, and rightfully so, but ye must allow others with less personal interest to find the answers." Murielle walked up to him and placed a comforting hand on his arm. "I will speak with her and report back. Ye ken I am on yer side, the side of the Picts. I ken what is at stake."

"Verra well. Go."

Murielle nodded and turned away, but before she left the longhouse, she looked over her shoulder with a mischievous gleam in her eye. "I noticed ye didnae disagree when I said ye love her."

Before he could give her a rebuttal, Murielle was gone, and Brodyn clenched his jaw. Heaven help him if Caitriona was his enemy, for his sister was not wrong. He was undeniably in love with his wife. How could she have so much power over him? He had bedded more women than he could count and never had he felt more than a passing need to slake his lust and move on with his business. But Caitriona showed up like a storm, knocking him on his arse. Just one look at her, and it was as if some missing piece of him had finally returned home.

Once Murielle was out of sight, Brodyn stood and turned to Goodwin. "I wish to see this strange weapon Ronan took from the man."

"Aye, 'tis kept safely in the armory under close guard."

Without a word, Brodyn left the longhouse and walked the few yards to the armory, ignoring everyone who attempted to gain his attention. The night had flown by and now, sunlight peeked through the clouds just over the horizon, and he squinted as his eyes adjusted to the light.

Arriving, he stepped inside and nodded at the guards. "Where is it?"

"Over here." Goodwin walked him over to a table in the back, where Brodyn saw the strange, black metal item. "Anya said 'tis called a gun, a verra powerful weapon that willnae be invented for several hundred years. Dinnae touch that trigger. If it goes off, well… ye heard what Anya said it can do."

"And ye believe this?" Brodyn asked, carefully looking over the oddly shaped object, avoiding the metal piece that appeared to set off the weapon.

"I dinnae ken what to believe, Brodyn. We have a man who looks like Talorc in the holding cell, and he speaks an odd language that only Anya and Caitriona understand. Both claim to be from a time much different from now and visit the fae cave. Either what they say is true, or they are from the Otherworld and have crossed the veil to torment us. I dinnae think this is Domnall's doing. He kens we can and would destroy him. And I saw ye kill Talorc myself. That man is not yer brother. At the same time, Anya trusts yer wife. Mayhap we should consider there are things we cannae understand."

Slowly, Brodyn placed the gun back onto the table, where he saw a few other strange items. "What are these?" Brodyn picked up a ring of oddly shaped pieces of metal, each one similar, yet slightly different. They jingled as he shook them, then spread them onto his palm to look at them more closely.

An emblem dangled from a small chain. It appeared to have a standard flying upon its metal surface, but not one Brodyn had ever seen before. Red and white stripes ran across it with a blue square in the corner filled with several white stars. A bright white piece of parchment was crumbled beside it with strange symbols that resembled Latin letters he had seen in some records his father once showed him from the monks. Despite his father's best efforts, he could never teach Brodyn how to read these letters, but these were different, not written with ink or by hand. Each symbol was the same size and identically printed directly onto the parchment.

None of these items could be from his time.

If only Anya hadn't disappeared again! Brodyn growled with frustration and slammed the wrinkled parchment onto the table.

He realized that as his temper had cooled, guilt had begun to niggle at him. He wasn't certain who that man was or what he meant to Caitriona, but Murielle was right. Brodyn was in love with his wife. Caitriona stole his heart and softened him in a way he never thought possible. And, he had fully believed her story about being from the future. So why was he suddenly questioning it?

Still, his mistrust of everyone around him was a survival skill that saved him many times, and Talorc's betrayal had only reinforced that nobody was beyond treachery.

But Cait wasn't Talorc, and Brodyn needed to set aside his jealousy, pride, and mistrust and speak with his wife. She claimed this man wasn't Talorc, and perhaps she told the truth. After all, Cait shared the same soul as the bride Domnall sent. Perhaps Taylor shared Talorc's soul. As odd as that concept was, Brodyn prayed she told the truth. There were things he didn't understand and even more things he didn't know. The one thing he did know was that he couldn't live his life without his wife.

He would find answers, but to do so, he had old demons to

face before he could face the woman who owned his heart.

WHEN A KNOCK startled her out of a staring contest with the low burning flames in her hearth, Cait's heart jumped into her throat, and she looked at the door, wondering if her impending doom stood on the other side.

"Caitriona, 'tis Murielle. I've come to speak with ye."

"You may enter if the guard at the door allows you to," Cait replied with spite lacing her tone.

The door's bar lifted from the other side before it swung open with a creak.

Murielle's head peeked around the corner, and Caitriona waved her in. "Despite what you've likely been told, I am not your enemy," she said with a sigh.

"I ken that." Murielle entered, but Ronan stood at the doorway with his giant arms crossed as he stared blankly ahead. "I spoke with Brodyn."

"Oh?" Cait quirked a brow and plopped on the bed, her mind tired of spinning circles as she tried to decide how to handle her situation. There was no escape as long as the door was barred shut and a guard stood by. Taylor likely remained below in the holding cell, and Cait felt terrible that he had come to find her and ended up here.

"Ye must understand that he never believed the tales of travelers that our people have told for generations, nor does he believe in the fae, or gods, or even a God. All Brodyn believes in is what he can see. Training for wars, keeping his people safe at all costs. He will take time to come around, but he will."

"Meanwhile, I'm a prisoner in here, and Taylor is a prisoner in the cell. He isn't your brother, Murielle. I wish I knew how to prove that, but I can't... especially from within this room." Caitriona paused and raised a brow. "Wait... you speak of travelers. Brodyn told you about me, and you believe it?"

"I ken ye tell the truth, aye. I've seen enough to believe the stories, and then I found this…"

Reaching into a pouch tied to a bronze belt around her waist, Murielle pulled out a familiar object that made Cait gasp. "My flashlight! I dropped it the night Brodyn found me on that shore!"

"Aye, I found it while walking along the shore last night. It didnae look like any object I've ever seen. What does it do?"

Murielle handed the flashlight to Cait, who clicked the round black button, grateful to discover the batteries still working. The heavy-duty flashlight held up to its waterproof promise. When its LED light shone brightly, illuminating the room with its white glow, Murielle's eyes widened, and she scrambled back with a squeal, avoiding contact with the light.

"The light won't hurt you," Cait said reassuringly, waving her hand through the beam.

"Ye've captured the sun inside this wee object?"

Caitriona giggled at Murielle's intrigue. "No, not at all. They are just small light bulbs. They won't be invented for over a thousand years from now. It uses batteries." Unscrewing the back of the flashlight, Cait dumped three large batteries into her hand to show Murielle.

Murielle stared in awe for several silent moments before shaking her head and taking a deep breath. "I would love to see this wondrous place ye come from someday! Cait, I wouldnae show this object to many people here. They may believe ye are the devil."

"Is that what you believe, Murielle?" Caitriona asked, clicking the light off and placing it on her nightstand.

"Och, nay! What if I told ye that ye are not the first traveler I ken, and this is not the first item from your world I have held in my hands?"

"I would be relieved to hear this, Murielle. Is that so?"

"Aye. I ken a traveler."

"Anya?" Cait asked slowly, and Murielle nodded.

"She comes and goes between this time and yers. I followed her to the caves when I was a wee lass. She bade me never to tell a soul that she passes through time here. When there is an illness, she retrieves medicines, though she doesnae tell anyone about it when she makes her potions and tonics. I never told Brodyn because I didnae think he would believe me. I love my brother, but he isnae as open-minded as I am. I kenned ye were not from here immediately when I saw ye. I ken Brodyn now believes ye and Anya are from the future, even if he is confused right now. He would never have accepted such a truth from anyone other than ye."

"I cannot tell you how much it means to have your support, Murielle. You're truly the sister I never had." Caitriona placed a warm hand on Murielle's and smiled, daring to let hope rise in her heart. With Anya and Murielle on her side, Cait hoped Brodyn would see reason.

"My brother loves ye verra much; I can see it."

Caitriona scoffed. "He has an odd way of showing it."

"This is his way of showing it. Ye understand that he saw a man who looks like the dead brother who betrayed him during a battle? That would shake anyone. Brodyn doesnae trust easily."

"Well, I cannot make Brodyn trust me if he refuses to speak to me."

"He will come to visit ye once he has had time to think. He is a fair man. I trust that my brother will come around."

"Time," Cait scoffed. "Time is what got me stuck in here in the first place!"

"Thank ye for entrusting me with yer secrets, Caitriona. I will stand by ye, always. I ken my brother believes ye, as well. But, first, he needs to come to terms with seeing Talorc's face again."

Cait let out a long breath, feeling lighter than before, thankful for her new sister. Caitriona felt like she was stuck in one of those time travel romance novels she used to read, but there was nothing romantic about Brodyn locking her away. Romance novels always had happy endings, except this story ended in death and heartache. She and the stubborn man she loved wouldn't get her happily ever after.

"Is there anything I do for ye before I go? I vow to come back as often as possible, but I must see to some of the villagers and their crops. We are preparing the fields for seeding, and the livestock is ready to leave the byre."

"No, I will be all right, one way or another. Thank you for being someone I can trust in this place and time. You cannot know what it means to me."

"Ye cannae ken what it means to me to finally have answers about the cave and where Anya's been going for years. I half thought I was insane for believing it."

"You are not insane, but I encourage you to keep it between us, for I doubt others will understand. I don't need anyone burning me at the pyre."

"I would never allow such a thing." Murielle squeezed Cait's hand. "Farewell, Sister. I shall return as soon as I can."

Hugging Murielle, Caitriona felt like she'd known her all of her life. She supposed her soul had known Murielle in many lifetimes, which was still hard for her to understand. Why could she remember some details but not others?

Caitriona sat on the floor and stared at the fire's flames, thinking of the life she once lived and the people she left behind. She missed Emilie and her parents. How she wished to pass through the cave once more to tell them she was all right. A tear slid down her cheek as she grieved for everything left behind while she sat here all alone, awaiting her fate and wondering what her warlord husband would do with her and Taylor. She prayed Taylor would leave with all his limbs intact and his head still on his neck.

Hearing the door open, Cait looked over her shoulder, scrambling to wipe away her tears before anyone saw her weakness. Anya stood in the doorway with a bowl of porridge, but Caitriona was too stressed and nauseous to think about food.

"King Brodyn bid me feed ye."

"How gracious of him," Cait mumbled. "I'm not hungry. What I want is to leave this room and go home."

"Ye are home."

"You know what I mean, Anya." Cait looked at the older woman and glared, never blinking until Anya sighed and nodded.

"Aye, I always kenned ye would arrive. And, ye ken why ye cannae go home."

"How could you possibly know I would arrive?"

Anya placed the bowl of porridge onto the small side table near the bed. "My dear Edwin was a Shaman and kenned what would come to pass. Some would call me a wise woman, others a witch. Perhaps neither is wrong," Anya said with a shrug. "Some of us are just born with a purpose that others cannae understand. Samuel is one of us, and we have danced this dance together over many lifetimes."

Swallowing, Caitriona shivered, wrapping her cloak around her arms despite the heat in the room. If she heard someone speaking about Shamans, witches, and time travel back in February, she would have dismissed them outright. Science had always been her guide, but she knew now that science couldn't explain everything as she once thought. "What time are you from, Anya?" she asked, desperate for more understanding.

"I passed through the cave during a blitz in 1941. We didnae have air-raid sirens, so when bombs fell, I sought shelter in a cave near my wee village. When I left the cave to find my family, I found myself on the shore just outside the cave here. Not only was I transported back in time, but I was also relocated here. This land is alive, lass. Ye may see us as pawns, but I prefer to consider us guardians. We serve a great purpose, often at a great cost."

Caitriona listened intently, soothed by their shared experiences. "You decided to stay here?"

"Aye. I met my Edwin and kenned I could never leave his side. My family perished in the blitz, and my town was destroyed. I had nothing to return to, and I could help these people more than I could help in 1941. I grew close to Brodyn's family and helped raise the children. I never had bairns of my own, and Edwin passed away two decades ago. Brodyn, Murielle, and Talorc were all I had left. I will be 99 years old this autumn and living between two times has allowed me to flourish. The air here is cleaner, and I have access to supplies from our time." Anya chuckled, and Caitriona enjoyed watching the elderly woman light up as she recounted her past with much joy.

"Is Taylor that similar to Talorc?" Cait asked. "Brodyn went out of his mind when he saw him."

"He looks verra similar to him, aye. He isnae identical but close enough to have Brodyn in a fit. Cannae ye blame him? He killed his brother two years ago after Talorc turned on him. It was the worst moment of Brodyn's life, and he has lived with the scar on his chest to remind him of that deceit. Plus, 'tis hard for a king to trust anyone, especially in this era. His father died by an act of betrayal, and Brodyn nearly suffered the same fate."

It was hard to remain angry with her husband when she understood all he had endured. Though she sympathized with Brodyn's physical and emotional scars, Caitriona couldn't shake her own feelings of betrayal. She had been honest and genuine, giving of herself entirely. Brodyn wasn't the only one who sacrificed for his people, and Cait didn't deserve to be cast aside. "I cannot make things right with Brodyn if he refuses to speak with me."

"Brodyn will come to his senses soon enough. He always does."

Sighing, Caitriona plopped onto her bed and cradled her face, having nothing else to do with herself but wait.

"Try to eat, lass. Ye need to keep yer strength." Anya stepped out of the room and slowly shut the door behind her, leaving Cait with nothing to do but repeatedly click her flashlight's button as anxiety roiled in her empty stomach.

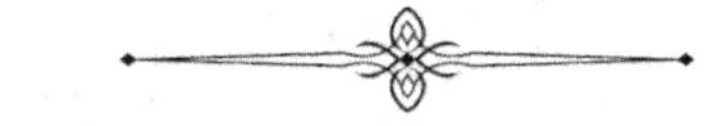

CHAPTER TWELVE

PACING IN FRONT of a large oak tree just down the hill from his village, Brodyn clutched his brother's ruby necklace—the last of Talorc's possessions—in his fist and stared at the soil. That necklace had been hidden away since the day Brodyn killed his brother. Given to Talorc by their father, Brodyn couldn't bring himself to destroy it, even if he couldn't stand the sight of it. He never spoke of it, keeping the bauble locked inside a wee chest beneath his bed, until now. It was time to finally visit Talorc's grave and make peace with his brother's memory.

Roots jutted from the ground, surrounded by small dew-covered blades of grass and one thistle flower that Brodyn assumed Anya planted, as she had done upon his mother and father's grave when they passed. He didn't blame the old woman for her continued love for Talorc. She had raised him since he was a wee lad. His betrayal broke her heart, but she'd found ways to honor the man, remembering a time before anger poisoned his soul.

Darkness and cold embraced him like old friends, reminding him of nights camped out with his men before a war. It had been a similar tree that he and Talorc laid beneath before that fateful battle. How had he not sensed the betrayal brewing within his brother's heart?

In truth, a part of Brodyn had always known his brother would turn, even if he didn't want to believe it. Now, Talorc's bones rested beneath this tree. Until now, Brodyn couldn't bring himself to visit Talorc's grave, nor had he been present to see him buried. He'd resorted to asking Goodwin for the gravesite's location, unwilling to say why he'd finally decided to travel there. However, with a man in his holding cell who looked exactly like Talorc, Brodyn had to see his brother's grave for himself, and he didn't relish the task at hand. Never again could Brodyn allow his brother's memory to affect his relationship with Cait.

His heart twisted when he recalled his rough treatment of her. He loved Caitriona more than he'd ever thought it was possible to love a woman. In his gut, he knew she hadn't betrayed him, and his gut seldom led him astray. However, his brother's treachery sat heavily on his heart, prompting Brodyn to second-guess everyone's motivations, even those most loyal to him. He'd learned the hard way that no one could be trusted, not when you're a king, and it was a lesson he'd never forget.

Still, after searching his heart during the long night, he'd finally realized that he was confident in Cait's innocence and that he owed her an apology. He only prayed she would accept it, and he wouldn't blame her if she didn't. But before he could address his wife, he had to seek closure from the ghost that haunted his days and the memory that tainted his nightmares.

Something wasn't right about the man Caitriona called Taylor. It wasn't envy that made the hairs of Brodyn's neck stand on end, nor was it even his strong resemblance to Talorc. His eyes held a darkness that Brodyn recognized—the same darkness that had been reflected in Talorc's black eyes just before he ran his blade through Brodyn's flesh. He knew that, given a chance, this man would do the same. He was a threat, not only to Brodyn but to Caitriona and Pinnata Castra.

Brodyn wished to turn away now and never return to this gravesite, but he couldn't. For two years, Brodyn had avoided coming here, and never had he expected his first—and last—visit to be under these circumstances.

The moon's blue haze shone down on the large oak towering overhead, the same tree he, Talorc, and Murielle used to climb as children. Now, its roots shared soil with his brother's bones. After killing his flesh and blood on the battlefield, Brodyn was too heartsick to bury his brother—the one cowardly act of his life, and he regretted it terribly.

Aye, he'd killed Talorc in self-defense, but the memory of his blade piercing his brother's heart would forever haunt him. The feel of his blade piercing his brother's flesh, the sound of bone shattering, and the sight of blood flowing from Talorc's chest as the life left his eyes would torture Brodyn for the remainder of his days. He'd left the task of his brother's burial to the priests, requesting he be laid to rest below his favorite tree, which had served to keep Talorc outside of the sacred burial sites reserved for royalty, yet offering him a respectful resting place.

"Brother… I do all I can to avoid thinking of ye because if I do, yer betrayal wounds me all over again." Brodyn clutched the gold necklace in a white-knuckled grip, clenched his teeth, and kneeled on the wet grass beneath the tree. "When the priest buried ye, he returned to me with this necklace, the one Father gave ye. Ye never removed it because it was the one thing ye owned that I didnae also own. Ye spent yer entire life wanting what I had, and ye died trying to take everything from me."

Brodyn cleared his throat, wondering if he sounded mad speaking to a tree, but this was his only option if he wished to seek closure. "I dinnae want yer necklace, and I never did. I loved ye, Talorc. I wanted ye to be happy, even if ye wanted me dead. Ye made me kill ye!" Brodyn roared, feeling years of anguish break through his hard exterior, shattering his resolve to remain calm.

"I never wanted anything from ye but a brother's love. I have come to return yer cursed necklace. I ken ye wouldnae want me to have it, nor did I ask for it. In exchange, I ask ye to stop haunting my dreams, and if ye have returned as this Taylor man, ye should ken that I will kill ye again if ye hurt my wife." Brodyn's fist shook, and he bit back the tears that threatened to fall. His brother was not worthy of his grief yet he received it because Brodyn wasn't heartless, though he wished he were. Guilt would not weigh so heavily on his soul if only he was the stone-hearted beast his brother had created in his sick mind. Sadness gripped Brodyn's heart when he considered what could have been if only Talorc had moved past petty desires and power struggles.

Digging his fingers into the soggy soil, Brodyn placed the necklace beside the thistle flower before covering it with dirt. "Now ye may rest for eternity with the only thing ye ever truly loved." Shifting, Brodyn pricked his finger on the thistle's thorny stem, and he jerked back when the sting caught him off guard.

A bright light flashed behind Brodyn's eyes, propelling him back against the tree's trunk. Mixed voices and blurry images flooded his mind. Cradling his head as pain seared his skull, Brodyn gritted his teeth and clenched his eyes shut as memories surfaced…only, they weren't his memories at all.

A woman who resembled Caitriona stood beside Domnall. Brodyn realized he was feeling Talorc's emotions, seeing through his eyes. Possession, greed, and envy brewed in his veins as he stared at the woman, desperate to have her for himself. But he couldn't have her because his whoreson cousin had offered her to his twin brother as a peace offering… Not if he could help it.

Resentment fed his need for revenge. He wanted what Brodyn had—the kingship, the power, and especially, the woman.

Brodyn had sent Talorc to Domnall's stronghold to negotiate peace, and instead, he started a war.

"Brodyn doesnae want peace. But I do," Talorc had told Domnall "Give the bride to me, and I will ensure Brodyn's death. With me as king, we will have peace." His brother's familiar voice echoed inside Brodyn's brain, making him shout out and grip his temples as pain slashed through his skull.

When the voices faded and the images dissolved, Brodyn roared his renewed pain into the morning sky, sending birds flying from the tree. Now, he understood what had motivated Talorc to turn against him. An agreement was forged in Brodyn's blood.

He'd already believed his wife, but what Brodyn had witnessed shook him to the core. Never did he know such forces existed beyond the natural world. Not only were his eyes opened to something bigger than he could possibly comprehend, but now he knew the truth about his brother's schemes, and he swallowed the bile burning his throat.

Talorc could have secured peace for his people, yet instead, he'd sought power and prompted a battle where dozens of Picts and Scots died needlessly. Talorc died serving his own desires, and Brodyn secured peace without him. Now he had Cait as his wife, and Domnall as his ally. Talorc had died in vain.

Brodyn couldn't blame Domnall for plotting with Talorc, for he understood that a man would stop at nothing to keep his people safe and victorious. Believing Brodyn was not open to peace, he'd had to make an agreement with the brother who was. Now, Brodyn understood more than ever. Cait shared a soul with the woman in Talorc's memory, and Taylor shared Talorc's soul. If Talorc was willing to kill for the bonnie bride, what was Taylor capable of?

The man was yet another part of this time loop, all their souls interwoven, and always coming together in every lifetime. Brodyn was part of an ancient love triangle between two brothers and one woman, and Talorc always lost. In the end, so too, would Taylor. He had to get back to Pinnata Castra and deliver Taylor back to the cave before the evil lurking in his soul broke free.

Climbing onto Tatha, who casually grazed while she waited, Brodyn sped back up the hill to his village, determined to make things right with Caitriona and get Taylor as far away from her as possible. Riding through the gates and past the stables, Brodyn stopped his horse directly in front of his home, dismounting and throwing the door open, then storming up the stairs.

"Ye may leave, Ronan," he said, dismissing his man who stood outside the door. Nodding, Ronan turned and left, heading down the stairs. Pushing the door open, Brodyn stopped short when he saw his wife sitting in the bed, holding a cylindrical piece of metal with the sun's power shining from one end.

"Have more to accuse me of?" she asked with narrowed eyes and reddened cheeks.

"What in the gods' creation is that object?" He reached out to touch it, pulling back just before his finger met with the ray of light.

"It's called a flashlight. Murielle found it on the shore. I dropped it when you found me there. I'd point out that it's evidence that I come from the future, not Domnall, but I'm not sure it matters anymore."

"Is it hot?" he asked, hearing her, yet still too intrigued to look away.

"Nope." She ran her hand through the beam before shining it into his face. He squinted as he looked into its light before blinking and shaking his head.

"How does it work?"

"Is this why you are here? To discuss how my flashlight works? This is very basic technology from my time. Should I explain modern aviation, how we have large metal birds that fly humans from one end of the world to the other in less than a day? Or discuss how we created a vessel to fly men to the moon? How about pipes that carry water to our homes and knobs that give us a choice of hot or cold or even lukewarm temperatures instantly before we bathe? We've already discussed vaccines. Is there anything else you want to know about where I came from? If it makes you stop accusing me of treachery, I will gladly retell the entire story of the Industrial Revolution. It seems I have nothing but time while I'm held captive in this room."

Brodyn did, in fact, wish to discuss much of the oddities she mentioned, though he shook his head and focused on the present rather than the future. "Caitriona, I ken I owe ye an apology. I was brash in my reaction. I am a man surrounded by plots, war, and danger every day. Ye wouldn't be the first person to betray me—if ye did. However, I ken ye didnae."

"I'm sorry your brother turned on you, but I will not pay for someone else's sins. I risked everything to tell you the truth! You said you believed me, then you locked me away." Her voice rose and quivered, and Brodyn saw her fisting the bedsheets as she harnessed her anger.

"Caitriona, Taylor is Talorc. He is dangerous. I visited his grave today for the first time, and… something happened." He paused, then dared to come closer to her. "I pricked my finger on the thistle buried over his grave, and suddenly I was thrust back in time, seeing the world through his eyes. Blinding rage and envy consumed me, and I witnessed the moment he conspired to kill me… It was for ye."

"For me?" Cait wrinkled her brow and frowned. "But…Talorc has been dead for two years."

"He wanted the woman promised to me. Her resemblance to ye is remarkable, though ye are far more beautiful."

"Don't bother sweet-talking me," she groused, crossing her arms.

Brodyn bit back a retort. He hadn't come here to fight, though the woman seemed to inspire passion in the men who loved her, and Brodyn was no exception. Even now, he wished to take her in his arms, to ravage her with kisses, to kneel before her and plead forgiveness. "I believe he is in love with ye in every lifetime. I am his enemy, for I am the one ye love… assuming ye still do." He offered her a contrite smile.

Blinking, Caitriona stared at him for a silent moment, processing his words. "There's a lot to unpack there," she mumbled. He didn't quite understand her meaning, though he assumed it meant she was overwhelmed by his information, and he didn't fault her for it. He himself still struggled to believe he had witnessed his dead brother's memories. In fact, over the past two moons, his entire worldview had changed drastically. And it was all because of this woman's heart. And soul.

"There was a thistle atop his burial site?" she asked, tilting her head with curiosity. He nodded, and she shifted in the bed. "There was a thistle atop your…" she stopped talking and eyed him, pursing her lips before her face flushed, and she cleared her throat.

"Listen, Taylor has a foul temper and can be controlling, even aggressive at times, but he would never hurt me. If you let me, I will get him back to the cave and away from here. You really believe he's Talorc?"

"Aye, I ken he is, and I ken he will kill me if he remains here."

"That is impossible," Cait said, shaking her head.

"Why is it so impossible to believe that a man in love with ye will kill me? He believes I've captured ye and hold ye against yer will."

Caitriona threw her hands up in the air and scoffed. "You have, Brodyn!"

"And I am here to remedy this. Ye must trust me."

"And you must trust that I know he will not kill you."

"Och, aye? How can ye ken this?"

Caitriona began to open her mouth but snapped it shut before saying something she obviously thought the better of. Brodyn took a deep breath and stared into her eyes. "Ye ken how I die, dinnae ye?"

She swallowed hard and diverted her gaze, staring instead at the wavering candle flame casting distorted shadows across the room.

"It's written in the books," she whispered finally.

"I dinnae ken what a book is, but I ken tales are often told incorrectly."

"I saw your bones!" she cried, hopping off the bed. "They were your bones that I touched, sending me back to this place! I saw the…" her voice shook before she finished. "I saw the evidence of a violent death myself. I know how this ends, and it's destroying me!" she sobbed, her legs giving way as she struggled to stay upright.

Brodyn strode over to her, placing supportive hands on her

waist and frowning when she pushed him away. "Don't touch me! Maybe it's better this way." Wrapping her arms around herself, she turned away from him.

He deserved her ire. The thought of dying didn't bother him nearly as much as the thought of losing her. Without Caitriona, he had nothing to live for. "I love ye, Caitriona. Unburden yerself. Tell me what ye ken."

She shook her head and kept her back to him, straightening her spine. "This isn't love."

Stepping closer, Brodyn grabbed her shoulders and spun her around, forcing her to face him as he pulled her close. He felt the warmth of her body through her thin undertunic and longed to show her how precious she was to him, how ashamed he was of his doubts. Looking into her eyes, Brodyn pressed his forehead against hers. "Caitriona Mac Cuill, my wife, my queen, my love. I was consumed not only by ghosts from my past but by jealousy for Taylor. I am fallible, and I will make more mistakes. I will never forgive myself if it's my pride that pushed ye away."

"You didn't trust me, though. You had to see the truth through your dead brother's eyes before believing me." Cait jerked away from him, and he let her go, dropping his arms to his side, keenly feeling the loss of her warmth.

"What I saw was a man possessed, determined to have ye by any means! That possession now resides within Taylor, and he may have a different body, but he has the same dark soul. He will try to kill me. I would see him dead here and now if I didnae ken ye will only hate me more for it. I will take him to the cave and make sure he goes safely back where he belongs."

"I will come with you," Caitriona insisted, glaring at him defiantly.

"Ye willnae."

"I am going with you because I am leaving with him."

Brodyn's heart stopped, and his stomach coiled. "Ye wish to go home?"

She nodded and looked toward the flickering candle. "I have

done what I was meant to do. You have your peace with Domnall. War is coming, and when it does, you will have the army you need. My presence is no longer required."

"I dinnae wish ye to leave, Caitriona."

Cait spun around to look at him. "You know nothing about my time or what I've given up to be here with you... for you... for your people and the future of Scotland! And for my efforts, for losing my family and friends, I get this..." she spun in a circle with her arms out. "Imprisoned by my husband because another man looked for me. At least Taylor found me. You locked me away! Women in your time may be expendable pawns, but they aren't in my time. I have a life and people who care about me. I'd like them to know I'm all right, and I deserve better than this!"

Brodyn nodded, feeling like his heart had just been ripped out, thrown to the floor, and stomped on. Regret roiled within his gut, and he wished to plead with her to stay, but he loved her enough to let her go if that was her genuine desire.

"I dinnae wish ye to go, but I willnae stop ye. I am sorry I failed to show ye the love ye deserve. Mayhap I am not like men from yer time. I am fighting one battle after another, and I willnae fight this one. If ye wish to go, we will leave in the morn."

Lifting his tunic, Brodyn flashed his scar to his wife. "Remember, I wear the proof of betrayal on my chest every day, a constant reminder that man is easily swayed by power. I'm sorry that my scars run deeper than the flesh."

He turned away before his strong façade crumbled. He had failed as a husband. However, with war on the horizon, she was safer away from this place. Still, every retreating step he took away from his wife felt weighed down by remorse and failure.

FREE TO LEAVE her room, Caitriona ran down to the basement, eager to first speak with Taylor. Her decision to leave Brodyn weighed heavily on her heart. She loved him, had dreamed of him for so long. Still, how could she know he wouldn't lock her away every time he was angry? She had no way to know except for blind faith, and right now, she needed more than that to stay here, especially knowing his death loomed. Perhaps leaving before he died in her arms would break the curse.

Brodyn's experience at Talorc's gravesite clearly shook him and opened his eyes. He'd believed her before, but witnessing time's oddities firsthand was life-altering. The thistle atop Talorc's grave reminded Cait of the thistle growing atop Brodyn's bones in the cave. She wanted to believe it was a coincidence, for thistle abounded in Scotland, yet something about the thorny flower growing atop both gravesites made Caitriona wonder if there was a connection. She'd thought the bones propelled her into the past, but perhaps it had been the thistle she'd removed from the ground. Brodyn touched it and saw the past through Talorc's eyes. Her removal of the thistle created a similar experience, only she heard many voices and saw many memories jumbled together while she fell through time.

When she opened the door leading into the dark underbelly of Brodyn's home, her nose wrinkled as the smell of dank water and mold hit her nostrils. Caitriona crept down the stairs toward the metal bars, clutching her flashlight tightly with an out-stretched hand.

"Taylor?" she whispered his name. "Are you here?"

"Cait!" Hearing her name and the shuffle of his feet against the dirty, cold earthen floor, she shone the light in his direction. He squinted and recoiled from the sudden brightness.

"Oh, sorry," she whispered and moved the light downward.

"Are you going to let me out, or what?" The dangerous edge in his tone reminded Caitriona of the possessive monster lurking beneath his handsome façade. Brodyn's warning rang in her ears.

"No. I am only here to let you know they are taking you back to the cave at dawn."

"Cait—"

"Don't argue. You have no idea what danger you are in if you stay. I appreciate that you came looking for me. Now, it's my turn to look out for you. When Brodyn releases you, you will cooperate, get on that horse, go to the cave, and return to our time."

"You say that so calmly, as if it is an ordinary thing to believe you traveled in time. Do you want to know what I believe?"

Cait huffed and placed a hand on her hip, knowing that Taylor imagined himself wiser than her in all things.

"I believe this is a re-enactment town, and that man has fooled you. Did you hit your head at any point? Have they drugged you or brainwashed you? Cait, there is no such thing as time travel. When I get out of here, I'm taking you home with me."

Cait opened her mouth to tell him she had already decided to return home, but something stopped her. Maybe it was the arrogance of his arched brow or the mockery glimmering in his eyes, but Caitriona realized in that second that she would rather live a thousand lifetimes here as Brodyn's wife than live in a time where Taylor believed he owned her, casting his shadow over her every move.

"Why did you come for me?" she asked. "You were stationed in California. If local search parties with intimate knowledge of the Highlands couldn't find me, what made you think you could?"

"They are obviously incompetent! I found you didn't I?" he said with that edge again. "I will always find you, Cait. We are connected."

Oh, they were connected, all right, far more than he knew. They were both a part of this twisted time loop that seemed to keep pulling their souls back here. Her purpose was clear enough. But why Taylor? Why was he sent here? To ruin her marriage or just make her miserable, she couldn't know, yet something about his determination to find her felt self-indulgent.

"You found me because you were pulled through time, just

like I was, Taylor. In the year 2023, this hillfort is a small town. All of this is long gone or buried deep beneath the earth. Do yourself a favor when you get home and Google Burghead. That's the modern name for this Pictish Stronghold. Brodyn is the king of the Picts. I'm supposed to be here. You are not. We will take you back in the morning, and I am not going with you."

"Like hell, you aren't! I found you! I'm a hero! And I will return with you, collect your parent's reward money, and use it to plan the wedding we always dreamed of! How about that, Cait?"

"Are you serious right now?" She scoffed and took a step back. This man was out of his mind. "I knew you had a selfish reason for coming to find me. You just want the glory and the money! Your family is wealthier than mine! You don't need my parents' money!"

Taylor shrugged. "They offered it. I see nothing wrong with a simple transaction. I find their daughter, and they pay $50,000. We all get what we want."

"You're an asshole."

"You're a bitch who left me to go dig in some dirt, then skulked off with some overgrown neanderthal who convinced you he's a king! I knew you liked dirt, but trash, Cait? That's all he is… and you are too, if you stay here with him."

Nothing he said could hurt her feelings. Over the years, Taylor had taken every opportunity to put down her career, dreams, style, and weight—in fact, pretty much anything he could use to make her feel poorly about herself. It was his coping mechanism. For all his pomp, Taylor had to bring others down to feel better about himself. He was a typical schoolyard bully, and Cait had emotionally closed herself off from him long ago.

"Think whatever you want about me, Taylor. I'm not yours, and I'm not coming home with you. I'm staying here with my husband."

Seething, Taylor gripped the bars until his knuckles turned white. "You… you married this man after days of knowing him, but you wouldn't marry me?" His booming voice echoed and reverberated off the dark stone walls, making her shrink back a step. "You bitch!" he roared, trying to shake the sturdy bars.

"What is going on down here?" She heard her husband's voice before she heard his footsteps storming down the stairs. He stopped when he saw Caitriona, sadness flashing in his eyes. "Caitriona."

"Brodyn."

"Is everything all right down here? I heard him shouting as I attempted to sleep… not that I can," he said in a tone that let Cait know he was just as heartbroken as she was. She had the power to make this right. They both needed to trust one another and stop making rash judgments without thinking.

"Everything is fine. I came down here to tell Taylor that we are sending him back through the cave and that I am staying here with my husband."

His brows rose before falling into creased lines. "Ye are staying?"

"If you will still have me, yes."

"Caitriona. I told ye, I love ye. But if ye wish to go back to yer own time, I willnae keep ye here."

Walking up to him, she held the flashlight to her side as she pressed against him, her lips curving into a small smile. "Brodyn, I don't understand what has transpired, but I do know one thing. I love you, and I always have. I've sought you out my entire life, and now that I have you, I won't walk away from this, from us. We don't have a lifetime together," she croaked, reaching up with her free hand to cup his strong jaw, running her thumb across his bearded chin. "But I want to share every moment with you that I can. I don't want to run away from this. Just know—you cannot lock me away whenever you are angry, and you cannot keep mistrusting me. We have to believe that we were brought together for a reason."

"There you go speaking that ridiculous language again!" she heard Taylor say from behind them. "Tell your 'husband' that I will kill him if ever I get the chance!"

"Is he threatening ye?" Brodyn asked, looking away to scowl at Taylor.

"He is threatening you," she replied.

Brodyn scoffed and took her hand. "He already tried to kill me once in this lifetime and failed. He will not succeed this time, either. Come… I prefer to continue this without my dead brother's new body listening in."

It was the oddest sentence Cait had ever heard spoken. Then again, none of this was typical. She let Brodyn lead her up the stairs before he slammed the door to the basement behind him, but Taylor's raging screams still filtered through the house.

"Caitriona, I'm verra sorry I treated ye as I did. I vow never to mistrust ye ever again."

"I'm sorry I asked to leave. I meant it at the time but speaking with Taylor made me realize I couldn't leave you. My life is here with you."

Brodyn pulled her closer. "I want to grow old with ye, lass. I will treasure ye until my dying breath."

His words were a punch to her gut, a blade twisting and tearing away at her flesh. With a sudden gasp for breath, Cait shivered as the anguish nearly made her collapse. Brodyn's strong arms held her up, though his smile turned into a frown as his beautiful eyes focused on her. "I will die soon, aye?"

Swallowing audibly, Caitriona closed her eyes and shook her head. "I cannot… I should not say what I know, Brodyn. It's too painful. Part of me thought I could avoid the pain of losing you if I left now. But it's too late. I'm in love with you and will only suffer your loss sooner if I go. I just want to enjoy every moment with you."

"As do I, my love." Leaning close, Brodyn kissed her neck, and another shiver raced down her body, her nipples tightening with need. "'Tis late, and I must ride to the cave in the morn. I wish to carry ye up the stairs, toss ye onto our bed, rip off yer clothes, and bury my face between yer thighs…" he whispered into her ear, making her shudder as his promises caressed her desire. She needed to feel him against her, inside her, over and over until there was nothing left but their tangled limbs and sweaty flesh—until her knowledge of what was to come was buried beneath her bliss.

"Well, then. What are you waiting for?" she asked. "Take me to bed."

Brodyn swept her off her feet and into his strong arms so quickly that she clung to his shoulders, squealing in shock and amusement as he ascended the stairs.

CHAPTER THIRTEEN

"NO! BRODYN, STAY with me! No, no!" Cait screamed and thrashed in her sleep, waking Brodyn up with a start as she yelled his name. Her forehead shimmered with sweat, and he gently shook her, though she failed to wake.

"Cait," he whispered. "Wake up, my love." He shook her a bit harder by the shoulders until she awoke with a yelp and sat up in bed, reaching to cling to him when she saw him. Her body shook, and before he could ask if she was all right, Caitriona began to sob, wrapping her arms around his neck.

He made shushing sounds as he rubbed her back, but he knew something plagued his wife. She didn't wish to speak of it, yet he couldn't help her if she kept it inside. "Tell me, Caitriona."

"I can't," she cried, burying her face into his neck. He felt her tears drip onto his skin, and he pulled away just enough to look into her eyes.

"Ye can. Ye had a nightmare and were screaming my name."

"It's been happening for a long time now," she whispered. "It's not just a nightmare. It's a memory from past lives. It haunts me!"

"Something happens to me."

"Yes!" Cait wailed, shaking with hysterics.

His heart broke as more tears streamed down her cheeks. She knew things no person should ever have to live with, and though no man ever wished to know how he died, he felt compelled to ask if only to relieve her of this pain, to help carry the weight of this burden. "Tell me, my heart. Is it my death?"

She nodded, remaining silent. "Tell me," he repeated, urging her. "I wish to ken."

"N-no… I cannot! How can you live, knowing how and when you will die?" she sniffled, wiping her wet, flushed cheeks with the back of her hand.

"What time I have left means naught if my wife is distressed with what's to come. I ken telling me willnae fix it, but mayhap I can avoid my death if I am aware."

"That's the thing. The legend of your wife burying you in the cave is what drove me to become an archaeologist, which led me to the cave where I found your bones. And your bones are what sent me back in time. Although, there was a thistle on top of your grave. When you mentioned the thistle on Talorc's grave, I wondered if the flower isn't the link. Either way, if I don't end up in that cave, then we never meet, the alliance with Domnall never happens, and you won't win the war with Northumbria. This battle brings all the remaining Celtic tribes together to defeat the Angles, securing a future for what will someday become Scotland."

"So, I must die to make this happen."

"I … I don't know, Brodyn! All I know is that I witness your death repeatedly in my dreams, and I cannot make it stop!"

"Do I die in battle?" he asked, hating to think about leaving this world now that he had found Caitriona.

"Yes." She swallowed hard and looked away.

"Which battle?"

She frowned at him, and another tear slid down her cheek. "There is no written record, but according to the same legend, you die in the battle against Ecgfrith. Although your men win the battle, you lose your life, and your wife—me!—buries you in that cave. Which I must have done if your bones are there. I re-live that scene in my mind. It haunts me!" Cait took his hand and clutched it. "I don't want to lose you, Brodyn."

Pulling her closer, Brodyn took a deep breath and let his

reality sink in. His days were numbered. He was a dead man walking. Still, he would succeed in gaining peace for his people and pave the way for his descendants to someday be free. That was a cause worth dying for, and he realized his only fear was the loss of his beautiful wife. But, when he was gone, his pain would end. Caitriona must live with the loss, and that thought pained him greater than his impending demise.

"I'm sorry ye must live with this knowledge. I wish I could take this pain away from ye. If I die victorious, then I will die a happy man, especially because ye loved me. Now…" Brodyn jumped out of bed, pulling her up with him. "We must be on our way to the cave. Goodwin will collect Talorc from the cell and meet us in the stables."

"Taylor," Caitriona corrected as she bent over to pick up her crumpled tunic from the floor. Brodyn eyed her arse and bit his lower lip, fighting off another wave of lust. They were short on time, and he'd just learned he was to die soon, but it didn't mean he couldn't admire his wife's fine form.

Brodyn shrugged and took the tunic from Caitriona's hands, slipping it over her head before tying the back. "He is the same man."

Slipping on his tunic and trousers, Brodyn laced up his boots before escorting Caitriona out of the room. Anya busied herself near the cauldron, crushing dried herbs in her pestle. "Yer man down there is verra loud and verra angry," she murmured without looking up. "Wakin' the dead, he is."

"He will be gone verra soon," Brodyn promised. "Where did ye disappear to last night?"

"Wouldnae ye like to ken?" Anya huffed sarcastically as she continued her work. Brodyn grunted with frustration, but he wasn't surprised by her response. Likely, she was angry at him for locking Caitriona away.

"Brother." Murielle entered the room next, giving him her cold stare and curt greeting. Apparently, all the women in his life were unimpressed by his behavior, and he couldn't blame them.

"No need to give him the cold shoulder," Caitriona said calmly, coming over to hold his hand. "I gave him hell enough for all three of us. Everything will be well once we take Taylor back to the cave."

Brodyn raised a brow at his sister. "See? I can be reasonable."

Murielle scoffed and rolled her eyes, but before turning away, she flashed him a smile, letting him know he was forgiven.

He hadn't seen much of Murielle lately, and she seemed to come and go as she pleased. He should keep better tabs on his sister, even if she was an intelligent woman whom he trusted to make her own decisions. Soon, he would need to find her a powerful husband from another tribe. She was a Pictish princess, after all, and it was her duty, as it was his, to marry strategically. Looking at Caitriona, his heart thumped wildly in his chest, aching with love for her. It spilled over, threatening to drown him with every new breath. He wanted that for his wee sister. He hoped he would find her a good husband to love once this war ended.

Caitriona's words suddenly sank in and cold dread tingled down his spine. He would not be around to see to her marriage. He hadn't long to live, and he had many affairs to set right before meeting Ecgfrith on the field—if the coward even bothered to fight beside his men.

The front door opened, and Ronan stepped inside, soaking wet from yet another downpour from the gray sky. "My king, Goodwin is ready to collect… the prisoner."

Brodyn nodded and sighed. He would need to explain things to Ronan eventually. He was a trustworthy man, and he knew Taylor couldn't be Talorc despite the resemblance. Still, the fewer people who knew that Cait was from another time, the better.

"I appreciate yer help, Ronan. Goodwin and I have it from here."

Ronan frowned and dropped his brows. "I expected to accompany ye to the cave."

"Ronan," Brodyn stepped forward and placed a hand on

Ronan's shoulder. "Ye and Goodwin are my two best men, ye ken this. I need ye to stay here and protect the village while we are away. We can handle this man, but Pinnata Castra can never be unprotected. I trust nobody else but ye to watch over Murielle and the rest of our people."

The disappointment in Ronan's eyes dissolved into a look of pride as he squared his shoulders and nodded. "I willnae let ye down, my king."

"I know ye willnae. Deliver the prisoner to Goodwin at the stables, and we will prepare to leave." Turning away, Brodyn dragged his palms down his face and fought the impending chaos that loomed. Now that he knew his days were numbered, Brodyn had a list of things to care for when he returned from the cave. In truth, his demise seemed less distressing than all the unfinished business he would leave behind. His men needed a leader. His wife needed safety. He had no heir, and he worried Murielle would be seen as a prize by neighboring chiefs and kings who wished to take hold of the Pictish seat of power through her, his only living heir. Murielle needed guidance.

However, none of this could be sorted until Taylor was gone. "Ye ready?"

Cait nodded and grabbed her cloak from the hook near the door, securing it with her brooch. Taking her hand, Brodyn pulled her closer to shield her from the onslaught of rain as they left the house. Thunder crashed in the distance, but Brodyn was determined to see this task done.

"Are ye certain ye wish to come with me? 'Tis a few hours journey. I shall be home by midday."

"I wish to come," she replied. "Besides Anya, I'm the only person who understands Taylor. You need me to translate."

"I care not about anything he has to say, but I will enjoy yer company."

Goodwin awaited them at the stables, gently brushing his horse while Ronan and another guard followed behind, Taylor positioned between them.

"I came here to help you, and you let them treat me like this?" Taylor spat at her.

"I am keeping you safe, Taylor! You have no idea what sort of danger you are in here. Brodyn is doing you a favor by taking you back to the cave!"

"Why the cave? I will just go back to town and fly home if you don't want me anymore." He struggled when the men grabbed his arms and forced him onto a large dark bay horse.

"You still don't get it, do you? There is no town to return to! This is the year 685, and a war will break out in a matter of days!"

Brodyn watched Cait bicker with her former lover, not feeling the slightest twinge of doubt or jealously. Though he understood nothing she or Taylor said, he knew she would never betray him.

Brodyn led Cait to his horse and helped her into the saddle before mounting behind her and wrapping an arm around her waist. Goodwin rode on one side of Taylor, holding his horse's reins in his left hand to prevent Taylor from fleeing. Brodyn and Cait rode on the other side, flanking the man in so he had no choice but to comply.

Brodyn's mind lay heavy in thought, his heart heavy with loss, and his stomach heavy with the reality he now faced. He knew too much to keep Caitriona here in his time. His mind was made up. When they reached the cave, he would let his beautiful wife go, even if it meant the destruction of his every happiness.

TAYLOR CALLED OUT to her a few times but soon realized she would not respond. Caitriona stared ahead, glad that the worst of the rain had finally subsided. Her woolen cloak worked wonders to keep her dry, though the biting wind numbed her hands and face as the horses galloped closer to the shore.

Looking around, Caitriona admired the lay of the land, untouched by men. Nature flourished in its natural habitat without pollution mudding the cerulean sky. Small animals scuffled out of the way as the horses clopped through the brush, and large fields of thistles scattered across the land, brightening the landscape with their brilliant purple flowers.

Once Taylor was out of their way and safely through the cave, Cait would be able to breathe again and focus on helping Brodyn prepare for battle. Food stores would need to be checked, and the women and men left behind would need to guard the stronghold while the warriors were away with Brodyn.

The closer the battle came, the less Caitriona understood. Why would Brodyn be in the cave if the battle was further south in Scotland? And why did the historic record claim that Brodyn's son succeeded him if he didn't have a son? She knew that the battle's details weren't recorded onto parchment until nearly two hundred years later; that could have led to inconsistencies.

Discovering the inconsistencies was intriguing, still, one detail remained the same: her husband would die soon. There was no blaming incorrect records, for she saw it with her own eyes every time the nightmare struck. Leaning back, Caitriona pushed herself closer to Brodyn, longing to feel his warmth, a reminder that he yet lived. She vowed to enjoy every remaining moment with him.

Perhaps, like Anya, she would stay in this time for the remainder of her life and use her knowledge to help these people. Still, her former life still awaited her. Friends, family, and a hard-earned career. If only she could see them all one last time, to say goodbye and tell them she was all right.

How would she ever explain disappearing without a trace? She couldn't explain to her parents that she never actually left but slipped into another time. And of course, by now, they all would think her dead, and that reality sat like a stone in the pit of her belly. Taylor's parents would be as worried as hers, and Cait idly wondered if his mom and dad resembled Brodyn and Talorc's. Did her parents resemble those of her soul-sister as well? Just how intricate was this web of connected souls?

Following the shoreline where a cliff rose about one hundred meters above sea level, the group stopped just before the cave's entrance. Waves crashed against the rocky shore, and gulls circled overhead, occasionally dropping into the water to hunt for surface-dwelling fish for breakfast.

A heavy feeling of dread enveloped her as she stared at the cave. How many people had disappeared here over the thousands of years?

Brodyn dismounted and helped Cait down while Goodwin grappled with Taylor, who shoved and cursed, staring daggers at Brodyn as he held Cait's waist.

"Taylor, this is for your own good! You need to go back!" Caitriona hollered over the howling wind.

"I won't leave without you!" he roared back. "You're mine, and you know it!"

Caitriona balled her fists and stormed over to Taylor. "I was never yours, Taylor! You don't own me! That was always something you couldn't understand! Now get into that cave and get the hell away from me! You won't get your reward money!"

He reached out to grab her cloak, and she gasped when he jerked her forward, making her fall to her knees on the wet shore. Climbing onto her feet, Caitriona shrieked when she saw Brodyn pressing a sword to Taylor's throat.

"I ought to kill ye where ye stand!" Brodyn growled in a tone so guttural that, even without understanding his words, Taylor turned white as the blade lay flush against his flesh. Cait held her breath as she stood and wiped the debris from her knees. Until now, she'd never seen the fighting side of Brodyn outside of the training field. He was swift and powerful, a formidable foe.

"I will guide him through the cave to make certain he leaves," a sudden voice spoke from within the cave, making Cait jump back and yelp in fright. Turning to follow the voice, Cait lit up with relief when she saw Samuel emerge from the cave.

"Samuel!" she cried and ran to him with arms wide open,

more thrilled to see her friend than she ever expected to be. "Brodyn sent for you! Taylor… my ex—"

"He came through looking for you. I know." Sam responded with his usual calm as he reached out to take her hand.

"I assume that always happens, as well?"

Samuel nodded. "I'm here to escort him back, though I cannot control where he goes from there."

Goodwin took Taylor by the collar and jerked him over toward Samuel. "What are we doing with this piece of shite?" Goodwin growled. "We cannae have these men coming through the cave and threatening us!"

Samuel nodded again. "There is nothing I can do to prevent that, I am afraid. Not everyone can pass through, but Taylor's soul is familiar with this time."

"How did you know to meet us here?" Caitriona asked. Samuel lifted a brow, and Cait understood her mistake. "Right. This isn't your first time experiencing this, is it?"

"No, it's not. Taylor always passes through, and I always escort him back. I'm sorry I couldn't tell you."

"Where's my gun? You took my gun!" Taylor struggled to escape Goodwin's grip with no success.

Cait glared at Taylor and lowered her brows. "You really think these men would give you a weapon?"

Samuel stepped up to Taylor and shook his head. "Your time here is up. I will take you home safely."

"I'm not leaving without Cait!" he protested, trying unsuccessfully to break free.

"I'm not going with you. My place is here now."

Caitriona felt Brodyn's hand slip around her waist, and she leaned in to relish the warmth of his large body. But when she looked up, his sullen face made her heart jump into her throat. Somehow, she suddenly knew what he planned to say next. "Caitriona, my love. I need ye to go back now," he spoke softly.

Shaking her head, she stepped away from Brodyn and furrowed her brows. "What? No… no, I need to stay here."

"Nay, ye needed to help us achieve peace with Domnall, and ye did. I love ye, Caitriona Mac Cull. Dinnae ever think I dinnae love ye with my whole heart. We both ken how this ends, and I willnae have ye stay here to watch me die. Ye have already re-lived that moment enough in yer life. Mayhap we can break the cycle. I cannae be saved, but ye can be saved from watching me die. I will make certain to be buried in the cave, so the legend continues, and ye find yer way back to me. Ye just willnae have the memory of watching me die."

"Brodyn, no! I won't leave! We still have time together!" Panic gripped her throat and constricted her lungs, and Cait gripped Brodyn by his sleeve. "I love you! I can't leave!"

"He's right, Cait," Samuel added, and she turned her head toward her mentor, a sick feeling rising in her belly.

"No! You can't send me back in time to fall in love with a man I know will die, then tear me away from him!"

"It's not safe here for ye. When I die, ye will be in danger without my protection," Brodyn stressed. "Every power-thirsty man in the land will wish to wed the Pictish Queen, and they will force ye if necessary. Trust me when I tell ye that most powerful men in this time willnae be gentle with ye. I cannae allow it. If I'm not here to protect ye, ye cannae stay."

"This is not like our time, Cait. You know that. A widowed queen is a sitting duck. Besides, Brodyn must prepare for this battle, and he can't if he is focused only on your safety. All of Scotland depends on this. History depends on it. It's best that you come with me now, Cait. You will be safer, and you will have fulfilled your destiny. Your friends and family await you," Samuel said with a gentle voice.

Caitriona knew she was losing this fight. She understood their concerns, even if leaving Brodyn was not something she'd expected to do. She'd thought she had more time.

Still, what the men said was true. As far as Domnall was concerned, the alliance was set. The tribes prepared to fight with their southern neighbors, and once they achieved victory, she would have nothing more to do here than grieve for her husband… and then what? Who would rule the Picts? Certainly not her. She had never seen any mention of a Queen Caitriona connected to Pictish history. She was nothing more than a woman who passed through time. Perhaps that was all she was ever meant to be.

A tear slid down her cheek as she realized she had no choice other than to return home, even if every cell in her body rejected the notion of leaving Brodyn behind. Still, she loved him enough to go so he could focus on the battle, because he'd know she was safe.

"If you wish me to go, I will go," she croaked, looking up at her husband. "But we didn't get enough time together. I'm not ready."

Pulling her close, Brodyn leaned in and kissed her softly, lingering for a second longer than usual. Pressing his forehead to hers, he whispered, "My wife, my love, my queen, my prickly thistle, so strong and beautiful. A lifetime would never be enough. I am sorry I cannae offer ye that. But this way, I get to say goodbye while I still have the breath to say it. I dinnae wish for yer nightmares to continue into yer next life when we shall meet again. Ye understand, aye?"

Cait nodded as more tears slid down her cheek. Grief clenched her heart in its merciless fist, and she gasped and clutched her chest when the pain became unbearable.

"I understand, but it isn't fair. I waited my whole life for you. Now, what will I do?" She wrapped her arms around his waist and clung for dear life, soaking in the feel of his warmth, his solid muscles, the rise and fall of his chest, his rapidly beating heart. Cait's hands shook as she realized she would never see his beautiful blue eyes again or hold his hand. He would be nothing more than a pile of bones when she returned home. How would she ever bear it?

"Ye will continue yer life kenning that ye were, are, and always be loved verra deeply by a foolish man, for I am a fool to let ye leave me."

"I am a fool for listening," she murmured into his chest. "I cannot bear to leave you, but I cannot bear to watch you die... I just... I can't." A sob caught in her throat, and waves of nausea washed over Cait. "Oh, God! I cannot bear it!"

Samuel stepped over and put out his hand, and Brodyn gently moved away, taking a step back. "Ye are the strongest woman I have ever kenned. Ye will bear it, and ye will survive it. Ye saved my people from an illness that would have wiped us out and potentially made us lose the war. Ye have saved me, for when I die, I will die kenning I was loved by ye. Ye still have much life to live and family looking for ye. Now, go, my love."

Caitriona clutched the brooch resting against her neck, its edges digging into her palm as she squeezed. When her fingers fumbled to remove it, Brodyn frowned and shook his head. "That is yer brooch, a symbol of our marriage and my love for ye. Ye must keep it."

Nodding, Caitriona sniffled and, with a strength she never knew she owned, stepped away from the man of her dreams and turned her back. "Let's go then," she forced through numb lips. Without waiting, Cait walked toward the cave, refusing to look back. If she did, she would run back into his arms and never let go, damn the consequences.

Goodwin shoved Taylor toward Samuel, who took him by the arm and guided him to the cave. He didn't struggle, for he had gotten his wish. He was leaving this place with Cait by his side.

Samuel and Taylor followed behind her, and she stopped. She didn't know how to get back without the bones that brought her there.

"We must hold hands, so Taylor doesn't run," Samuel whispered to Caitriona.

Slowly but hesitantly, Cait took Samuel's outstretched hand, then Taylor's, taking a shaky breath. When sharp pain struck her skull, and bright lights flashed behind her eyes, she knew the time had come. She was leaving the year 685 and would never see Brodyn again, except in her dreams.

Gritting her teeth, she squeezed Samuel and Taylor's hands as the ground rumbled and voices surrounded her.

With an explosion of energy, all three of them fell backward onto the cave floor. Pressing her fingers into her throbbing temples, Caitriona slowly opened her eyes and found herself in pitch black. Samuel clicked on his flashlight and shined it around the small side chamber of the cave where she had found the bones. Blinking, Cait noticed bright yellow caution tape surrounding the large rectangular hole in the ground where Brodyn's bones once rested.

An overwhelming sense of loss choked Cait, making her throat sting as she swallowed the grief and tried to remain calm. Taylor got to his feet and looked around, confusion furrowing his brows. "What the hell just happened?" he asked, frantically spinning in a circle as he observed his surroundings.

"We are back in 2023," Samuel replied casually. "You two stay here. I need to check the area to make sure it's clear."

Taylor looked at Caitriona and put out a hand, as if nothing unusual had just occurred. She recognized that fake smile of his—the same smile he flashed every time he hoped to manipulate his way into someone's good favor. Ignoring him, she turned away, remembering all the times he'd stalked her or yelled so much she worried he would hurt her. His temper could go from zero to sixty, and he'd used his charm and good looks to get his way, but it wouldn't work with her. Not anymore.

"After all I've done for you, you turn your back on me? When will it sink into your thick skull? You. Are. Mine!" Taylor grabbed her arm and forced her to face him.

"You're insane! And I'm married!" Cait hissed and tried to pull away, but he tightened his grip. She knew Samuel would be back soon, so she wasn't in danger, even if his aggression was alarming. Had going back in time triggered any of Taylor's memories as Talorc? His behavior was more erratic than it had been before, but then again, he was never good at accepting rejection.

"If this time-travel shit is real, your husband died 1,400 years ago! I think it's safe to move on. You knew him for what, two minutes?"

"I literally just lost him!" she cried, shoving at his chest. "You cannot possibly understand this situation, and I don't owe you any explanation. There are forces at play beyond anything you—or I—will ever understand."

"I came for you!" he roared, making Cait shrink back when she saw the vein protruding from his neck.

But then, she narrowed her eyes and stepped toward him. She was the wife of a warrior and a king. She was queen of the Picts, and she feared no man. "You didn't come for me; you came for the money. I'm not fooled by you. I want nothing to do with you, Taylor!"

Samuel's voice echoed off the walls, signaling his arrival before he rounded the corner. "The coast is clear. Nobody is around, and we have a low tide." Taking a fortifying breath, Caitriona slightly relaxed when she saw his face. "I can't just show up here after all this time." Cait looked toward Samuel for guidance. He had done this before, so surely, he had a plan. People didn't just reappear after three months of missing without a good reason.

"I will alert the authorities to your arrival and bring you to the hospital for an exam. That's just protocol, but there is something I need to explain to you. While time has passed on this side of the cave, it passed at a much slower rate. Essentially, only a fraction of the time has passed while you were away."

Cait tilted her head and pursed her lips. "Exactly how long have I been missing, then?"

"It's been two weeks. Taylor has only been gone for four hours."

"I want my reward money," Taylor spat, not caring about anything else Samuel said. "I found you. Without me, you'd still be with him in that barbaric place! I deserve that money."

"You deserve nothing, Taylor," Caitriona shot back. "I need you to leave me alone—forever. Go back to California."

Taylor glared at Cait and clenched his jaw. His nostrils flared. Then his gaze shifted to Samuel. "You haven't heard the last of this." Storming out of the alcove, Taylor rammed into Samuel's shoulder as he passed.

"Taylor," Samuel turned and spoke calmly, stopping the man heading for the entrance of the cave. "There will be grave consequences if you ever approach Caitriona or this place again."

"Are you threatening me? I always knew you were in love with her," Taylor growled.

"You're ridiculous," Cait spat. "You think everyone is in love with me."

"And you're ignorant, Caitriona! You're so coddled that you can't even see when you're being groomed. But you're not my problem anymore." Taylor turned and left the cave, and Cait sighed, feeling another heavy burden lift from her shoulders.

"Okay. I can work with two weeks," Caitriona said, returning to her conversation with Samuel. "I will figure out how to explain where I've been later. I can't think right now."

Sam nodded and ran a hand over the back of his neck. He sighed. "It's good to have you back, Cait. I'm sorry you've endured so much and that I had to lead you into it. It weighs on me every time."

Caitriona took his hand and looked at his familiar face. His Italian heritage showed in his olive complexion and dark features, but beyond that, Cait saw a man worn down by worry and time.

"You have nothing to apologize for. I'm sorry you must endure this over and over. But think of it this way—I got to spend time with Brodyn. I wouldn't change a thing. Let's bring me home."

She squeezed his hand and smiled warmly at him. With that, Samuel escorted her out of the cave and back into the 2023 sunlight.

CHAPTER FOURTEEN

"Yes, Mom. I know… Yes, I was careless… Yes, you did well to teach me survival skills." Caitriona huffed and rolled her eyes as her mom chattered away on the other line, somehow making herself the hero of the story. Now that Cait was back safely and had answered all of her mom's many questions, the lectures began. As usual.

"No, don't do that. Yes, I appreciate that you rented a flat nearby and posted a reward while looking for me. I understand. No, don't leave your annual vacation in Puerta Vallarta. I know how much you pay for that timeshare. I understand that you were very stressed and needed to get away… I'm fine here, and Emilie is on her way. Taylor? No! He did not find me, Mom! Do not give him a penny!" Caitriona insisted in between her mother's blabbering. "Send Dad my love. Enjoy the rest of the vacation… I love you, too."

Hanging up with a sigh, Caitriona just shook her head and smiled. Her parents had been beside themselves with worry and grief and were thrilled when she'd called. Once she'd explained where she had been and insisted she was fine, everything went right back to normal, and she was good with that. Having her parents fuss over her was not ideal and very unnatural. It was better for them to remain blissfully unaware within their own world. She rarely saw them anyway with the amount of time they spent traveling. Money was a crutch, and while she appreciated the award they'd offered, it was surprising that they'd done little else but assume she'd been careless and sent Taylor to find her.

Awaiting discharge from the hospital, Caitriona sat on the exam table in her faded cloth robe tied in the back, swinging her feet impatiently. All she wanted was to find a motel room in the area, take a long, hot shower, and cry until she fell asleep. But even in her sleep, Cait wouldn't be safe from the painful memories.

A knock on the door made her head pop up, hoping it was her blood work so she could go home. The doctors poked and prodded to check for injuries or internal bleeding, and a final blood analysis was ordered to check for anemia or any signs of infection. Not knowing what else to say, Caitriona told the doctors she'd been hiking alone and fell into a ravine. She'd told them she'd climbed out but was lost this entire time and living off the land. That was the closest to the truth that she could offer. She had lost a few pounds due to a change of diet, which helped to validate her story. So far, nobody had asked too many questions, and her exam showed no injuries, so the police report was easy enough to make believable.

When the exam room's door opened, Emilie's familiar face poked around the door frame. "Oh, my God!" Caitriona's best friend hurried to her side and embraced her, dropping the red duffel bag slung across her shoulder onto the floor. "I never thought I'd see you again!" Tears sprang to her eyes, and she wiped them away, her cheeks growing red as emotion overwhelmed her. "I thought you… you were dead!"

"I'm so sorry you went through that, Emilie." Cait's heart sank when the pain her friend endured finally became a reality.

"No, I'm sorry you went through this. I should have been there! I shouldn't have let you wander off alone!"

"I'm a big girl, Emilie. I'm not your responsibility." Cait hugged her and hoped her assurances were enough.

Emilie huffed and stepped back, then took her hand. "Where were you, really? I know this area as well as you do. There is no way you got lost for two weeks."

"It's a pretty bad cover story, isn't it?" Cait sighed and frowned. "I just don't have a story to tell that anyone else would believe."

Looking at the pile of fabric on the chair beside the exam table, Emilie walked over and picked up the top item, a faded blue tunic with front ties of thin leather. "Woad dye. Thick, rough linen. Where did you get these tunics, Cait?"

"From the year 685 AD."

Emilie paused at Caitriona's blunt response, then nodded. "I wondered as much."

"You believe me?"

"Cait, what do I do when I'm hunting information? I obsess over every detail. There have been several stories about people disappearing and reappearing around that cave. It's well-regarded as a portal to the fairy world by the locals. Your reappearing only solidifies what I thought. I wasn't sure if I was insane for believing you had passed through some portal, or if my grief was so intense that I wanted to believe you were safe elsewhere. And these tunics are more evidence. You went back in time?" Emilie gently placed the tunic back onto the table. "Can I examine those, by the way? They are officially the only remaining tunics on the planet from that time."

"Have at it. But, the brooch is mine," Caitriona said, opening her palm to show Emilie the shiny gold oval brooch with intricate carvings around the perimeter.

"Wow! Where did you get that?"

"King Brodyn Mac Cuill, my husband."

Emilie froze, and silence captured the room. The wall clock's second hand ticked away, counting the passage of time, but time would never be linear to Cait again. "You married the man you've dreamed of your entire life?"

Cait nodded and tried to remain calm until tears suddenly blurred her vision when she knew she had to talk about Brodyn. Emilie stepped closer and wrapped her arms around Cait, listening intently as her friend told her all about her time in the year 685, her marriage to the Pictish king, Samuel's role, saving the village from smallpox, and Taylor's arrival, leading up to this moment.

"I miss him, Emilie. My heart is breaking. I cannot breathe. He is dead, nothing but a pile of bones probably now inside a lab. He is more than that, damnit! He is my husband, my soulmate! He didn't want me to witness his death all over again, so he bade me leave… and I did… because deep down, I knew watching him die would only destroy me all over again! I was there for three months, Em!"

She cried until her eyes stung and her vision blurred. Emilie stayed by her side, the calm strength that Cait needed more than anything. Samuel had gone to speak with the team about her reappearance. They all wanted to celebrate her return, though all Cait wanted to do was curl up in a ball and disappear. None of this mattered without Brodyn. Hot showers, fresh coffee, modern conveniences—she would give them all up to be back with Brodyn. But to what end? If she went back now, she would only lose him again.

"I won't ever see him again!"

Emilie hesitated and took a deep breath, her nose wrinkling like it did when she was in deep thought. "But, if you aren't there to bury him in the cave when he dies, who does bury him? And how do you have the memory of him dying if you leave before it happens?"

Cait frowned and slowly shook her head as she thought about that. "The memory is from a past life. Hopefully it will be erased if I'm not there this time. That's Brodyn's hope. He knows everything, and promised to be buried in the cave, so we still find his bones. I should be able to return, but without the painful memory of his death."

"Have you asked Samuel?"

"All he says is that I still have free will. I don't always make the same decisions, but the main events have to happen, like the alliance formed by our marriage. He agreed that I must leave, which tells me everything will continue as needed without me."

"Hello, Miss Murray?" A tall man with dark hair and a long white coat walked in after knocking on the door.

"Yes, that's me," Cait responded, squinting as she looked at his ID tag. "Doctor Singh."

"I have your lab results. Is it okay to discuss them in front of your friend, or shall I have her leave the room?"

"She knows more about me than I do sometimes. She can stay."

With a little chuckle, Dr. Singh stepped in with her lab results in his left hand. "You've been through quite an ordeal, Miss Murray. I heard about you on the news. I'm very glad you were unharmed, and you're extremely fortunate. Your blood work looks pretty good so far. You are borderline anemic, nothing too serious. We can send you home with some iron pills from the pharmacy and have you on your way. There are a few other lab tests awaiting results, but I see no reason why you can't go now. We will call you when we have the rest of the tests back later today. Shouldn't take too much longer."

"Okay, thank you," Cait replied, anxious to be out of this room and alone in any other room she could find in the area.

Once he left, Cait looked at the tunics folded on the chair and cringed. "I can't wear those again… for many reasons."

"Agreed. Here…" Picking up the red duffel bag she'd dropped in her excitement upon entering the room, Emilie rummaged through it, removing cases of makeup and travel toiletries. "Will this work until we can get you something better?" She pulled out burgundy yoga pants and a faded gray sweater that read, I'm into Fitness… Fitness Taco in my Mouth, across its front.

Cait laughed and nodded. "Oh my God, yes. I remember this sweater!"

"You bought it for me freshman year. Still my favorite— hence why it's in my overnight bag."

"Yeah… why are you carrying that around, anyway?"

"Because I wasn't sure if I would be staying in the hospital with you tonight," Emilie said with a shrug. "I'm glad I don't need to, only because it means you're healthy. Also, I have your purse and cell phone. I collected your things from camp and kept them safe."

"You are the best friend ever, Em. I missed you so much. How about we find a motel nearby, veg out, and have a girls' night. Though, I will warn you now that I will likely cry… like, a lot."

"I'm in for all the laughter, all of the tears, all of the venting you need to do, or all of the silence you want. We can stream Dirty Dancing and eat nachos?"

"It's like you know my soul." Cait took the clothes from her friend, but before she put them on, she hugged Emilie, feeling her stress melt away as she embraced her.

"I do know your soul, and I love it. Get dressed. I'll step out and find us a motel in the area. We could use the place I'm staying, but the team is on the same floor, and I know you need some space."

Emilie slung her bag back onto her shoulder and left the room. Silently, Cait looked around, paying close attention to the modern amenities surrounding her. Buzzing overhead lights, running water, temporal thermometers, blood pressure cuffs, and brightly colored posters about nutrition. How very different this place was from where she was just hours ago.

Quickly dressing, Cait tossed the worn-out hospital robe into the laundry bin in the corner, then grabbed the tunics for Emilie. Though she had wanted time alone, being with Emilie would be much better for her. There was nothing she couldn't say to her best friend, and ugly crying was nothing new between them. She needed to share all of her thoughts and get Emilie's perspective.

When she stepped out of the room, Emilie took her by the hand and started toward the parking garage.

"I booked us a room with two double beds and a minibar. I think you need it."

"More than you know. Let's go."

The motel was only fifteen minutes up the road, and when they arrived, Cait plopped onto the mattress and groaned loudly into the sheets. "I forgot how good a modern bed feels," she mumbled into the Egyptian cotton. "I may sleep and never wake up."

"You do you, girl. What did you sleep on… erm, back then?" Emilie scrunched her nose again, knowing it was an awkward question.

"A mattress stuffed with itchy straw and topped with lots of animal pelts and wool blankets."

"And how was sex in this ancient bed?"

"Are you really asking this?" Cait asked, rolling over to eye her best friend.

"Can you blame a girl for asking? My best friend married a Pictish king. Holy balls. You're a queen!"

"I was, yeah. How can I feel so lovesick for this man I've only known for three months?"

"You've known him your entire life, technically. Dreams can be very real. I had a dream once about Jon Bon Jovi, and I swear I was in love with him for months afterward. You've dreamt of Brodyn like hundreds of times. He's your soul's mate."

"And now, I've lost him." Cait forced back her sadness and decided to roar instead, letting out all her angst as she clenched her hands into the cool, pure white sheets beneath her. "And, yes, we quite enjoyed our time in bed, and the cave, and the forest…" she said with a sigh. "Everything was wonderful until all hell broke loose in the form of Taylor."

"You little minx!" Emilie said excitedly, clapping her hands. "How did Brodyn act when he showed up?"

Caitriona briefly explained everything to Emilie, including how Taylor was the modern version of Brodyn's brother, Talorc, who was in love with the version of Caitriona from that time. "Basically, it's an ancient love triangle that I'm stuck in forever."

"Taylor is always destined to love you and lose you. It would be sad if he wasn't such an ass."

"Yeah, he is an ass, and I don't think love is what he feels for me or anyone but himself. He only wanted my parent's reward money. Taylor thought it was a renaissance town and that everyone was acting. He didn't understand the truth until we went back through the cave. Hell, I still don't understand how it works, so I can't blame him for that."

"Maybe it's magic," Emilie said with a shrug. "Or maybe there is a science behind it, a thinning of the veil, or a wormhole. In my obsessive research while you were gone, I read about a woman who disappeared during WWII air raids. People report seeing her roaming the area to this day, only she ages, so they don't know if she is a ghost or somehow living in between worlds."

Stunned that Emilie had found information on Anya, Caitriona paused and gaped before smacking her palm on the bed. "That's Anya!" Cait replied, excited. "She's the most loyal servant in Brodyn's household. She helped raise him and his siblings and is a traveler, just like Samuel." She paused, remembering all the people she'd met and lived with over the past months. "I will miss Murielle, his sister. You'd love her. She is a modern woman trapped in an archaic world. But I have a feeling she will make her way. It's sad to know I won't ever see her again."

"I'm sorry. I wish I could make it better, Cait."

"Maybe you can. Tomorrow, will you take me to see Brodyn? Is that weird to ask?"

"I think I will be redefining my definition of weird after all of this, but yes. I'll take you to the lab tomorrow. Today, they told me they had some findings for me, but I was in a rush to get to you." She looked at Cait and wrinkled her nose. "My question is… Will it help you or hurt you, though?"

"I can't even begin to say. For now, I need a shower, then a healthy dose of Swayze's dirty dance moves and some minibar treats before I pass out. Processed sugar! I haven't had it in months."

"Deal. Hop in the shower while I find the movie."

Cait did as Emilie commanded, though she knew there was no number of movies, hot showers, or booze to repair the heartache she would endure for the rest of her life.

"You made her leave?" Murielle shouted at Brodyn with wide eyes and hands on her hips. "Why would you do that?"

"To keep her safe," he said as he stormed toward the training grounds. He needed to let out all of his pain and rage. "Goodwin, grab yer sword," he commanded when he spotted his best warrior gathering men onto the field.

"She was safe here. The battle willnae happen within these walls. Are ye saying we are in danger here?"

"As my only living heir, ye are in danger if I die. Every man across the land will do everything they can to wed ye, including kidnapping and murder. I dinnae have time to find ye a husband before the battle. If I fall, I am appointing Goodwin as yer guardian. He will keep ye safe until ye find a husband."

"I dinnae want a husband," Murielle said, panting as she matched his swift stride.

Brodyn stopped and glared at his stubborn sister. "I dinnae care what ye wish for, Murielle! We all must do what's needed to survive! I gave up my wife! Do ye understand the importance of this battle?"

Realizing this would be one of his last conversations with his sister, Brodyn took a deep breath to steady his nerves. Then Brodyn reached out to grab Murielle's hand. "Ye ken how much I love ye, aye?" he asked softly.

Frowning, she nodded. "And I ye."

"We ken much more about the world now than we did before Caitriona arrived. There are things we can control and things we cannae. I cannae control my fate, however I can make certain ye are safe when I'm gone."

"Ye sound like a man preparing for death," she whispered, squeezing his hand. "Caitriona didnae say ye die, did she?"

Deciding it would do no good for his sister to fret more than necessary, Brodyn shook his head. "Nay, but I must prepare for every battle and assume I may never return. Ye are well beyond a marriageable age. Most lassies yer age are wedded, bedded, and have bairns. I have over-indulged ye, allowed ye to live life on yer terms, but we have people to protect and land to hold, lest our enemies take it from us. I married a woman within hours of meeting her. She was dirty, wet, and angry. I thought she would make me miserable every day of my life, and I married her anyway because it was my duty. Now, she is the love of my life. I am devastated to have lost her. We make hard decisions for those we love. I had to make certain she was safe, just as I must do for ye. I will wed ye to a good man who will treat ye fairly and keep ye safe. Mayhap ye will grow to love him as I did Caitriona."

"I dinnae like it when ye use logic against me," Murielle said wryly. "I agree to allow Goodwin to be my guardian should anything befall ye, and I agree to wed whichever man he believes is best for the tribe. I trust him as I do ye. Although, I would prefer my elder brother to return safely to me."

"I would prefer that, too. I will do all in my power to make it so." Leaning in, Brodyn kissed Murielle on the forehead. "Now, go see about yer duties. I must train with my men. There is much to be done around the village. Make certain the food stores are safe. If there is a siege, we should have enough to wait it out."

Nodding, Murielle did as he asked without arguing, which was very rare these days. Still, she was a good lass with a good head on her shoulders. He knew he could trust her to watch the women and children while the men were away.

He made his way to the sparring field until he spotted Goodwin. "Goodwin!" Brodyn hollered. "Grab yer sword. I need to spar, and I warn ye that I will be giving ye all I have."

Flashing a smile, Goodwin unsheathed his sword from his hilt and rotated his wrist a few times to warm up as he walked over. "Give me all ye got."

With a roar, Brodyn swung his sword with all his might, feeling the reverberations run up his arm as Goodwin blocked the blow with matched strength. His friend allowed him to lead, to swing as he wished while Goodwin blocked and parried. Sweat dripped down Brodyn's face as he moved, blessedly hiding the tears that tracked down his cheeks with every swing of the sword. When finally his emotions cracked, Brodyn dropped his sword to the ground with a clatter, kneeling at Goodwin's feet.

"Tell me," Goodwin demanded, putting out a hand to help his king onto his feet. "I ken something is eating at ye."

"I willnae survive the battle. Caitriona says we will be victorious, but I perish. She claims to have nightmares of my death, for she witnesses it within the cave just before I die. I will need ye to be Murielle's guardian and arrange her marriage to a neighboring tribesman of royal blood. She will be a target to all men if she isnae betrothed."

"Ye... ye die?" Goodwin shook his head in disbelief. "Nay, I refuse to believe such nonsense."

"'Tis not nonsense. Am I not a man of flesh, blood, and bone? 'Twas my bones buried in the cave that Caitriona found in her time."

"If ye die in battle, how do ye make it to the cave? We are due to convene south from here."

"Mayhap I sustain injuries and am carried back there. I ask to be buried there, Goodwin. Even if I die on the battlefield, ye must take me back to the cave. 'Tis where my life began, the moment I spotted Caitriona, and 'tis where I wish to die. If my bones arenae buried there, Cait cannae find her way back to me."

"'Tis madness, Brodyn. All of it." Goodwin ran a hand through his shoulder-length brownish-red hair and shook his head. "Ye sent her away, so she doesnae witness yer death, aye?" Brodyn nodded, and Goodwin pursed his lips. "If ye can change the course of history in one way, ye can change it in another way."

"What do ye mean?"

"I mean, ye can trust me to lead the army and defeat Ecgfrith. Ye stay behind and guard the stronghold. Then ye will survive battle because ye arenae there."

"Ye wish me to be a coward? Nay!" Brodyn groused. "I will die with a sword in my hand, defending my people before living in the shadows like a coward!"

"Ye need to think, Brodyn! Ye are better off for yer people, alive! As ye say, ye have no heir, and yer sister will be hunted as a prize. Ye ken I will keep her safe, but Brodyn, men dinnae get to ken when and where they die. Mayhap ye can place yer fate into yer own hands. The gods gave ye Caitriona for a reason, and she gave ye the knowledge to avoid death. Dinnae be a fool!" Goodwin paced back and forth, and Brodyn hoped he hadn't made a mistake telling him the truth.

"There is no honor in sending men to fight a war for my grandfather's lands if I am not there. I willnae send men to die while sparing myself. 'Tis out of the question. I will be at the battle and live or die as my fate decides."

Goodwin stopped pacing and narrowed his eyes, pointing a finger in Brodyn's face with the other hand still gripping his sword. "And ye say yer sister is the stubborn one! Curse it all, Brodyn!"

"Would ye stay behind if ye kenned ye would die?" Brodyn asked, crooking a brow.

"Nay, of course not. But I'm no king."

"That is not the reason, and ye ken it. Ye would never take the coward's way. We always expect death when we leave for battle. This time, I expect it more than usual. But I will die an honorable death, and my wife willnae be present to witness it. I made certain of that."

After a moment of silence, Goodwin nodded, accepting his king's decision. "I will be beside ye at the battle, guarding ye with my life. If ye are injured, I vow to get ye to the cave."

Brodyn placed a hand on Goodwin's shoulder and bowed his head. "Ye have been a fine friend, Goodwin. The best I have ever kenned."

"Dinnae speak with such finality, Brodyn. Ye yet live and may continue to do so."

"We will see. Gather the men and run drills. I have other tasks to trouble myself with. We leave in three days. The full moon will guide our path with its light."

"As ye wish." Offering a stiff bow to Brodyn, Goodwin turned and walked toward the other men as they spared, shouting for them all to gather.

A boulder weighed down Brodyn's stomach, but he sheathed his sword, clenched his jaw, and strode toward the armory to take inventory of the weapons, despite knowing precisely what was there. Staying busy was the only way he wouldn't go mad with grief. Already, he missed Cait with a soul-deep ache, and he wondered what she was doing and if she was all right.

Without Cait in his life, he welcomed death. There was nothing more for him. He longed to see her face one last time, even if it was during his last breath. Then, he would die a happy man with his wife by his side.

Entering the armory, Brodyn noticed Taylor's gun and pondered the weapon, carefully testing its weight in his palms before placing it back onto the table.

Caitriona lived in a bizarre world, though his wasn't much better. Apparently, men would always wage war on one another, and rather than achieving peace, they created new ways to kill proficiently.

With days left to live, Brodyn found himself lost and wandering, feeling like a feather caught in a wind storm—helpless to control the direction of his life.

CHAPTER FIFTEEN

SLEEP ELUDED CAIT. She missed Brodyn's strong arms around her and the familiar scent of his skin. His impending death still haunted her dreams, and she wondered if leaving Brodyn mattered if she still couldn't escape the pain of losing him 1,400 years later.

Rolling over in bed, Cait stared at the motel room's outdated floral print wallpaper and wondered what Brodyn was doing now, in his time. Likely, he was scrambling to prepare his people for the battle. What would the people think of her abandoning them in their time of need? Caitriona grappled with the temptation to return. Would the veil of time allow her to pass through again?

Guilt wrestled with her logic. Coming back here was worth her while if only to notify her friends and family that she was alive and well… or at least still breathing. She couldn't say with any amount of honesty that she was well. Her stomach churned, and she battled nausea from the stress and anxiety.

"Cait?" She heard Emilie whisper her name into the sun-speckled room as the morning rays pushed through the window slats.

"I'm awake," she groaned and rolled over to look at her friend in the other double bed.

"I received a message from the lab. They've finished analyzing the bones found in the cave and have created the facial reconstruction."

"What?" Cait popped up in the bed and swung her feet over the edge. "What does it look like?" She was curious to see how closely they matched Brodyn's features.

"I don't know, but I was thinking… if you're up for it, we can head over there and find out. You wanted to see him anyway, and this feels less morbid than just staring at… bones."

Closing her eyes, Cait sucked in a deep, calming breath to staunch another wave of nausea. The thought of seeing him through reconstruction was a sweet torture that she both wanted to run away from and run toward as fast as possible.

"Cait?"

"Yeah… yeah, sorry." Cait wiped her hands down her face and scooped her messy hair over her shoulder. "I didn't sleep much last night. I want to see him, I do. It's just really hard. Yesterday, I was in his arms. Now he's a pile of bones in a lab, and his face is nothing more than a piece of CGI art. It makes me feel sick to my stomach."

Emilie nodded and frowned. "I wish I could think of something to do or say to make you feel better."

"You are, Em. You believe me. How many other people would? You and Samuel are the only people I can talk to. I missed you so much. I'm glad I came back, so you knew I wasn't dead."

"It's been horrifying, Cait. And then Taylor showed up looking for you, then he disappeared. It's been chaos. That man is unstable. I want to believe he came looking for you because he was worried, but I think it was his next moment to play the hero. The more he holds over your head, the more he thinks he can guilt you into going back to him."

"With him looking so much like Brodyn and his twin brother, there is no way I could ever be with Taylor again… not that there was ever a chance."

"I know that. Taylor needs to get that through his thick skull."

"Speaking of skulls…" Cait slowly stood up and fought back another wave of anxiety. "Let's get ready to head to the lab.

Maybe I will feel better once I'm there."

She didn't feel better—not even a little. When they arrived at the lab, scientists shuffled around them, but she saw no sign of Brodyn. Everyone went about their day, but Cait's mind was stuck in the past while torturous thoughts ravished her present.

The lab scientist working on the facial reconstruction sat down on a swiveling chair and turned on his computer screen, clicking the mouse button while Emilie and Cait stood behind him, anxiously awaiting the results.

"Here you are," he said with one final push of a button. "Technology is an amazing thing. We used his skull's structure for the facial features, though there are always small variances like muscle and other tissue." He turned the screen toward Cait, and her heart jumped into her throat. The image resembled Brodyn, only with a slightly weaker chin, higher cheekbones, dark hair, and dark eyes. As familiar as it was, it wasn't the stark likeness she had expected.

Leaning into Emilie, Cait whispered, "Brodyn has dark blond hair and blue eyes. It's close… but not quite it. It's still amazing they can accomplish this."

Without hearing her words, the lab tech picked up a pile of papers and handed them to Emilie. "This just arrived today, and I have to say I find it baffling. We have a scientific anomaly on our hands with this one."

"What do you mean," Emilie murmured as she flipped through the stack. Cait saw sheets with genome sequences, followed by a write-up on the results.

"We collected the DNA to see if new technology could more accurately predict hair and eye color, but also to see if any trace of disease or illness could be found. The results show a high probability of dominant features like dark hair and eyes, which is rarer in Celtic people, however the thing that stumps me is on page 24 of the report."

Emilie furrowed her brow and glanced at Cait before thumbing through the report. Emilie's lips moved as she silently read, her head shaking as she scanned the document. "How is this possible?"

"What does it say?" Cait took the report from Emilie and looked it over, frowning at the findings. "They found evidence of modern dental work and... screws in the left fibula?" Cait shook her head and looked sideways at Emilie. "Did you know about this?"

"No way, I had no idea. While the bones were being excavated and readied to transport, I was part of a search team looking for you. I haven't exactly been able to focus on work while you were missing. Why didn't Samuel mention this to me?"

Cait's hand shook as she held the papers, her throat constricting. "Samuel doesn't say much about any of it. What does this mean? How is this possible?"

The lab tech stepped closer and looked at the report. "We're looking at a male, roughly twenty-five to thirty years in age, based on the radiocarbon levels in his tooth enamel. I'm stumped. I've never seen anything like this, and to be frank, I can't send this report off without looking closer at the findings. The radiocarbon in his bones says he perished roughly 1,500 years ago, yet the modern use of dental fillings and screws in the bones... it's not possible."

"Have you shown this to anyone else?" Emilie asked.

"Just the supervisor of your dig, Samuel. Oddly, he didn't seem so concerned about the findings, almost like he suspected it. But I've never found an ancient body with tooth fillings and screws in the bones. We even tested the hardware. It's modern. Next, you need to test that cave's soil. I have no answer for what we've found, but there is always a scientific explanation."

Cait's head spun, and she stumbled over to the rotating seat near the computer, plopping down before she collapsed onto the floor. Did the bones not belong to Brodyn? Hope blossomed in her chest, but she dared not accept it. Even if these were not his bones, it didn't change his fate. She'd witnessed his death many times over. And legend still claimed that his wife buried him there. If this wasn't Brodyn, who was it?

Dark hair, dark eyes, silver fillings, and pins in his fibula… who was this man who looked like Brodyn but had access to modern medicine? Jumping from her seat, Cait looked at Emilie. "We have to go! Thank you for showing us the report!" she shouted to the lab scientist as she grabbed Emilie's hand and dragged her away.

Once they were outside the lab and walking down the street, Cait looked at Emilie, panting as she sprinted toward the motel. They had no car rented here in Scotland, and she was suddenly too jittery to sit in a cab. "You know that isn't Brodyn."

"I don't know who it is, but yes, it can't be. Though, if not, how… who?" Emilie stopped walking and waited for Cait to notice. Once she did, Cait turned to look at her friend as panic seized her insides, and she had no idea how to articulate the fears running through her mind.

"A time traveler passed through the cave and died in Brodyn's time. That's the only explanation," Emilie suggested, looking uncertain.

"It's Taylor. I need to find him. Oh, God!" Cait spun in a circle and yanked on her hair, wondering which way would bring her to Samuel the quickest. He would know what's going on.

"Your ex-fiancé? Didn't he cross back over with you?"

"Yes! So, how and when does he return? I hope I'm not too late!" Reaching into her crossbody bag, Cait searched frantically for her phone, cursing when she grabbed her wallet, glasses, and keys first. "Dumb bag… it's so small and yet… ah!" Pulling out the phone, she swiped it open and clicked on recent calls. When Emilie had returned all of her belongings, Caitriona's phone was brimming with calls and texts from Taylor, each message more aggressive than the previous one.

The phone rang several times, but he didn't answer. Maybe he was on a plane home or already back on base in California. When Taylor's voicemail picked up, she cursed again and looked at Emilie. "This is bad."

"You're sure it's him?"

"When he was in high school, he and his brother got into an accident. His brother Brian died. Taylor was banged up badly and needed screws put into his severely fractured fibula because he had his leg up on the dash when the car collided with a truck. He was never the same emotionally after that. Physically, it never slowed him down, even in the military. The reconstruction of his face, the dark hair and eyes found in the extracted DNA? Brodyn has light hair and eyes. And he certainly has no dental fillings and pins in his ankle!"

"Okay, let's take a beat and think this through. First, we need to locate Samuel."

"Ach!" Cait hollered and stomped her foot. "I know Samuel can't tell me anything, but this is killing me! If that body is Taylor, where is Brodyn buried?"

"Maybe because you came back here, you aren't there to bury him in the cave, so he is placed elsewhere? Maybe the records are wrong. History still says his son takes over for him after his death, but unless you're pregnant, he has no son."

Cait stopped and stared blankly at Emilie, widening her eyes as blood rushed to her face.

"You aren't pregnant, Cait, are you?"

"No? I mean, no. I'd know, right? I've been nauseous, but my husband is going to die soon. That is causing me a bit of stress!"

"Follow me."

Emilie took off down the street like a woman on fire, and Cait blindly followed, not sure where they were going but too frazzled to care. After a few moments, Cait stopped to catch her breath and grip her side. Running was never her best sport. "Can you tell me where we are going?"

"Over there." Emilie pointed at a little pharmacy across the street before stepping into the crosswalk and entering the store. Cait entered behind her, her stomach flipping with nerves as her best friend grabbed a pregnancy test kit.

"Here." Ripping the box open, she handed Cait one of the

two tests. "You pee. I pay."

"You're serious right now?"

Emilie pointed to a sign on the wall. "The bathroom is just down there." She walked away with the open box in her hand, leaving Cait to fend for herself with the small, wrapped stick.

"This is ridiculous," she murmured once inside a bathroom stall as she hastily tore away the wrapper. She'd never taken a pregnancy test before, and Emilie had the instructions, but how hard could it be? Pee, wait, read.

Once she finished, she sat in the stall alone, watching the timer on her phone, awaiting the results. Within two minutes, the word "pregnant" suddenly lit up on the screen, and Cait's heart plummeted to her toes. Perhaps it was a false positive. As she stepped out of the stall, her phone rang, flashing an unknown call from the local area.

"Hello?" She said while washing her hands before walking out of the bathroom. "This is Cait Murray. Oh… hi, Doctor Singh."

She listened in silence as the doctor spoke. "Sorry to bother you. You sound a bit winded. Is this a good time?"

"As good as any," she offered. Her life couldn't get more complicated unless they found tapeworms in her system.

"Great. I'm calling because the rest of your lab work came in. We wanted to check everything thoroughly. Your white blood cell count is great, and I wanted to congratulate you personally on your pregnancy."

"My… my pregnancy?" she looked down at the small stick in her hand and leaned against the wall for support.

"Yes. Based on your hormone levels, you appear to be about eight weeks along, which means you should come back soon for your first ultrasound. Were you aware of your condition?"

Was she aware that she carried a Pictish king's baby inside her womb? "No, I wasn't," she whispered.

"Lucky you. Many women would feel ill by now. When you come in, we will give you a list of all the foods and drinks to avoid, the classes we offer, and other resources. Congrats again,

Miss Murray."

"Thanks… bye." She hung up and shoved her phone into her bag, feeling like her spirit somehow floated about her body. She was detached from reality, from the world, from herself.

Emilie walked over to her with a curious look on her face, and Cait, not having the words, thrust the pee stick close to Emilie's face before shoving it into her purse and walking away. She wasn't sure where she was going for now, but Caitriona knew, eventually, she had to go back to the year 685, for she was pregnant with the next king of the Picts.

WITH DOUBLE THE men in the longhouse, it was nearly impossible to hear anything Domnall said above the raucous laughter. He and his large army of well-trained warriors arrived in the afternoon, weary, starving, and filthy from the journey. Brodyn had never seen so many men running into the nearby loch bare arsed after a battle. Now that Domnall's army was clean, Brodyn broke out their best ale, mead, and meats to offer Pictish hospitality. The women in the village enjoyed the extra men and most assuredly enjoyed the sight of them bathing. Brodyn made sure his sister was scarce, for he had yet to decide on a husband, and he hoped to arrange that tonight without her distracting the men. She was a bonnie woman, and most assuredly, any man would give his left testicle to be her husband and become heir to the Pictish kingdom of Fortriu, but he needed a proper match based on power and protection.

"Did ye ever expect us to break bread in yer longhouse without us breaking one another's necks?" Domnall asked with a chuckle before downing another cup of ale.

"Nay, I never thought to see the day, though I am grateful, for we need to unite as one and fight our true enemy."

"Here, here!" his cousin toasted as he raised his mug. "Where is the bride I sent ye? I had thought to find her by yer side. Is it not a love match?"

"Och, 'twas a fine match, indeed. She is a true Celtic beauty, hard-working, intelligent, and good with our people. However, with the battle looming, I tucked her and my sister away to keep them safe. Should I fall, they will become targets." Brodyn's heart clenched as he thought of Cait. If only she was here…but his decision was the right one. He knew that for sure.

"Aye, I ken this all too well. I have also advised my sister to stay well-hidden until we are assured victory."

"And, how fares the wife we sent ye? I hope she is serving yer people as a fair queen of the Scots," Brodyn asked, doing all he could to change the subject away from Caitriona. His heart ached every second she was gone.

"She is a fine wife and carries our first child. He is due in the early winter. I am grateful that ye sent me a fine wife, indeed."

"I am verra glad to hear this." Brodyn sipped his ale to hide his pain, wondering what it would have been like to know Caitriona carried his child. To know he had an heir on the way would make death an easier fate to accept, and to see the woman he loved carrying his bairn would be a blessing greater than any other. But, she was gone, no babe grew within her womb, and he would be dead in two days' time.

"Domnall, there is a matter I would like to discuss with ye before we travel, and I wish for the truth. I vow that the past will remain in the past, for I have no wish to quarrel, but I seek clarity. Did my brother plot against me to take over Fortriu and wed my bride when ye suggested peace through marriage alliance?"

Domnall's features sobered, his hazel eyes growing wide as he slowly lowered his mug and ran a hand through his reddish-brown beard. "Aye, this is so. Before our battle two years ago, I hoped to prevent bloodshed and asked him to relay the message to ye. I would agree to stand down from this fight over our grandfather's lands if we could create an alliance. I am not a greedy man, Cousin. My lands are plenty, and my people are happy… or they were before these battles over territories. Grandfather would not have wanted his grandsons fighting over land. He wanted us to each have our piece and rule fairly. He captured those lands through many bloody battles and did not wish the same for us."

"Ecgfrith made that impossible when he started sending men to our lands to collect tribute, denying our people the fruits of their labor," Brodyn groused.

"Aye, that he did. And I believed him when he turned me against ye, telling me ye wished to take my lands to make up for the tribute losses. 'Tis why I wanted to speak with Talorc and come to an agreement. But he told me ye didnae wish for peace. Ye wanted my lands, not a wife. So, he offered to take yer place as king, marry yer Scot's bride, and kill ye during battle. I am sorry for believing him and conspiring. 'Tis one of my greatest regrets."

Somehow, hearing the truth from Domnall didn't hurt like it once would have, and Brodyn sighed, finally having his closure. "The need to protect our tribe can make us trust the wrong people. Ye didnae turn Talorc against me. He chose that path, and he paid the ultimate price," Brodyn said over the sounds of a mug shattering and women cackling at bawdy jests. "We have done well to unite the remaining Celtic tribes, and when we meet up with the others, we have our chance to overthrow Ecgfrith."

"Our cousin is a fool to disregard the counsel of his advisors," Domnall said. "Even the bishop Cuthbert has decried his desire to attack Fortriu. He will find himself in the harsh Highland terrain, outnumbered and surrounded. 'Tis his downfall he will find and naught more."

"Aye," Brodyn replied, knowing full well that Northumbria would lose the battle. "It didnae have to end this way, yet the greed of men kens no bounds."

"I will drink to that." Domnall whistled, and one of his servants came over to refill his mug.

"Ye will drink to anything," Brodyn said wryly, pushing to his feet. "I leave ye and yer men to feast, for I have some matters to finalize before we head south on the morrow."

"We thank ye for yer hospitality. Please tell yer bonnie wife that her king wishes her well."

Brodyn felt a knot of emotion in his throat, wishing to relay that message more than Domnall could ever know. Nodding, Brodyn left the longhouse and its celebrating people to sit alone in his home, staring blankly at the fire.

Footsteps made Brodyn look over his shoulder to see his sister standing behind him in her undertunic, wringing her hands with distress. "Sorry, brother, I dinnae wish to disturb ye."

Brodyn waved Murielle closer and forced a smile. "Ye never disturb me, Murielle. I am merely thinking about the battle that awaits."

"Me, as well. Ye sent Caitriona away, and I didnae get to say goodbye. Did ye send her… home?" She came closer and sat down beside him, wiggling her bare toes by the fire.

"I did, aye. It was the safest place for her, and I would send ye away as well, if I dinnae believe ye would prefer the future and never come back," he jested and bumped her shoulder with his.

"I would never leave yer side, and I believe the same of Caitriona, which is why I ken ye are telling me lies."

"I havenae lied, only omitted details ye need not fret over."

"She told ye some awful news, didnae she? Is that why ye are desperate to marry me off? Ye told me it was 'in case ye perish,' but now I am worried ye ken more than ye say."

Brodyn sighed and wiped his hands down his face, scratching at his untrimmed beard. Sleep alluded him since Caitriona had left, and his mind would not stop playing over battle strategies repeatedly. The last thing his weary mind and bleeding heart needed was to crush his sister's spirit with the truth. "The outcome of war is never known, Murielle."

"'Tis in the future, isnae it?" she pressed.

"Aye, I assume as much. Caitriona didnae tell me anything about it." Now, he was lying, though sometimes lying had its merits. "'Tis best to always leave yer loved ones before a battle as if 'tis yer last time with them. Let us simply enjoy this time together while we have it, my dear wee sister. I hope ye ken how much ye mean to me."

"Now, yer scaring me," she chuckled. "Ye never compliment me so."

"Well, 'tis time I do. I see how intelligent ye are, and I ken ye will make a fine wife, mother, and ruler wherever ye go. I am a man of many regrets, and I do wish I hadnae spent so much of my life fighting and had settled with a family long ago. Then I would have an heir, and ye wouldnae be in danger if I perish."

"But, then ye wouldnae have married Caitriona," she said with a frown and looked at his profile while he stared into the dancing flames within the hearth.

"Mayhap that would be just as well."

"I ken ye dinnae mean that. I see the love ye bear her," Murielle insisted.

"I will never deny my love for her, but what good is love if it is torn away from ye, leaving ye to die inside slowly?"

Having nothing to say, Murielle leaned in and wrapped her arms around his waist, tilting her head against his shoulder. "Let us just sit in the silence tonight. I fear words cannae mend yer pain."

Kissing her forehead before resting his head atop hers, Brodyn allowed his wee sister to comfort him in his final hours, for aside from Caitriona, there was no other woman who he loved better, and he would miss them both dearly.

CHAPTER SIXTEEN

"Come on, pick up!" Cait shouted when Taylor's phone went to voicemail for the dozenth time. "Taylor! Where are you? Do not go back through that cave! You have no idea what you're dealing with!" She left her message, then ended the call, nervously tapping her foot and biting her lower lip.

"Now what?" Emilie said as they walked along the road leading back to the motel.

"I have to go back."

"What?" Emilie tugged on Cait to slow her down. "Not right now. There's a battle about to go down!"

"It's not happening at the cave site, and I need to find Taylor before he ends up as a pile of bones. Maybe I can see Brodyn one last time and let him know I'm pregnant. If he's going to…" She swallowed hard. "If he doesn't survive, he will at least know he has an heir."

"It's not safe! You will be a target as a widowed queen!"

"Emilie," Cait turned to look at her friend and shook her head. "I don't have a choice. This child belongs in that time. He will have sons who have sons. His entire line will cease to exist if I don't get him back. There are enough people in Fortriu to protect me. I trust Goodwin."

"Who's Goodwin?" Emilie asked, panting as she jogged behind Cait once again.

"Brodyn's best friend and champion warrior. He knows the truth about me, as does Anya. They will know what to do."

"Is Goodwin hot?" Emilie asked, tilting her head.

"Are you serious right now?"

Emilie shrugged. "It's a fair question, but I'll let it go."

Cait shook her head and grinned. "He is, but not as hot as Brodyn."

"Aw, man." Emilie shrugged.

The road sloped down the hill and turned to the right, where the motel stood in its dilapidated glory, reminding Caitriona of a hotel she once saw in a horror flick. Luckily, the inside was clean enough, and she hadn't time to be picky. Crossing the street, Cait ran through the main entrance and headed straight for the elevator, frantically pushing the button to go up. She knew that hitting the button a dozen times wouldn't make it arrive faster, but it kept her shaky hand busy while her mind raced.

The door dinged and opened, allowing Cait and Emilie to slide inside and head to their room on the fifth floor. "If my parents happen to call, tell them I moved to a remote village in Scotland with no cell service, and that I'm fine."

"I will. I'm sure they wouldn't be surprised to hear it, anyway." Emilie nodded.

Once they reached the room, Cait scrambled to pack what little there was and looked at the pile of tunics. "I'm sorry, Emilie. I need to return wearing these. I can't show up in 685 wearing a shirt about fitting tacos in my mouth."

Emilie cracked a smile and nodded. "I understand. I would be hard-pressed to answer questions about where I found pristine linen tunics from the 7th century, anyway."

"I called Samuel, but he didn't answer either. I assume he will be awaiting me near the cave since he seems to know my every move," Cait murmured wryly. "Apparently, I'm predictable in every lifetime."

"You're not predictable; you're caught in a time loop, hun. I can't believe I just uttered those words. This is so bizarre."

"You're telling me." Cait threw her clothes onto the floor and pulled the tunics over her head. "Can't wear underwear either.

They haven't invented butt floss yet."

Emilie's laughter raised Cait's spirits, making her smile once more before looking around the room. Everything was hitting her all at once. She was leaving this time again and may never return. No more in-door plumbing, hot showers, or sushi dinners. No air conditioning on hot days or airplane trips to Hawaii. No more expeditions around the world.

No more Emilie by her side.

Placing a hand on her stomach, Cait closed her eyes. She grew a baby inside her—Brodyn's child, the future king of the Picts. No record remained about Brodyn's wife, which Cait appreciated, for she preferred not knowing her fate.

"I'm going to miss you."

Cait looked at Emilie and nodded. "I'll miss you more. I won't ever forget that you helped me with all of this. I don't know what I would do if I didn't have you, Em."

Emilie leaned in and hugged Cait. "You will always have me, even if 1,337 years exist between us."

"But, who's counting?" Caitriona said with a chuckle, feeling that familiar constriction in her throat as she fought back her emotions. She wanted to say so much to her best friend, but there would never be enough time, and Taylor was in grave danger. Time was of the essence.

Sensing her hesitation, Emilie nudged Caitriona toward the door. "Come on. We need to get to the cave."

"We?"

"Um, yeah. I'm coming with you. Not to the seventh century, but I will see my best friend off. It's like waving on a dock when someone leaves on a cruise."

"Yeah. The Titanic," Caitriona sighed as they left the room.

The sun was beginning to disappear over the horizon when their cab dropped them off in the sleepy village nestled atop the seaside cliff dotted with random drops of purple from the wild thistles, and the women hopped out before the driver could ask more questions about Caitriona's odd clothing. Thank goodness for Renaissance fairs. People might think she was nerdy, but they didn't think she was insane.

Without the rental cart Samuel had supplied for the team to take them down to the shore before she disappeared, Cait and Emilie shuffled down the half-mile path, and Cait lifted her long skirts to avoid snagging on the low brush and prickly thistles along the way. Her leather slippers did nothing to shield her feet from the gravelly earth, but she carried on, step by step, until they reached the shore.

Cait looked at the cave and groaned with frustration. "It's high tide! Why didn't we think to check before heading here? There is no way to get to the cave until low tide."

Emilie pulled her cell phone out from her small backpack and looked up the tide schedule with a frown. "Looks like we won't be accessing it until six o'clock tomorrow morning."

"No! That's… that's too late!" Cait wailed, feeling her panic rise. "I don't know where Taylor is yet, and Brodyn will be leaving for the battle if he hasn't already! Time moves faster on his end, but I cannot calculate it. I shouldn't have left him! I wanted to tell him…"

Emilie silently watched with a frown, her sympathy evident, yet there was nothing to be done except to wait.

"Em, I appreciate you being here, but there is nothing else for you to do here, and you have your own life to manage. I'll walk back up with you to get you a cab."

"I'm not leaving you here! Are you crazy? It's nearly dark, and soon it will be nearly freezing, as well."

"This cloak will keep me warm," Cait said, running her fingers over the gold brooch that held the heavy cloak around her neck.

"I'm still not leaving."

A rustling sound from behind made both women gasp. "Taylor?" Cait asked before turning, clutching the cloak to her chest as her heart rate sped up.

"Taylor is gone." Samuel walked up with a serious expression on his face. "You arrived earlier this time. No accounting for traffic with these things."

"I knew you would be here. Which means—"

"Taylor went back, yes," Samuel finished for Caitriona.

"He's going to die! Those bones we found are Taylors, not Brodyn's!" She paused and studied Samuel's calm expression. "Wait. You know this already, don't you?" Caitriona fisted her tunic skirts and gritted her teeth to keep them from chattering. Her nerves threatened to undo her, but she fought to stay outwardly calm. She knew Samuel couldn't tell her any details. Still, she was tired of his aloof attitude. Her entire world was upside down, and Samuel just showed up everywhere with all the answers.

"Yes, I am aware, sadly." He nodded.

"Why are you just allowing this to happen? Taylor isn't involved in any of this!"

"Cait," Samuel said, stepping closer. "I told you that everyone has free will. You were early arriving here because of decisions others made to leave their houses at certain times or because a light turned green on one street earlier than if you took a cab from another street. It's always the same outcome, though the details vary. The bottom line is—Taylor has free will. He chose to go back. I cannot intervene. I've told you this."

"Is it too late? Can I find him and convince him to go home?"

"You may try, and I'm sure you will. You always do try."

Another vague answer. Does she ever succeed? She didn't bother asking. Maybe she didn't want to know. Obviously, last time she failed, if his bones were in that cave...but why is he buried there? Based on the skeleton's position, he was carefully placed there. By whom?

"I need to go back!"

"I know, Cait."

"Well, I can't!" she yelled, feeling her frustration bubble over as she stomped her foot and pointed to the cave. "Low tide isn't until morning! It will be too late by then!"

Samuel remained silent, but his lips drew down, and his forehead furrowed, showing that he honestly did care. It must be equally hard, perhaps harder, for Samuel, going through this every lifetime and not being able to intervene. He was held captive by time just as she was, and Cait's frustration wasn't helping.

"I'm sorry, Sam. I know this isn't your fault."

"What can we do?" Emilie interjected. "Is there another way?"

"Until low tide? I'm afraid not. It's too dangerous to attempt wading into the cave. The waves crash against the cliffside, and you will be bashed against the rock with the water. I'm sorry, Cait. We have to wait until then."

"He'll be dead by then, won't he?" Cait asked, feeling ice flood her veins. It was futile. Taylor had made his decision, and she couldn't save him. Somehow, she felt even more helpless than before.

"Cait…"

"I know. You can't tell me," she huffed.

"All you can do is go back to town until morning. In your condition, you shouldn't be out here. I will accompany you. I have anthropology papers to grade anyway," he said with a crooked smile.

Of course, he knew she was pregnant. Cait wanted to protest, but Samuel was right. There was nothing to be done, and she had a life growing inside of her. He was her priority now, and no good would come of her staying here in the cold and darkness for another twelve hours.

Reluctantly, Cait and Emilie silently walked back up the trail with Samuel by their side. Cold dread sat like a stone in the pit of Caitriona's stomach, nausea once again roiling in her belly. She wasn't sure if it was caused by the baby, fear for Taylor's life, knowing Brodyn may die before she made it back, or the weight of the world's timeline on her shoulders, but never had she felt more helpless. She was in Time's hands, and she prayed it showed her mercy.

STANDING IN THE middle of a vast field, Brodyn looked at the thousands of men gathered at the camp from the Picts, Scots, and reluctant Britons. Their king, Caedan, marched up the northwest coast, bypassing the Northumbrian Angles to join the highland tribes for the battle, but he made no promise of further cooperation. The Britons preferred to work alone, though Brodyn was grateful for their efforts in this battle that would define the rest of their history, even if the thousands of men on this field didn't know it.

Being assured of both victory and death was an uneasy combination. He still had many other men whose lives depended on him to lead them to victory. Still, many would fall beside him on this day. Oddly, knowing he would die on this field left Brodyn with a sense of closure. His destiny lay before him.

Just over his shoulder, Brodyn saw Caedan, the illusive King of the Britons, approaching with a disgruntled look on his face. Brodyn nudged Domnall in the shoulder and braced himself for an unpleasant experience, remembering Caedan as a man full of constant gripes, even if he was an ally. "Ye sent Domnall a bonnie bride, and he sent ye one in exchange, so I am told. I wonder that I was not included in this bargain for peace," Caedan said, crossing his burly arms in front of him. His long reddish-brown hair was braided, matching his beard. He was a decent-looking man, and Brodyn hadn't heard any reports of him being a tyrant. To Brodyn's best knowledge, the man was simply guarded and hesitant to trust others.

"Aye, because ye refused to let our messenger into yer stronghold when we came with the offer," Brodyn said. "Ye made it clear ye work alone."

"Yet, here I am," the man said, widening his eyes and stretching his arms. "I brought a thousand men with me for yer cause, did I no?"

"Indeed, and we are grateful. We all benefit from this cause. Dinnae ye forget that, Caedan. When we defeat my cousin, ye willnae have to send tribute to him any longer, and then ye can crawl back into yer hole and pretend we dinnae exist." Brodyn smiled and slapped the man on his broad shoulder.

Caedan ran a hand over his braided beard, deep in thought. "I would consider taking a bride and creating an alliance with ye… for my people, ye ken."

Pride radiated off his entire being, making Domnall and Brodyn bite back bemused smiles. They had heard that King Caedan sought a bride but had rejected more than one offer, preferring a noble and bonnie lass. "Well then, ye should've opened yer gates to us," Domnall added, raising a brow.

Caedan glared at Domnall for a second before clearing his throat. "My gate is open now. If we live to see another day, I will discuss a more permanent arrangement between our tribes. I willnae owe ye tribute. We will be equals. But this doesnae mean I wish to host ye and yer men, wasting my resources on yer lot. I will answer yer calls to arms, and I willnae start conflicts. 'Tis all I can offer."

Brodyn ran his tongue along his top teeth and regarded this king. He didn't blame the man for being brusque or unaccommodating. His lands spread across the island, but his territory of Gwynedd was much further south than the Picts and Scots, and the kings of Briton had learned to rely on no one but themselves for many generations. Brodyn hoped to change that, for Caedan, for all of his bluster, would make a fine ally.

"The Picts are open to discussions," Brodyn replied. "If I dinnae survive this battle, my counsel will send a messenger to conduct my business." Tentatively, Brodyn wondered if Murielle would make a good wife and queen for Caedan. She knew her role and duty, but now was not the time to mention such things.

Goodwin and Ronan came up from behind on their horses,

dismounting quickly.

"Ecgfrith's army approaches just beyond that ridge, my king."

"Good, then our plan is working," Domnall said, looking at Caedan and Brodyn.

"Aye, let him come to us. He doesnae ken the difficulties of this land. When they are within sight, we shall do as we discussed and feign retreat until we are flanked by the mountains. Most of our men are positioned within the trees and will emerge when commanded. Let them believe they outnumber us. When their guard is down, our first line will attack."

"Archers are positioned in the back," Goodwin said with a nod. "Spearmen and swordsmen are centered on foot, and our calvary is mounted and ready at yer command."

Brodyn nodded, doing his best not to think about Caitriona or that he would never see her again. He felt at peace with his death, but never would he feel at peace with the time lost with his beloved wife.

The sun was at its highest point in the sky, its rays stretching out in every direction, sending speckled light across the field where clouds shifted and danced between the glow. Green grass, still wet from the last night's rain, spread beneath their feet, smelling sweet, loamy, and fresh. Soon, red blood would soak much of this land, and the stink of war would consume it. The familiar gut-twisting dread settled into his bones, hardening him for the battle ahead.

"Ready yerselves, men! Our enemy approaches on the horizon!" he shouted, catching all the warriors' attention. The chatter stopped as men straightened their backs and gripped their weapons. Swords and axes glittered in the sun, and spears pointed toward the sky. "Today, we fight for our ancestors, our land, and our families. Today, we fight against tyranny!"

Men pounded their weapons against shields and roared their approval as they stood their ground, wanting to attract the enemy's attention so they could properly trap them. The gleam of metal in the distance, caused by the Northumbrian's familiar helms, allowed Brodyn's army to spot their foe even from a distance. No helms adorned the heads of this Celtic army. They relied on their skill with weapons, strategic moves, and knowledge of the land. Most men wore only their linen and wool daily clothing, but the Pictish men stood out above the others with blue paint smeared across their faces and bared chests. Varying tattoos adorned their chests and arms, representing their family, old gods, or battle honors. Brodyn's bull tattoo, a target the enemies would recognize as belonging to the Pictish King, was proudly exposed.

He welcomed Ecgfrith's men to single him out. The sooner they located their target and killed Brodyn, the fewer men would die. He was no coward like many Angle kings who hid behind helms and fought in the backline, if at all. Nay, he would lead his men into battle, preferring his to be the first face the enemy saw.

With only a few hundred Celtic men visible on the field, the approaching army appeared destined to swallow them whole, a strategy Brodyn had used before against a different enemy. Let their enemy's confidence grow with every step. That confidence would wane once the thousands of men beyond the mountains revealed themselves.

"Retreat!" Brodyn shouted once the encroaching army was about a hundred yards away. "We are outnumbered!" he shouted in the Angle's language so they could hear his words floating on the wind.

At his command, his army turned and ran toward the valley where mountains flanked either side. Already bolstered by a sense of victory, the Northumbrians roared and charged forward, chasing the Celts across the land—land they knew better than the backs of their own hands. Domnall and Caedan stayed beside Brodyn as they waited for all three lines of men to disperse before mounting their horses and riding behind them. If arrows flew, the kings would be the target, leaving the men to run to safety.

"It's working," Domnall said as they rode between the mountains. "They are following us into the valley."

"Ecgfrith would do well to better train his men in the ways of Celtic warfare," Caedan chuckled as he pushed his brown and white speckled horse harder.

"My cousin may never get that chance, for he is the target of all three thousand of our men." Brodyn looked over his shoulder to view the enemy, his blood rushing as it did before a battle. If this plan worked, the Angles stood no chance, and victory would be theirs, as Caitriona had said. Thinking of her disoriented Brodyn, so he hardened his heart, took a deep breath, and stared straight ahead as he entered the valley. Mountains lined with trees flanked them, and he knew the time for battle had arrived.

As planned, their army disappeared behind a bend, so when the Angles approached, they would find the valley empty and believe they had chased away the Celtic army.

"My king." Brodyn looked at Goodwin, who guided his horse toward Brodyn's. "I wish I had the words to say how much I honor ye. I vow to make certain Murielle and all the others are safe. No other king will ever be half the man ye are."

Brodyn placed a hand on his best friend's shoulder and nodded. "'Tis been an honor to fight beside ye and an even greater honor to call ye friend. I trust ye will uphold yer vow."

Goodwin nodded and swallowed his emotions, looking away to break the awkwardness. "They are approaching."

"Aye. When they reach the valley, I will give the signal."

"We will be ready." Goodwin looked Brodyn in the eye one last time, cracked his signature dimpled smile, and turned away, joining the men in the first wave.

How thousands of men could blend into the world around them and remain silent was a skill honed by generations of Celtic warriors. The shiny helms worn by the Angles might have served as extra protection, but they also reflected the sun's rays, lighting up the horizon. While they relied on brute force, numbers, and intimation, Brodyn and his warriors understood the benefit of stealth and strategy.

When the valley echoed with the sounds of clanking metal

and cheering Angles who believed they'd won an easy victory, Brodyn signaled to the archers in the trees, raising his sword high for them to see. Goodwin repeated the gesture so the men on the other side of the valley would see it, as well. In tandem, they lowered their swords, and a swarm of arrows loosed from invisible men, flying through the sky like locusts sent to signal the apocalypse that the Christian monks in his village discussed.

The apocalypse wasn't what Brodyn's people feared. Instead, it was the constant threat from tyrants who preferred power to peace and refused to listen to the best counsel of his advisers—tyrants such as Ecgfrith.

Men shouted and scattered as they ran, dozens falling with dull thuds on the ground, sparking the start of the battle. Men from both sides surged forward, and Brodyn's cavalry charged from behind trees and shrubs, his finest fighters wielding swords and large spiked shields. Their battle cry rang out as they swiped at the men below, cutting a bloody trail between them as the second round ran down from the mountain, covered in blue woad and screaming as if the devil himself commanded them. Angles turned to flee, finding themselves cornered between the hills and the Celtic warriors. When fewer men came, it became clear to Brodyn that the Angle army was significantly smaller than his. Still, Ecgfrith's men filtered through the gaps, desperate to defend their king, who had yet to appear.

Brodyn had never relished killing. It never sat easily with his soul, and he longed for a world where men could resolve conflict without bloodshed. Unfortunately, based on Caitriona's accounts of the future, the world will see endless wars. Anya had arrived in his time because she hid in a cave while her village was attacked from the sky. Knowing that man would one day create flying devices that dropped weapons, killing dozens of men, women, and children at once, only made Brodyn question the true spirit of men. As humans advanced, so too did their methods of killing.

Men rushed toward him, and he dismounted, preferring to fight on foot. Unsheathing his sword, Brodyn stood ready. He might die today, but he would die fighting for his people. Stepping left to avoid an enemy's blade, Brodyn spun around, locking swords with a man whose face was obscured by the long metal nose piece on his helm. Just as well, for Brodyn didn't wish to see his eyes as he drove his steel into his belly. With a grunt, the man fell, and Brodyn pulled his blade from his body, having no time to think about the blood pooling at his feet. Another man came, then another, and Brodyn stayed focused, his movements fluid and practiced, like second nature.

Victory came swiftly, a clear sign that Ecgfrith had misjudged the Celtic people again. His desire for power only led to his defeat. Still, with his army either lying dead in the valley or scattered in every direction as they fled, Ecgfrith still hadn't shown his face.

"Where is yer king?" Brodyn roared. "Tell the coward to face me!"

"He is already dead." Brodyn followed the familiar voice, looking at Goodwin, who panted and stepped forward. "He attacked yer back like a true coward. I ran him through. His body lies just there." Goodwin pointed to a body that Brodyn hadn't noticed until now. There was no other indication that he was a king aside from the crown laying atop his askew helm.

"He sat in hiding the entire battle and waited until ye had yer back turned before he slithered out like the snake he is. I'm sorry, for I ken ye wished to end him yerself."

Slowly, Brodyn approached Goodwin with narrowed eyes, placing a hand on his friend's shoulder. "Ye saved my life. Never apologize for that." He paused as elation—and sorrow—washed over him. "I… I survived the battle."

"It appears ye have, aye," Goodwin said with a nod. "Ye already had to kill yer brother in battle, so I determined to kill Ecgfrith myself to save ye from killing more of yer kin."

"Then it appears I owe ye my life and my honor."

"Ye owe me naught, my king. 'Tis an honor to serve ye always. And now, I get to continue my servitude because ye yet live." Goodwin kneeled before his king and lowered his head. Brodyn hated to see his friend kneel to him, though he understood the gesture. Several of his men followed suit, kneeling before Brodyn on the valley floor, littered with the blood of their enemy.

"Victory!" King Caedan shouted as he approached and stood beside Brodyn, caked in mud, blood, and sweat. His victory cry echoed throughout the valley, inspiring thousands of men to repeat the gesture simultaneously, raising their weapons in the air as they celebrated.

"We are free, thanks to yer efforts," Domnall said as he walked up to Brodyn and smacked him on the shoulder. "I am proud to be yer ally, and especially proud to be yer kin."

Brodyn put out his hand and clasped wrists with his cousin, doing the same to Caedan when he came to stand near the other two kings.

"Today, the Celtic tribes from across the land came together as one, and we have won our freedom!" Brodyn bellowed, eliciting cheers from thousands of men. His head spun as he wondered how he survived. Were the history books incorrect about his death? Caitriona said minimal records existed from this time since his people hadn't yet adopted the use of letters like the monks had. The first man to write down the events of this day would do so fifty years from now. Brodyn knew well that half a century was enough time for tales to be passed down and embellished. His wife had told him that her people call it "playing telephone" … whatever that meant.

Caitriona. He missed his wife with a relentless ache that often threatened to undo him, and he had sent her away for nothing. That reality slammed into him harder than one of the enemy's swords. She was gone and would never return because she thought he was dead.

Could he bring her back? The idea struck him like lightning. Mayhap he could go to the cave and try to retrieve her. He knew not what he would find, nor did Brodyn understand their odd language, but he knew her name. If he could find her, they could be together again, perhaps even start a family.

With nothing else to lose, Brodyn made up his mind. He would go to the cave. If he failed, he would seek Anya's help, but the fastest route to Caitriona was to go to her himself before anything else.

"Goodwin," Brodyn whispered when he stepped closer to his friend. "I have some business to attend to… alone."

Goodwin's brows dropped in confusion before shooting upward in understanding, and a smile spread across his lips.

"Aye, ye do. I will tell the men that ye placed our queen in hiding and must retrieve her."

"Pray that I do. Should I come home without Caitriona, I dinnae ken what to tell our people about their queen. I had not thought beyond getting her to safety and avoiding my death."

"We will figure it out if needed. I pray ye find her. I vow, ye've made me desire a wife to love as ye love our queen."

"Then we shall find ye a match, my friend." Brodyn nodded and turned to find his horse grazing on the brush along the valley's edge. "For now, I have a wife of my own to find."

CHAPTER SEVENTEEN

CAITRIONA SHIVERED AND wrapped her arms around herself as she walked down to the shore. The sun rose just above the horizon, and streaks of purple and orange lit up the sky. If her heart wasn't so heavy and her stomach not so nauseous, maybe she could appreciate the beauty of this Scottish sunrise.

Every step she took felt like she walked a tight rope as she carefully navigated the wet trail, concentrating on every move to keep her mind busy. Loose gravel crunched and shifted beneath her feet, but Emilie walked in front of her to ensure she didn't slip. It had only been a day since they found out she was pregnant, and her friend was already the overprotective aunt, packing enough prenatal vitamins in Cait's satchel to last through three pregnancies.

"Watch your step. Almost there…" Emilie murmured, and Cait just smiled, grateful for her friend. There was no need to remind Emilie that Cait had already traversed this trail on her own many times. Everything changed the moment she began to grow a small human, and suddenly Emilie acted as if Cait was made of glass.

"Here we are." Emilie put out a hand to help Caitriona with the last step before finding herself on flat land.

"You're a good friend, Em."

"Only because you're the best friend, and I'll miss you like crazy. I wish I could go with you. I've been thinking about it. We could live together. I can help with the baby."

Cait's heart warmed, but she shook her head. "Don't give up your life here for me, Em. You have your whole life and your hard-earned career. Trust me, I will be just fine, and you will want to leave the first time you have to bathe in well water that was snow only days before. It's not pleasant."

"None of that matters without you, Cait."

"It does matter. Anyway, Anya and Samuel pass back and forth. Maybe I can, too. I expect the prenatal care of 2023 will be a bit better than in 685. If I can continue my care in our time, I plan to. I will reap the benefits of both times, and I will get to see you again, I'm certain."

Emilie didn't seem so sure, even if she didn't argue. On time as always, Samuel arrived from the opposite side, where a steeper trail led up the cliff. He always preferred the road less traveled, as did Cait, but when it came to hiking, she admitted she would take the easier route every time.

"Good morning, ladies," he said with a yawn. "My apologies. I was up all night grading papers. Barely slept. You ready, Cait?"

"As ready as I'll ever be. Though, now that I'm thinking about it, how will I pass through time if the bones are no longer there? Actually, how do you, Anya, and Taylor pass through?" This entire time, Caitriona believed she needed Brodyn's bones to connect to the past, but Anya and Samuel had been passing through for years, as had many before them. The bones weren't even Brodyn's, so that theory wasn't accurate.

"Caitriona, the portal wasn't the bones. There are other factors, such as your soul's intention, the thinned veil, and whether or not your soul already resides in the time you'd enter. However, the cave ultimately determines who passes. If your intention doesn't serve a greater purpose, you cannot pass through."

"But what's Taylor's intention for going back if he knows I'm here?" Caitriona had been thinking about that question all night, and still, the answer escaped her. There was nothing for him there. He knew no one and couldn't communicate with anyone. What could he possibly seek?

When the answer suddenly hit her, she gasped and clutched her chest, looking at Samuel with horror glistening in her eyes. "Brodyn! Do you think he went back to find Brodyn?"

When Samuel didn't answer her immediately, Cait stepped closer to him. "I wondered why Brodyn was in the cave when he died and not on the battlefield, a day's march south. The bones we found weren't Brodyn's, but I'm still certain it's Brodyn I see dying in my dreams."

Icy dread trickled up her spine as she suddenly understood Taylor's intentions, and nausea roiled in her coiling stomach. "Does Taylor kill Brodyn? No… he wouldn't… I have to go! Now! If I'm late because I missed the low tide last night, I will never forgive myself!" Cait spun in a circle, beside herself with fear and worry. "Why would the cave allow him through for such a dark purpose?" she cried, flailing her arms as panic dug its claws into her flesh.

"Because Taylor serves a greater purpose," Samuel calmly replied. "Remember, it was your desire to find Brodyn's bones that led you to the cave. Allowing Taylor to pass, even with evil intentions, leads you back every time, which is the very point of this time loop. You cannot save Taylor, Cait. He used his free will to return, and now his fate is sealed."

"I may not be able to save Taylor, but I need to find him before he gets to Brodyn!" Turning to face Emilie, Caitriona hugged her friend fiercely. "Thank you for all you've done. I wish I had more time to say goodbye, but I fear the worst."

"Go… go. We will see each other again. I know it. Take care of the little bean and tell it stories about Auntie Emilie, but only the good stories."

"All I have are good stories. Tell my parents I love them, and I will contact them if I ever reach civilization. I love you." Letting go of Emilie, Cait ran straight for the cave now that the water had receded enough for them to reach its entrance. The familiar buzzing sound radiating off the cave instantly shot waves of pain straight to her brain, but she gritted her teeth and pushed through, determined to find her way back to Brodyn.

Once inside the cave, she ran to the small alcove, praying she arrived in time to talk sense into Taylor before he did something she couldn't fix. Though, if she had been able to fix it before, his bones wouldn't have been buried in the cave to begin with. Maybe it was all a predestined loop that she had no control over, but she had to try.

Samuel entered the cave just behind her. "Cait. I will walk Emilie back to the car, and then I will meet you on the other side."

"How do I get through?" she asked, looking around the small, dark alcove. Something metal and shiny caught her attention, and Cait bent over to examine the rectangular object. Gasping, she picked it up, realizing it was Taylor's phone, its glass screen shattered beyond repair. Part of her had hoped she was wrong about his whereabouts, but now she knew for sure Taylor had gone back in time.

"Just think about your purpose, and the cave will do the rest," she heard Samuel shout from the entrance before he left with Emilie.

Alone, she did as he said, closing her eyes and imagining Brodyn holding their son. Tears flooded her eyes as the image materialized in realistic detail despite its unlikely reality. A sensation ran through her palm and up her arm, like waves of energy tingling every nerve ending.

Sparks flashed behind her eyelids, and a static charge built, making the hairs on her nape stand on end. Like before, voices buzzed in her mind, and images of people long gone developed in sharp detail before fading into darkness. Crackling sounds popped and hissed, and before she could brace herself, an energy surge swept her off her feet, sending her sailing backward, unable to brace her fall.

Grunting, Cait scrambled to her feet and spun around, wondering if it had worked. Her hip ached from the fall, and she touched her belly, hoping the baby wasn't affected. "Did it work?" she whispered to herself, leaving the alcove to enter the central area of the cave. Fewer carvings covered the cave walls than before, letting Cait know she was back in Brodyn's time. Was the war over? Was he already gone? Adrenaline rushed through her veins as she bolted toward the cave entrance. She wasn't sure where to go first, but the desperate need to learn Brodyn's current whereabouts drove her to move without thought.

"Cait?"

Stopping in her tracks, she turned, finding herself face to face with Taylor. Gasping, she clutched her chest and tried to control her breathing when she saw the gun in his hand. "Wh-what are you doing, Taylor?" she asked, fisting her skirts to still her shaking hands. "You shouldn't be here. This won't end well for you," she tried to reason.

"Why are you here?" he asked with a scowl and narrowed eyes. She had only seen that wild look in his eyes once before when he spoke about his brother Brian, who'd died in a car crash. She had always wondered why he looked more angry than sad when he spoke of his brother, but she never questioned it. Now, that same look warped his face, and she could see he was in fight mode.

"I came to find you," she said, taking a step closer. "Taylor, there is a war happening. It's dangerous to be here."

"I am familiar with war, Cait. Or have you forgotten everything about me now that you married that Scottish barbarian?"

"I remember," she whispered. "Why did you come back? If you plan on hurting Brodyn, you're too late." Her words nearly made her crumble to the ground, acknowledging that, somewhere right now, Brodyn might lay dead in a field, and she stood here in his time, carrying his unborn child, and arguing with her ex-fiancé.

"You told me about your dreams, Cait. I remember where he dies. You aren't the only one stuck between worlds. You dragged me into this, and now I'm going to finish it. I have to. It's my destiny. I'm going to kill Brodyn, then you and I will stay here together where we will raise the baby ourselves… away from those heathens!"

Taylor waved his gun like a lunatic, and Caitriona shrunk back, instinctively clutching her belly. She'd forgotten that Taylor owned an arsenal of guns. "How do you know about the baby?"

With lightning-quick reflexes, Taylor grabbed Cait's arm and dragged her back into the cave. "I know more than you think."

"Taylor! Stop! You're hurting me!" she cried as she tried to break free without success.

"You hurt me when you broke off our engagement!" he roared. His voice echoed off the walls, amplifying his rage, reminding her that she'd never felt truly safe when his anger flared. He had never hurt her before, though she'd seen him lash out at men if they simply looked at her, and his sudden fits of rage had always frightened her. Seeing her with Brodyn and knowing they were married must have made him snap.

"I came for you, and for what? To find you with another man? Coming through that cave triggered something in my head… images… memories… I can't stop them. I see things that I know I did, things I know I will do."

"Taylor… put down the gun. You can change this. You still have free will!"

"No! We don't! We are prisoners to time, Cait! No matter what we do, this all happens the same way every time! I don't blame you for coming here and marrying him. I get it now. You had to, and you have to have this baby. But your job here is done. He forced you to marry him! I know this now! I will free you from him, and we will make a life together."

"Taylor, what is it you've seen?" She needed to distract him, to somehow get that gun from him. Still, curiosity tugged at her. Did Taylor remember things from a past life as she had?

Still gripping her arm, Taylor held the gun in his other hand with a white-knuckled grip, his voice gravelly as he recalled his memories. "I could speak that odd language, understand every word. I plotted to kill Brodyn, so I could be king and marry you… or a woman who looked just like you. Then another memory of attacking Brodyn during a battle. But he ran me through with a sword, and everything went black."

"Taylor… I understand what's happening, okay?" Cait tried to look him in the eye, tried to reason with him. "My soul is the same one that belongs to the woman in your memory. She was promised to Brodyn but always died before arriving in his lands. Their marriage alliance was important to Scottish history. It's like the timeline corrects itself by pulling me from our century. I can't quite explain it, but Taylor, you're experiencing the memories of Brodyn's twin brother, Talorc."

"It seems your husband and I are fated enemies," Taylor said with a scowl. "I began to remember everything on the way back to the cave. It struck me like lightning in my skull. I knew what I had to do then."

"It doesn't have to be this way, Taylor." Cait put out a hand to touch his arm, attempting to reason with him. "You will die if you continue. I'm not sure how you die or when, but it will happen if you don't turn around now and leave."

His gaze focused on her throat, and his eyes narrowed. "You have Mother's brooch."

Cait furrowed her brows and shook her head. "I have Brodyn's mother's brooch, yes. It was a wedding gift." She placed her hand protectively over the precious item, worried he would try to steal it.

"His mother is mine, as well!" At that moment, Cait realized Taylor was speaking the Pictish language fluently, and chills ran up her spine. It appeared that Talorc's memories were melding with Taylor's, and Caitriona worried she'd run out of time to convince him to leave before it was too late. "I was going to marry ye! I was going to gift ye that brooch! Brodyn stole everything from me!"

Cait shook her head. "I was never meant for you. Not in this time, or ours."

"He was born only minutes before me, and because of that, he has won every honor. I was heir to nothing. Husband to nobody. A second son gets nowhere in this world unless he makes his own path."

"You call killing your brother 'making your own path'?" Cait asked incredulously.

"It worked with my brother, Brian." His deadpan response sent waves of fear and disgust through her body, and she gasped, trying to break free from his relentless grip. He spoke of murder so casually, and Samuel would arrive soon. She prayed Taylor didn't turn his gun on her mentor.

"Your brother died in a car crash when you were in high school," she said slowly. "You injured your ankle in that same accident."

With a salacious grin, Taylor shook his head. "Ye never met Brian, and I made certain of that. He was just like Brodyn—he was Brodyn. The better version of me in every way. He received higher marks in school, performed better in sports, and was always better liked by our parents. I'd never had a girlfriend who didn't prefer him. One day, he saw a photo of ye in my car. The look in his eyes when he saw ye..." Taylor trailed off as he thought back on that day. "He asked who ye were and if I would introduce ye. He kenned ye were my girlfriend, but he wanted to take ye from me like he took everything else. I couldn't allow that. So, I grabbed the steering wheel and plowed the car into a tree. My injured ankle was worth the cost. It also made the crash look accidental. After all, nobody would suspect I put myself in danger."

"You... you killed your brother?" Panicking, Cait jerked her arm out of his grip once he was distracted, staggering backward until the cold cave wall touched her back.

"It wasn't planned, Cait. Ye look at me like I'm a monster..." Taylor stepped closer to her, placing his hand on her throat. "He's the monster, Cait! Not me! In every life, he overpowers my existence! I killed my brother to make a better life for us without his interference, and I plan to kill him again. He won't win this war!"

His fingers dug into the soft flesh beneath her chin as he forced her to look at him. "Remember how it felt when we made love, Caitriona?" he whispered against her ear. "We can have it all. One bullet is all it takes."

"You're insane!" she cried, turning her head aside before he squeezed her throat harder, making her cough for air.

"Wake up! Do ye think your perfect husband never killed a man for gain? He's out there, right now, killing dozens of men for his own gain! 'Tis the way of the world. Ye cannae have power without taking it. He'd do the same if needed."

She shook her head and swallowed. "You're wrong. Taylor, this won't end well for you. I'm trying to help you, to save you! You will die if you don't return home!"

"I'd rather die than let my brother have ye!" he spat, and she felt the spray from his saliva land on her face, making her flinch back and bang the back of her head on the stone.

Footsteps sounded from the cave's entrance, and a large shadow blocked out a portion of the sun's rays. Tightening his grip on her throat, Taylor pinned her against the cave and turned to see who approached. Unable to turn her head, Cait prayed it wasn't Anya coming through the cave to get supplies.

"Caitriona?" That voice. That familiar, beautifully deep brogue that she never thought to hear again made her stomach flip and her heart drop at the same time.

"Brodyn," she gasped, unable to turn her head with Taylor pinning her against the wall. "You're alive…"

"Get yer hands off my wife!" Brodyn's roar echoed through the cave, and she felt the reverberations through her spine as it pressed against the stone.

"He… he has Talorc's memories," she sputtered. "The battle doesn't kill you… Taylor does!"

She heard Brodyn step closer, and she panicked. "He has a gun! The same weapon he brought the last time. One shot will kill you from a distance. Please… go!"

"I came here after battle to find ye, and I'm not leaving ye ever again!"

"Brother…" Taylor said with a calm that made Cait's skin crawl. "I kenned ye would show up if I waited long enough. 'Tis a fine thing to have memories from both of my lives. Now, I shall kill ye, then have yer wife and yer child. If only ye would be alive to witness how well I will treat them." His hold on Caitriona's throat tightened, belying his words.

"Child?" Though she couldn't see Brodyn, she heard the tenderness in his voice, and she wished to run to him and feel his strong arms embrace her.

When Cait saw Taylor raise his gun in Brodyn's direction before cocking it, she screamed in terror as her knees weakened and threatened to give way.

"No, Taylor! P-please! I will marry you! In our time! We will raise the baby together just as you want! Just, please… don't do this!" Cait begged as tears slid down her face, her throat constricting with panic.

"This is our time, Cait. We will start over here, together," he whispered, leaning in to place a gentle kiss on her quivering lips. "But he must die. There is no way around it. There never was…"

"No… Taylor!"

A shot rang out, reverberating off the walls and deafening Cait to her own screams. Her throat burned, her head rattled from the explosion, and numbness spread down her limbs as shock enveloped her.

Taylor released his grip on Cait just before she collapsed to the ground and scrambled over to Brodyn. Small, jagged rocks dug into her knees as she scrambled to reach his side. A second shot rang out, and Cait yelped and cringed, looking over her shoulder, afraid Taylor was aiming at her back.

When Taylor toppled to the ground with a blank look on his face and blood rushing out of his chest, Cait looked up to see Samuel behind him holding a gun.

Taylor was dead, but Brodyn's groans of agony proved he wasn't… not yet.

"Brodyn!" Cait shouted, reaching his side just as another groan of pain tore from his cracked lips.

"Don't leave me," she whispered and drew closer to him.

Blood dripped from his bared chest, just above his bull tattoo, ironically obscuring the scar from Talorc's first attack. Cradling his head, Caitriona noticed another wound caused by his fall to the ground. A large, jagged rock lay at his feet, covered in blood from the impact with his skull.

His injured head thrashed from side to side. Wet tendrils of dark blond hair stuck to his forehead, and a loud crack of thunder shook the cave. The sky opened up, and the drizzle became a torrential downpour as if the earth mourned beside Caitriona.

"I warned you… not to…" she wailed, pain searing her heart as she bore down on his chest wound, attempting to staunch the bleeding. "You didn't listen!" she wailed just as another flash of lightning lit up the cave's interior.

Looking at Taylor, whose blank face stared back from the cave floor, Caitriona released a scream so loud, so deep from within her soul, that she felt as if her heart ripped from her chest. "I told you to go back home!" she screamed to Taylor, knowing he could no longer hear her.

Looking down at Brodyn's pained face, covered in dirt and blood, Caitriona knew she had reached the end. This was her nightmare. Despite their attempts to avoid this moment, it had arrived anyway. Brodyn would die here in this cave as she cradled his body, and there was nothing she could do to save him. Samuel silently walked over but did not speak a word. No words were required, for his sorrow showed on every crevice of his tired face. He, too, bore the weight of this time loop's manipulation. He, too, was a victim to the circumstances, forced to watch events unfold, forced to know the results in advance, forced never to intervene… and yet, he did. He shot Taylor before he could follow through with his threats to steal Caitriona away. Samuel couldn't save Brodyn, but he'd saved Caitriona.

With a gasp, Brodyn's eyes flew open when a clash of thunder reverberated off the cave's walls, and she saw the beautiful blue of his irises one last time before his eyes slid shut.

She shook his shoulder with one blood-stained hand, shrieking when a final gasp of air left his lungs. A visible wisp of breath curled into the chilled cave's air.

"No! Don't leave me!" she shouted, collapsing onto his still body as sobs wracked hers. "I loved you… I'm so sorry…" Laying her head against his chest, she allowed her tears to coat his skin, too weak and numb to bring herself to move from this spot.

"Cait…riona…" Her name was a mere whisper upon his lips, but it enveloped Caitriona like a beacon of hope.

"Brodyn? Brodyn! He is alive! Samuel!" Cait looked up at Sam with hope blossoming in her heart just as a small shadow entered the cave.

Anya walked in carrying a large leather bag, humming to herself. Seeing Brodyn on the ground, she gasped and dropped the bag onto the cave floor, shuffling toward them as fast as her old bones could bring her.

"What has happened?"

"Taylor shot him…" Cait managed to say through her constricting throat and lack of breath. "I tried to stop him… I couldn't…"

Anya kneeled beside Brodyn, running her hand through his hair with a mother's affection. "I was bringin' my bag through the cave to gather more supplies. Thank the Lord I came when I did." Reaching into her bag, Anya grabbed an opened pack of sterile gauze and carefully opened it with surprisingly steady hands.

"Grab the bottle of alcohol from my bag, dear. Oh, and the long forceps." Brodyn groaned and moved his head when Cait shifted, proving he was still alive and conscious but unable to open his eyes. Anya pressed the gauze against the chest wound and examined his head.

Handing Cait another wad of gauze, Anya moved to the chest

wound. "Wrap that around his head to staunch the bleeding. I will tend to that once I remove the bullet. It appears to be only a flesh wound, but 'tis sizeable to be sure."

"Will he be all right?" Cait dared to ask, dared to hope.

"I have seen much worse than this in my time," she murmured. "During the war, I tended to many injured men. Shrapnel, shell casings, blown-off limbs. 'Tis but one reason I chose to stay in this time. War is a messy business no matter the time, but bombs and guns dinnae exist here." She looked at Taylor lying on the cave floor and scowled. "Or they didnae, until now." She worked diligently while she spoke, and Cait wondered if blabbering helped Anya stay calm while she worked, for her ancient hands remained steady as a young surgeon's as she poured alcohol on the forceps, then his chest.

Brodyn let out a guttural growl when the alcohol hit his skin and roared like a beast when Anya dug into his chest wound with the forceps. Caitriona stayed by his side, cradling his head in her hands, praying he did not die, not now. He'd survived the battle. He survived Taylor's attack. He had to survive the removal of the bullet. Dabbing his sweaty face with her tunic's skirt, Caitriona ran her fingers down his cheek, whispering encouraging words, so he knew she was with him.

"I love you, Brodyn. Do not leave me. I am carrying your child… an heir. We can be a family…" Her voice cracked as emotion overcame her. The thought of living alone in this time without him was too much to bear.

Anya pulled the forceps out of his wound and made a sound of triumph when the bullet successfully dislodged. More blood oozed from the gaping wound, and Cait grabbed more gauze and applied pressure to the area.

"The bullet hit his upper pectoral muscle. He should survive if we stave off infection." Anya looked at Caitriona, and hope glittered in her eyes, raising Cait's hopes, as well. "I just need to stitch him up." Moving back to her bag, Anya searched for her sutures and a curved needle, both within sterile packages. Clearly,

Anya had sources in 2023 that gave her modern-day medical supplies, and Cait was grateful for them and for Anya showing up when she did.

A few minutes and stitches later, Anya moved to his head wound, unraveling the gauze to observe the gash caused by hitting a rock as he fell. "His wound is deep but should heal well enough as long as we keep it clean." Removing the alcohol vial's cork, Anya poured some on Brodyn's wound, making him groan again, though much less than before.

Despite Brodyn remaining alive for the moment, an uneasiness sat in the pit of Caitriona's stomach like a stone. Perhaps he did not die in the battle, but historical records still claim that he died on this day. He wasn't out of danger, and should an infection set in, Brodyn could succumb to his injuries.

"What was Brodyn doing in this cave? The other men arrived back from the battle without him. And ye… ye're meant to be back in yer own time. Ye say ye are with child?"

Still cradling Brodyn's head in her lap, Caitriona wiped away a fresh set of tears and nodded. "Yes, Brodyn sent me away to avoid this very moment, yet it appears to be my fate to always relive this. I discovered I was pregnant once I was back, and I knew I had to return when we discovered Taylor had disappeared. It's a long story. I returned and found Taylor here with a gun, determined to kill Brodyn. Then Brodyn showed up, hoping to find me. And then…" She trailed off, unable to say the rest, and she knew it was unnecessary. Anya could piece together the rest. "Thank you for helping him."

"He is as much a son to me as any man could be. I ken ye will take good care of him." Now that Brodyn was patched up, Anya's hands trembled, and Caitriona knew the woman hid her fear until her work was done.

Sniffling, Anya began to gather her supplies, but Samuel took her hand and helped her to her feet before placing the medical items into her bag.

"I will get some antibiotics while I'm in yer time. Get him

home and make him rest. I shall check in on him later." Anya squeezed Caitriona's hand and forced a smile before walking into a dark alcove of the cave.

"Are you all right?" Samuel asked Cait.

"No! I'm not!" Anger bubbled to the surface. She was tired of the emotional trauma and the secrets. Looking up at Samuel, Cait ran her hands through Brodyn's hair while his breathing lulled to a steady pace. She looked at his serene features while he slept, and she refused to move even if her legs were falling asleep from having his weight on them for so long.

"I am tired of not knowing! Damn it, Sam! Is Brodyn going to die? If so, tell me now because I cannot hope for recovery just to lose him again."

Sighing, Samuel frowned and closed his eye. "He will live, Cait. I can tell you that now. He will survive this. That is all I know, for my work is done here. I can come and go as I please, for I have done what is expected of me."

Relief washed over Cait, and peace washed over her as she absorbed his words. Brodyn would live. All of the anguish had been for nothing, but she didn't care because he would live. Looking at Taylor lying dead on the ground, a different form of grief took root. Taylor was a monster, a murderer. How had she never seen it? Still, he didn't deserve to lay lifeless here for much longer.

"Why did you kill Taylor, Sam? I thought you weren't supposed to intervene?"

"I had to, Cait. I always have to. Remember, I have free will just as you do. There have been times when I did not kill him, and... things do not go well, especially when Anya arrives. You must understand I did that because I knew if I did not, more people would die."

Cait swallowed her disgust, understanding what Samuel couldn't bring himself to say. If ever there was a reality where Taylor shot an innocent old woman, then his soul was truly tainted with evil.

"Sam, I need you to run to the village and get help. We need to get a cart to bring Brodyn home, and Taylor must be buried."

"He will rest here for 1,400 years until he is found again."

"And so, the time loop starts once more."

"As always," Samuel said wearily. "I will get help and be back as swiftly as possible."

Samuel took off, leaving Cait alone, cradling Brodyn in her arms. Placing her finger on his throat, she felt his pulse, weak but present, and that was all she could hope for right now.

"I will get you home, my love," she whispered. The wind howled outside the cave, and a gust blew in through the entrance. Unclasping the brooch around her neck, Cait removed her cloak and laid it across Brodyn's bare chest, careful to avoid his wound. The blood flowing from his head wound had slowed down, and Cait couldn't help but exhale a deep, relieved sigh.

Together, she and Brodyn awaited help, and Cait filled the time by counting his pulse and tracking every breath, thankful for every rise of his chest and beat of his heart.

CHAPTER EIGHTEEN

CAITRIONA WALKED INTO the dimly lit room carrying two mugs of herbal tea. Wisps of steam floated to her nose, and the scent of lavender and honey made her smile. Lit candles around the room cast dancing shadows across the walls. Carefully, she placed a mug down on the table beside Brodyn as he sat before the hearth, bare-chested, as he rocked their new son in his arms.

Sitting back, Cait observed her two favorite men in the world, finally at peace now that they were both safe and well. Brodyn's recovery from his wounds went well, thanks to Anya's access to antibiotics and modern ointments, though she did well to disguise them in other containers, so the villagers didn't call her a witch any more than they already did. If not for Brodyn's protection, Anya would likely have been accused long ago, and Caitriona herself wasn't convinced that the woman wasn't a bit of a witch. Either way. She used her skills to help others, and now Brodyn was alive because of her.

The scar left behind from the bullet wound puckered just above his bull tattoo, directly over the original scar from Talorc, and her heart sank each time she saw it and remembered the fear she felt as he lay dying in her arms. But now her heart soared because he was whole and well, and so was their son, Lucas, who had his father's beaming blue eyes and his mother's reddish-blond hair.

Snow fell just outside the walls of their thick-walled home, and the village prepared to celebrate the Yuletide season. Swaddled tightly within a warm linen blanket that Murielle knit for her nephew, Lucas cooed contently as he seemingly stared at the shifting shadows of the fire dancing over his father's face.

"I brought you some tea," Cait whispered, carefully handing the hot mug to Brodyn, making certain not to spill any on Lucas.

"Thank ye, love. Ye ken, I had an odd dream last night."

"Oh?" Caitriona raised a brow and took a sip of her tea. She missed hot coffee in the mornings, but tea made with herbs she grew herself gave her great satisfaction. Life was more complicated in many ways here, yet simpler in others.

"I dreamed that ye birthed us a wee bonnie lassie."

Cait creased her brow and pursed her lips. "You mean, instead of Lucas?"

Brodyn shook his head and smiled. "Nay. I mean another child."

"Good thing your dreams don't reflect the future like mine do."

"Ye dinnae want another?" He frowned.

"Brodyn. I just birthed Lucas three weeks ago, and my nipples are raw from nursing him. Maybe give me a few months?"

"But yer wanting more bairns, aye?"

The look in her husband's eyes as he asked that question while holding Lucas in his arms made her heart nearly burst with love. She had been very certain that he would die during that battle. His survival was evidence that history books were often mistaken about the times of the Picts. The past few months had Cait on pins and needles waiting for disaster to strike, but only blessings had occurred thus far. As for the rest of their lives, it was in fate's hands, and Cait was glad not to know the rest.

"I would love more bairns, but you must give me some time," Cait said, chuckling before sipping more tea.

Slowly, Brodyn rose from the seat and stepped closer to her. The fire's light reflected off his chest, highlighting his scar again, and Caitriona slowly ran her finger over its rough surface, reliving the horror all over again.

"I'm here, my love," he whispered. "I willnae leave ye."

"You cannot promise that" she said with a sigh. "I just want to treasure every moment we have."

"Then what do ye say we give this bairn to Murielle for a wee spell, so we may treasure more moments together in our chamber."

Cait flashed him an incredulous look and gently smacked his shoulder, making sure not to disrupt Lucas. "I told you; I don't want another bairn just yet. Don't try to seduce me!" she chided.

"Ye ken I can please ye in plenty of ways that willnae lead to a bairn." Brodyn gave Caitriona that wicked smile he flashed when his mind was full of dark deeds.

"You tempt me, but we don't have much time before the Yule feast begins."

"They can start without us..." Brodyn whispered, leaning in to kiss her neck, sending warmth throughout her body. His merest touch lit up her whole being, and it was a sensation she might never adjust to. Not that she wanted to adjust.

The front door flew open, making the candles flicker as a gust of frigid wind swallowed their flames. Brodyn groaned and scowled at the intruder, but Cait laughed when she saw her sister by marriage walk in with a knowing look on her face.

"I dinnae mean to interrupt ye." She closed the door against the chill.

"Then why do ye?" Brodyn shot back with a hint of irritation in his voice.

"Have ye forgotten that it's the first day of Yuletide? The feast is soon to begin, and we require our king and queen to light the Yule log."

Murielle walked over and stole Lucas from her brother's arms, her face alight with joy as she looked down upon her wee nephew, who opened his eyes and began to wail.

"Look what ye've done," Brodyn chided halfheartedly.

"Bairns never did warm to me. Mayhap he senses my deviance." Murielle made her best attempt at a scary face, but she only succeeded in making Caitriona laugh.

"You couldn't be scary if you tried. Deviant, however, I believe." Caitriona looked at Brodyn and touched his arm. "She is right. The people await their fearless leader. We have much to celebrate this Yuletide. In my time, we'd have a tree inside the house, decorated with shiny balls and lights."

Brodyn and Murielle both looked at Cait as if she had grown a second head.

"Ye hang shiny balls on it? What in the world is wrong with yer people?" Murielle asked.

"Ye put lights in the tree?" Brodyn clipped. "Ye will burn down the entire village!"

Caitriona laughed and shook her head. "I'll explain it to you both when we have more time. Go put on a tunic. I do not want the other women looking at your half-naked body any more than necessary."

"I certainly dinnae wish to see his chest," Murielle scoffed. "Meet me at the longhouse and be quick about it… my queen." Murielle winked and reached out to touch Cait's arm. "I ken it's been a few moons, but I truly am glad ye are back. I was worried I'd never see ye again. We have been blessed."

With that, Murielle handed Lucas to Caitriona and left the house. Brodyn disappeared to ready himself for the festivities, and Caitriona stood alone in the peace of their small, simple home, holding her newborn son in her arms, and listened to the tranquil sound of the crackling fire.

"Indeed, we are blessed," Caitriona whispered as she kissed her son's forehead.

WITH THE ENTIRE village stuffed into the longhouse, Brodyn sat in the front of the room with his queen by his side and his son in her arms. The Yule log burned in the center of the room and would be kept burning through the next twelve days. Many things had changed since his people converted to Christianity, yet the Yule log and several other traditions from his people's pagan days still persevered, connecting them to their ancestors.

Brodyn hadn't expected to make it another year, and he nearly hadn't. The time his wife came from was undoubtedly filled with many wonders that he'd never understand, but the most wondrous thing from Caitriona's time was his wife herself, and she sat beside him now. He wasn't sure what the future held for them, nor did Cait, for there was no record of his life beyond the false reports of his early death in the battle against his cousin. Not knowing what to expect was far better than the dread of knowing what was to come. Every day was new, unexpected, and held unlimited possibilities.

Murielle and Samuel stood with Goodwin near the fire, and Brodyn marveled at people from different times gathering here under one roof, proving that time may pass and things may change, but people would always connect on a deeper level, always find ways to relate.

Brodyn frowned when he realized one important person was missing from the gathering, as usual. It was a Solstice day, which meant Anya would be missing for a while. He only wished he knew where she disappeared to and what she was doing. The woman had raised him as a child and then saved his life. He owed her everything. She was a mystery that he might never understand, and he had accepted that. Anya could have gone back to her own time and stayed, but she chose to be here, and though she felt as ancient as the sea and as constant as the tides, he knew she wouldn't be here forever despite her moving like a woman half her age. He often wondered if Anya was more than just a healer, though he never asked, and she'd never told.

Plates topped with boar, venison, and boiled cabbage with leeks were quickly eaten before rounds of pies and tarts were brought out from the kitchens, filling the room with the scents of cinnamon, cardamon, and buttery crusts. Mead and ale disappeared from clanking mugs soon to be refilled as his people celebrated the season. Brodyn watched with both amusement and wonder that so many mysteries surrounded this earth, and yet he had simply existed, blind to anything but the need to survive. He'd survived by the skin of his teeth, and his people had rejoiced in his recovery every day since.

Looking at Caitriona, Brodyn watched as she chatted with Sorcha and other women from the village as they fawned over wee Lucas, passing him around and bouncing him in loving arms. She had truly integrated herself into his world and become highly regarded by his people. It had been less than a year since she'd arrived, a stranger in this land, turning heads with her odd speech and manners. Some had accused her of witchcraft and adultery, but Sorcha was forever grateful for Caitriona's care of her father, and the two women seemed inseparable these days.

With a grateful sigh, Brodyn sipped his ale and stood from his seat, ready to celebrate the Yule with his people, those who shared the blood within his veins, shared his dreams and goals… and he would never let them down.

Walking over to his wife, Brodyn touched her shoulder and looked down at her, admiring the skilled braids lacing her otherwise flowing blonde hair, a stark contrast against the green velvet tunic she wore with a simple golden circlet upon her head that he gifted her once he healed from his wounds.

She looked up at him with adoring eyes and a smile that sent his heart aflutter no matter how many times he saw it. As he smiled back at her musicians began to play flutes and horns and couples took to the floor.

"Would ye care to dance, my queen?" Brodyn put a hand out to Caitriona, who quirked a brow in response.

"I thought you didn't like to dance?"

"I like to do all manner of things with ye… as ye well ken."

Caitriona flushed and looked at Sorcha, who held Lucas in her arms.

"Shoo, go. I have the bairn. Go enjoy yerselves."

Taking his hand, Cait walked with him onto the floor and allowed him to spin her in his arms. As they swayed, he enjoyed the sound of her laughter and the sweet floral scent floating in the air around her.

"I can't tell you how strange it feels every day to be here with you after years of dreaming about you. But, I could not be happier, Brodyn, and I hope you always know that."

"I cannae tell ye how happy I am to hear that, for I want only for yer happiness, my love. I ken ye left a far different world behind to be with me."

"This is my home. You and Lucas are my home."

Brodyn stopped his feet from moving and pulled her into his arms, leaning in to kiss Caitriona deeply, slipping his tongue between her sweet lips, feeling his blood rush and his heart pound. Villagers whooped and cheered as they passed, making bawdy comments about another bairn coming soon.

Cait pulled away and laughed, her cheeks flushed when she looked up at him. "Where is Anya anyway?" she asked. "I haven't seen her all day."

"'Tis a Solstice Day. She is likely off doing whatever she does on these days when the world is said to be charged with magic."

"Well… we know full well that there is no such thing as magic," Caitriona said with a wry smile.

"Whether 'tis magic, fate, or divine intervention, I cannae ken, but I am glad of it, for it brought ye to me." Brodyn kissed her again, this time gently, before spinning her in his arms as another song began to play.

THE WIND HOWLED, whipping Anya's cloak into the air as she made her way to the shore. Looking out onto the horizon, she smiled at the dancing stars. It was a night much like this when she first found herself in this strange time.

A howling sound had guided her steps on that fateful day, but it hadn't been the wind that called to her. How she missed her beloved husband, Edwin. Sometimes she cursed her ancient body for being so sturdy, for she longed for the day she could unite with her life's love. That day would come in time, but tonight, the solstice had arrived, and the cave thrummed with energy, opening its arms to the woman who passed through its walls so frequently.

Stepping into the darkened cave, Anya reached into her bag with fresh dirt beneath her short nails. At the ripe age of 99, she never knew when the earth would call her home, and there was still much to be done. Looking at the cave walls, Anya regarded the freshly etched symbols of a bull and thistle, representing King Brodyn and Queen Caitriona of Fortriu. In a few hundred years, these etchings would mean nothing when the Picts disappeared, fading into the lands without a word, leaving nothing but mysteries for the future generations. For now, they represented an unbreakable bond and one that Anya helped to create.

Grabbing a flashlight from her bag, Anya flicked it on and held it before her as she walked to the back alcove where Taylor was buried. Her heart ached for the young man she helped raise. He had been a lovely lad, if not thoroughly envious of his brother in every way. Slowly, that envy grew into a seething, writhing hatred that consumed Talorc's soul and turned him into a man she could not recognize or protect, for his treachery ran too deep even for Anya to fix. In a way, it helped Anya to know his soul would live on, evidenced by Taylor, but the anger and envy he carried in his soul tainted every body it resided in. Taylor never stood a chance, and for that, Anya grieved.

Who knew if Anya would live to see another solstice, for she could not say with much certainty that she would. It was time for her to place the final symbol into the soil, the symbol that would bring Caitriona back to them when the time arose.

Getting onto her knees, Anya looked at the mound of dirt

before her, the sacred soil of the cave that held ancient secrets and shared them with only a select few. Many would pass by or through this cave over the centuries, never recognizing it for what it was: a portal through time. But more than that, it was a guardian of the land, and she and Caitriona were only a part of its story.

Gently, Anya pulled a freshly unearthed thistle from her bag, careful not to damage its roots as she buried it into the soil above Taylor's grave. She did this not only out of love for the lad he once was, still fresh and innocent, but as the final piece of the puzzle that would lead Caitriona back to them. Pulling out a vial of water, Anya slowly poured it over the thistle, saturating its roots as she murmured a prayer that many would consider a spell—the same spell she placed on the thistle buried over Talorc's grave. Witch, wise-woman, seer... she'd been referred to as many things over the years. What she was, she didn't quite know, but from within this cave, Anya had a connection to the earth, and she would use it to do its bidding.

The thistle could not survive all these years, nay, but every winter, from this year forward, it would grow and blossom on this spot, lasting through the season, only to ever be located by the traveler meant to discover it... Caitriona Murray—the one soul who could save Scotland simply by loving King Brodyn Mac Cuill throughout every lifetime.

AUTHOR'S NOTE

Hello, lovely reader! Thank you so much for choosing to read *Where the Thistle Grows*! I truly hope you enjoyed your journey through time!

I am often asked where I get my book ideas from, and the answer isn't always the same. Sometimes reading old historical articles makes my imagination wander, and other times it's simply watching others interact as I'm sitting in a park. Inspiration can spark in any manner of ways, but with this book, the inspiration hit me like an anvil over the head when I read a news article about the discovery of a Pictish burial site in Scotland.

It wasn't only the discovery of the ancient man's bones or their theory that he was royal due to the style of burial site, but the reconstruction of his face done in a lab. To gaze upon the face of a man long dead is truly a wonder of modern science. My mind started wandering, as it so often does, and I started researching the Picts, their history, hillfort locations, everything associated with them. As the book explains, little about the Picts has survived the hands of time, and they did disappear from the historical record after Kenneth mac Alpin became the first King of Scotland.

King Brodyn mac Cuill is very closely based on the real Pictish king, Bridei III, who did fight in the battle of Dun Nechtan in the year 685 against his cousin, Ecgfrith. King Bridei, like Brodyn, was victorious and, indeed, that battle is regarded as a turning point for the separate Celtic tribes that spanned the land we call Scotland today. It secured them against the constant threat of Northumbria to strengthen the Celtic cause. If you've read my first ever published series, The Sisters of Danu, you may recognize the surname "mac Cuill" as belonging to my very first ever hero, Liam, from Forbidden Fate. I like to pay tribute to my other characters now and again!

Across Scotland, ancient stones etched with Pictish symbols abound, and I was fortunate enough to see many firsthand when I traveled to Edinburgh in the winter of 2021, as many of the stones reside inside the National Museum of Scotland. I gained a lot of wonderful knowledge on that trip, even if it was also my honeymoon!

The most famous stone, found in Moray, where this story takes place, is thought to depict King Bridei as he arose victorious after the Battle of Nechtan, and the famous Pictish bull symbol is sometimes attributed to King Bridei. However, nobody truly knows what many of the symbols mean as the Picts had no written form of communication, like many Celtic cultures.

Burghead, a small village at the northern tip of Scotland in Moray, is where the hillfort I refer to as "Pinnata Castra" once stood. King Bridei was the king of all of Fortriu, the kingdom of the Picts, and though nobody knows exactly what the Picts called that hillfort, some historians have considered the name "Pinnata Castra" so I decided to stick with that. Its remains reside beneath Burghead today, and you can still see the silhouette of their familiar triple-walled defenses.

As for the cave, there is a set of caves off the coast of Moray, not far to the East of Burghead, that have Pictish symbols carved into their walls. One cave in particular is called Sculpture's Cave, and after studying the area and the cave, I knew this needed to be the epicenter of my story.

So much research and love went into every aspect of this story, and I truly hope you enjoyed it! Next up on deck is Emilie and Goodwin's story, *Where the Stars Lead*, and if you want to read Anya's story, you can find her in *Where the Wolf Howls*, a novella first published in the Dragonblade anthology called *Midnight Requiem: The Ghostly Hour*.

You can find links to all of my books at www.miapride.com

Thanks again for reading *Where the Thistle Grows*, book one of the Pict by Time Series!

Cheers,
Mia

ABOUT THE AUTHOR

Mia is a full-time mother of two rowdy boys, residing in the SF Bay Area. As a child, she often wrote stories about fantastic places or magical things, always preferring to live in a world where the line between reality and fantasy didn't exist.

In High school, she entered writing contests and had some stories published in small newspapers or school magazines. As life continued, so did her love of writing. So one day, she decided to end her cake decorating business, pull out her laptop and fulfill her dream of writing and publishing novels. And she did.

When Mia isn't writing books or chasing her sweaty children around a park, she loves to drink coffee by the gallon, get lost in a good book, hike with her family and drink really big margaritas with her friends! Her happy place is the Renaissance Faire, where you can find her at the joust, rooting for the shirtless highlander in a kilt.

Website: www.miapride.com
FB: facebook.com/miaprideauthor
Amazon: amazon.com/Mia-Pride/e/B01M6VEWGX
Instagram: instagram.com/mia_pride_author
Twitter: twitter.com/mia_pride
BookBub: https://www.bookbub.com/profile/mia-pride

www.ingramcontent.com/pod-product-compliance
Lightning Source LLC
Chambersburg PA
CBHW071231210726
48293CB00002B/662